The DIVA Delivers on a Promise

Krista Davis is the author of:

The Domestic Diva Mysteries:

The Diva Cooks Up a Storm
The Diva Sweetens the Pie
The Diva Spices It Up
The Diva Serves Forbidden Fruit
The Diva Says Cheesecake!

The Pen & Ink Mysteries:

Color Me Murder
The Coloring Crook
Color Outside the Lines
A Colorful Scheme

The DIVA Delivers on a Promise

KRISTA DAVIS

Kensington Publishing Corp.
www.kensingtonbooks.com

KENSINGTON BOOKS are published by

Kensington Publishing Corp.
119 West 40th Street
New York, NY 10018

All Kensington titles, imprints and distributed lines are available at special quantity discounts for bulk purchases for sales promotion, premiums, fund-raising, educational or institutional use. Special book excerpts or customized printings can also be created to fit specific needs. For details, write or phone the office of the Kensington Special Sales Manager: Kensington Publishing Corp., 119 West 40th Street, New York, NY, 10018. Attn. Special Sales Department. Phone: 1-800-221-2647.

The K and Teapot logo is a trademark of Kensington Publishing Corp.

Library of Congress Control Number: 2023930890

ISBN: 978-1-4967-3279-8

First Kensington Hardcover Edition: June 2023

ISBN: 978-1-4967-3281-1 (e-book)

10 9 8 7 6 5 4 3 2 1

Printed in the United States of America

Dedicated with love to
Nancy Rasper Hanson and Chew-Mee Kirtland

Acknowledgments

Each book I write requires a good amount of research and a little help from my friends! I had heard of ghost kitchens but had to dig a little deeper to understand exactly what they are. As I did so, an interesting idea emerged. It might be legal, and it might not. I'll let you decide.

Thanks to my editors, Wendy McCurdy and Elizabeth Trout, for all they do. So many details go into publishing a book and they are always on top of it all. Thanks also to my patient and very wise agent, Jessica Faust, who always steers me in the right direction.

Amy Wheeler and Vickie Green shared fun stories with me about new and different ways to deliver insults about attire and housekeeping. Naturally, Natasha adopted them immediately. I think they're funnier to read about than to experience!

Very special thanks go to my godson, David Erba, for his delicious Deep Blue Cream after-dinner drink that can also be served as a dessert! Thanks to his mom, Susan Erba, for recommending it. And as always, thanks to Betsy Strickland for her encouragement and for listening to me when I need a friend.

Cast of Characters

Sophie Winston
    Mars Winston—Sophie's ex-husband
Nina Reid Norwood
Bernie Frei—restaurateur
Natasha
    Charlene Smith—her half sister
Geraldine Stansfield, known as Gerrie
    Edwin Stansfield—her deceased husband
    Jim Stansfield—her son
    Todd Stansfield—her son
        Colleen Stansfield—her soon-to-be former
            daughter-in-law
        Penelope Stansfield—Todd and Colleen's daughter
        Irv Baskin—driver for Dinner at Home
Russ Everett
Senator Albert Keswick
    Henrietta Keswick—his wife
    Emily Keswick—Albert and Henrietta's daughter
Nicci Mancini
    Dale Mancini—her brother
Jenna Ryder
Detective Wolf Fleishman
Officer Wong
    Eddie Wong—her ex-husband

Chapter 1

Dear Sophie,
My brother's girlfriend invited my family to a birthday dinner for him at her house. She doesn't like me because I am the holiday hostess in our family, a position she would like to usurp. When I asked what I could bring, she laughed and said she was ordering everything from a ghost kitchen. It's not Halloween. What does that mean?
    Not Eating a Bite in Sleepy Hollow, New York

Dear Not Eating a Bite,
Your brother's girlfriend won't be cooking. The latest trend in dining, ghost kitchens are also known as virtual, dark, cloud, zombie, and shadow kitchens. The principle behind them is food by delivery only. They don't have dining rooms or tables where customers can eat. It's sort of like ordering from a restaurant and having them deliver the food to your home.
    Sophie

The glowing and quite lengthy obituary of Edwin Stansfield painted him as a defender and guardian of the needy, as well as a paragon of humanity. We all knew we weren't supposed to be critical of the dearly departed, but the excessive glory with which he was described prompted a great deal of eye-rolling and droll comments in Old Town.

His wife, Geraldine, Gerrie to her friends, and a domestic diva by anyone's standards, had thrown herself into funeral preparations worthy of the pope. She had inherited an enormously successful restaurant supply company from her parents, and she hadn't spared a dime in celebrating Edwin's life.

We all noticed, though, that Edwin's recent demise hadn't seemed to leave Gerrie particularly bereft. I suspected that the myriad details of his funeral had distracted her from the day-to-day reality of his absence.

Besides, not everyone played the forlorn widow publicly. It seemed more in character for Gerrie to spend those lonely, weepy hours in the privacy of her own home.

Three months had passed and Gerrie had surprised us all by calling the annual meeting of A Healthy Meal, a local organization that provided meals for less fortunate children.

Although I made my living as an event planner, and quite often have charities as clients, some causes are so dear to me that I don't charge any fees for my contributions. A Healthy Meal was among them. One of the perks, though, was the annual luncheon meeting at Gerrie's house. She certainly knew how to throw an elegant ladies' luncheon.

Shortly before noon, I met my best friend and across-the-street neighbor, Nina Reid Norwood, in front of her house. As we walked along the brick sidewalk, I was glad

I had pinned my hair up in an easy chignon. The August sun blazed down on us.

"Should have worn a hat," Nina griped.

"It's not that far." At that moment, the two of us stopped abruptly and watched as a plump, petite woman dashed across the road dodging traffic. She wore a gauzy red, pink, and yellow dress with a pleated skirt that swished around her legs.

"Was that Gerrie?" asked Nina.

"Do we have the wrong day?" I asked. Nevertheless, we continued on our way to her house.

Half-a-dozen other women clustered before the front door of Gerrie's white Federal-style home. Pots of lush hot-coral geraniums, a shade squarely between screaming pink and vivid orange, flanked the three stairs to her door. The oval plaque on the wall denoted it as a historic building. Four stories tall, it was bold and impressive. But it had absolutely no front yard and abutted the sidewalk.

The other women greeted us warmly. One of them said, "I don't think Gerrie's home. It's not like her to make us wait."

Minutes later, Gerrie, her hair perfect as always, opened the front door and invited us inside. She must have entered the house through the kitchen door in the back. She didn't look flustered or hurried, but the one thing she couldn't disguise was her rapid respiration.

We entered the cool foyer, a long hall on the right side of the house. White-on-white wallpaper and judiciously placed tall gold-framed mirrors helped it feel larger. It ended at stairs and a door.

Gerrie smiled brightly and held out a tray of icy pink drinks with a twist of cucumber on the rim. "They're mocktails. So refreshing in this heat."

Nina wrinkled her nose. "No booze?"

In a most earnest tone, Gerrie said, "Nina, they're the latest thing."

Each of us took one and Gerrie flitted away to offer them to other guests.

Nina took a sip. "Not bad. But if this is the trend, I'm going to become one of those women who carries a little flask in her purse."

I laughed at the image, and we chatted with friends as we entered the living room. The walls were a dusty Williamsburg blue that was picked up in the furniture fabrics, along with generous hints of gold.

An oil portrait of Gerrie and Edwin hung over the marble fireplace mantel in an ornate frame. I guessed it must have been painted about ten or fifteen years ago.

"It was definitely Gerrie we saw crossing the street. That dress is unmistakable," murmured Nina.

"I wonder where she bought it. I love the colors."

"I'm starved. Do you know what she's serving?" Nina edged toward the dining room.

Williamsburg blue continued as the dominant color, with white wainscoting around the bottom half. A cozy window seat should have been the main architectural attraction, but the far wall, where open French doors led to a lush patio, was full of glass and white molding that offered a welcome interruption to the blue. The upholstered seats on the dining chairs matched the blue walls. A blast of heat radiated in through the open doors, though I could feel the relief of air-conditioning behind me in the living room.

Gerrie had outdone herself on the tablescape. Fresh roses, irises, white columbine, and coral butterfly weed added a punch of color to the table. And she had used no less than three tablecloths. A gold one peeked out at the bottom. It was covered by a tablecloth in shades of blue, and that was topped by an elegant white embroidered square. The luncheon dishes had a beautiful blue floral pattern on white and were rimmed with a band of gold around the edges. A rose lay on a napkin at each place setting.

A horrific scream interrupted my thoughts, and the din of voices was abruptly silenced.

Chapter 2

Dear Sophie,
My mother-in-law nearly had a cow when I plopped flowers in a vase. She said that's not how it's done! C'mon, flowers are flowers. She's picking another fight with me, right?
Baffled Daughter-in-law in Roseville, California

Dear Baffled Daughter-in-law,
Your mother-in-law wants your flowers to last longer. Remove low leaves and cut the stems on a diagonal. It's also wise to add plant food or a drop of vodka to help keep the water fresh. A base of foliage goes in first, and then the flowers.
Sophie

At the other end of the table, near the French doors, Mindy Parsons cupped her hands over her nose and mouth in horror and whimpered.

Nina and I rushed to her side. Nina squealed and clutched my arm.

At Mindy's feet, a man lay on his back with a blue knife

handle jutting from his chest. A growing red stain marred his crisp white button-down shirt.

Gerrie peered past me and shrieked before howling, "Noooo! Russ!"

The dining room was filled with her luncheon guests, who also screamed in various pitches, adding panic and chaos to an already bad situation.

I pulled my phone from my purse and called 911. "Gerrie, what's your address?"

She told me, and I repeated it to the dispatcher, then handed my phone to Nina, while I kneeled on the floor beside the small man.

He looked vaguely familiar to me. I had probably seen him around Old Town or at events I arranged. His straight sandy hair had fallen back off his face, accentuating his open eyes, wide with terror. His long sleeves were rolled back, and his shirt was open at the neck. I slid my fingers under the collar in search of a pulse.

Sirens wailed in the air. One of the advantages of living in a small community was that it rarely took long for help to arrive. But I felt no pulse.

"Should we pull out the knife? Do CPR?" Gerrie's shaking hand wavered in the air above the blue knife handle.

"Don't touch the knife!" I tried to sound calm. "He could bleed out. He needs professional help." I thought he was already beyond the help of anyone, but there was no point in saying so. Maybe the rescue crew could jolt his heart into beating again.

I breathed easier when I heard Gerrie's front door knocker bang.

I rose to my feet and watched as the guests parted to let Officer Wong through. Like me, Wong was partial to good food, especially of the cupcake variety, which was probably the reason for her snug uniform. She wasn't very tall for a cop, but she made up for her lack of height with serious smarts. The African-American Wong had chosen to keep her former husband's name, but she'd told me she hadn't regretted kicking him to the curb.

Her eyes narrowed and she murmured, "Russ Everett. Well, well."

As she took in the situation, I did, too. I hadn't noticed some items that were definitely out of place. A green baseball cap lay on the floor. It was embroidered with the words *Dinner at Home*. On the table lay a small robin's-egg–blue box of cookies. The words *Natasha's Cookies* glittered on it in gold lettering. A ribbon that had probably been tied on the box unfurled on the table. Cookie crumbs lay scattered on the pristine tablecloth.

I longed to pick the package up and take a closer look, but I didn't dare touch it. I knew Natasha very well and there wasn't a doubt in my mind that the cookies must be her latest project. Natasha and I had grown up together in the same small town, which was the reason I knew her last name was Smith, even though she insisted on using one name, like Cher. And now, through a quirk of fate, we lived on the same block and wrote competing advice columns about the domestic life, a phrase that had fallen out of favor and was being replaced by *everyday living*.

Natasha liked to brag about everything she undertook. Yet I hadn't heard so much as a whisper about a line of cookies, which I found odd.

Much as I had, Wong kneeled beside Russ and checked for a pulse. "What happened here?"

"Mindy found him like this. We were on the other side of the table." I looked at Mindy. "Right?"

Her hands trembled. "Y-y-yes."

Wong's shoulders stiffened. I had known her for years, but had never seen her uncomfortable like this. She always took the worst in stride. She hadn't hesitated a second to help me carry my old beau out of a burning building. Wong gazed up at me. Her voice tense, she asked, "Did you see who knifed him?"

"Not at all. I didn't even know he was here."

"How about you, Mindy?"

She shook her head, her expression fearful.

The sirens grew louder, which only served to heighten tension in the room. Wong appeared to be out of her element.

"Why don't we all move back into the living room?" I held out my arms like I was herding them.

"I think we should all go home." Jenna Ryder clutched her purse tightly, as if she thought someone might grab it.

Wong got to her feet. "Not so fast, ladies. You need to stay here. Y'all have a seat." Wong followed us into the living room and eyed them, one by one, as if assessing them. She sounded gentle and kind when she said, "I know most of you. There's nothing to be scared about. But we need you to stick around so we can get some information from you. Okay?"

It was a rhetorical question, but a number of them nodded their heads.

I rushed to the front door and flung it open in anticipation of the emergency crew's arrival. Jenna dashed past me, and out the door, leaving only a whiff of Miss Dior behind.

Emergency medical responders calmly walked inside.

Wong greeted them and led them to the dining room.

A man stood outside watching. He was tall and dressed in a striped golf shirt and white trousers. As he neared, I recognized his aristocratic face. I had arranged many functions to which U.S. Senator Albert Keswick had been invited.

"Is Gerrie all right? I'm her neighbor. I live just across the way." He pointed to an equally large house distinguished by a small balcony on the second floor that hung over the main entrance.

"Gerrie is fine."

"I worry about her, now that Edwin isn't with us anymore."

"That's very kind of you." I wondered whether to invite him in. The fewer people, the better, I thought.

"Albert!" Gerrie cried as she came toward the door. "What are you doing here?"

I eased out of the way and watched as Wong filled in the rescue team with what little she knew. Then leaving them to their work, Wong returned to the living room and looked at the women gathered there in silence. "Was Russ invited to whatever y'all are doing here?"

Nina shook her head. "No! It's a luncheon meeting of A Healthy Meal."

Mindy added, "For needy children. No sodas, chips, or pizza."

Wong grunted "uh-huh," as if she wasn't impressed. "I'm going to have to get your names and addresses." She cast a quick glance my way when she added, "But first I have to call Wolf."

Years ago, I had dated Wolf Fleishman of the Criminal Investigations Division of the Alexandria Police. Things had been a little awkward between us after we broke off our relationship, but at least we had stopped avoiding each other. At times like this, I was very happy to see Wong and Wolf because I knew how competent they were.

Gerrie pulled me aside. "What should I do?"

"Why don't you sit down and wait for Wong? I'm sure she'll want to speak with you."

"What if one of the guests is diabetic or something and needs to eat?" She didn't wait for a response. "I'll bring more drinks. Yes, that's what I'll do." She flitted away eagerly, as if thrilled to have something to keep her busy.

Nina scowled at me. "I'm *always* hungry, but who can think of food at a time like this?" Nevertheless, she drifted in the direction Gerrie had gone.

Gerrie was neither unkind nor stupid. I guessed she simply didn't know what to do and felt too unsettled to sit and wait.

The emergency medical responders didn't linger. Everyone stopped talking and watched with horror as they wheeled Russ through the living room. The knife handle still jutted from his chest. I followed them and observed from the doorway as they whisked him into the waiting ambulance in record time. I didn't know if he could be resuscitated, but I knew for sure that his best chance was in an emergency room and that minutes mattered.

Wolf had arrived and was speaking with the emergency responders. He looked a little trimmer than the last time I had seen him. The sun glinted off silver strands that increasingly crept into his hair along the edges of his face. He watched as the ambulance rolled away.

Wolf turned and hesitated for just a beat when he saw me. "Hi, Sophie."

"Can they save him?"

He shook his head. "Doesn't look like it. A doctor will probably declare him dead on arrival at the hospital."

Wolf entered the house and Wong led him to the scene of the crime.

Gerrie reappeared with a pitcher. "Refills, anyone?"

I'd never seen anything like it. A man had just been stabbed in her house and Gerrie was being a proper hostess, as if nothing untoward had happened! But as I watched her, I realized that the pitcher was shaking so violently that she had to steady it with her other hand. Everyone coped differently.

Nina had returned and now nudged me toward the dining room. "Gerrie was looking in her knife drawer," she murmured.

"That's curious. Wouldn't she have known from the handle if it belonged to her?"

"Maybe she recognized it and was hoping her knives were all accounted for?"

Wong passed us and pulled out a small notebook and pen. She glanced around the living room. "Who's missing?"

The silence that followed reminded me of kids who had been rounded up because one of them had done something wrong.

"Jenna Ryder," Mindy whined.

"Mindy!" scolded Gerrie. Turning to Wong, Gerrie babbled, "I'm sure she had an emergency at home."

Wolf approached me and asked in a low voice, "Where's the kitchen?"

At one of her parties, Gerrie had needed a hand and directed me through the door at the end of the foyer. So I happened to know that it led through a narrow butler's pantry to a second door. Beyond that, one stepped into a short passage, which contained a door to a powder room, and finally opened to the kitchen. That section of the house appeared to have been an addition. Unlike most homes, there was no easy connection between the kitchen and the dining room, which was to the left of the foyer. To serve a meal, one had to carry the food through the butler's pantry, into the foyer, and then through an archway to the dining room. Alternatively, one could step outside the kitchen and walk through the elegant private patio to the French doors of the dining room. Clearly, not the best alternative in inclement weather. It struck me as oddly cumbersome, but it was the norm to Gerrie. The house had been in her family for decades. She had grown up with

that crazy arrangement. And even I could see that changing it would mean ripping off the entire four-story rear of
the building and losing the gorgeous private patio.

I showed him the way through the butler's pantry and
into the kitchen.

"That seems awkward. I thought those pantry things
usually led right into the dining room." He peered out the
French doors at the patio.

"Old homes can be hard to update." I was itching to
open drawers in search of Gerrie's knives, but didn't want
to leave my fingerprints in the kitchen. The countertop
was fairly tidy for a luncheon about to begin. A quart of
half-and-half sat next to a creamer that contained a white
liquid. Half-and-half, I assumed. A strawberry cake roll
had been dusted with powdered sugar. Ruby-red strawberries threatened to fall off the white cream at the coiling
end of the roll. "It's part of an addition. I guess there
wasn't a better way to do it."

"What do you know about Gerrie?"

I peeked in the trash. She was using a lot of half-and-
half. An opened container of it lay on the top. "Her husband died a few months ago. She has two sons, Todd and
Jim. Both of them live in Old Town. Rumor has it that
Todd is divorcing his wife, Colleen, with whom he has a
daughter."

Two trays sat on a counter, one loaded with teacups and
a stack of dessert plates, the other packed with matching
coffee cups, a china teapot, and a coffeepot. They were so
perfect and pretty that they looked like a setup for a magazine photograph.

"Were the French doors open in the dining room?"

"Yes."

"What happened?"

"We were making our way into the dining room for

lunch, when Mindy Parsons screamed. The body was on the opposite end of the table, so we hadn't noticed it. He must have lain there while we mingled in the living room."

Wolf opened the French doors of the kitchen and stepped outside. I followed him into the perfect patio. High brick walls around the edge provided privacy. Short brickwork enclosed garden beds of carefully selected bushes and trees that provided a background for red geraniums and golden black-eyed Susans. It reminded me of the way a flower arrangement is created. Greens first as a background for the flowers.

The large, weathered lanterns would shed a peaceful glow during evening dinners al fresco. A wooden door with a curved top was the only way to exit without going through the house. If we assumed Russ was murdered where we found him, the killer could only leave the house one of three ways. He could have gone through the front door, but a gaggle of women were out there and surely *someone* would have noticed him leaving. He could have fled to the kitchen and exited through the French doors, as we had just done, or most likely he was the one who opened the French doors of the dining room to depart through the patio.

I stepped back and gazed up at the windows. "He could be hiding in the house right now. Are you going to search it?"

Wolf stood beside me and looked up. "The perpetrator is probably long gone, but we'll do a sweep. Just in case."

"Wong seemed to know the victim. Russ somebody?"

Wolf nodded. "Russ Everett. He is well known to the police. I'm sorry to say that I'm not particularly surprised that he came to a bad end. But it's quite curious that it happened here." His hands in his pockets, he observed, "No sign of breaking and entering."

I knew what Wolf was getting at. It wouldn't have been difficult to break the glass in the French doors. But neither

Russ nor his killer had done so, which meant the doors weren't locked or someone had let them in. And that, while not conclusive, likely indicated that Gerrie or someone in her household knew Russ well enough to invite him into the house.

"Are you familiar with Gerrie's kitchen knives?" Wolf raised his eyebrows.

"No. But I saw the handle of the murder weapon. I could probably tell you if it came from a matching set."

"Thanks. We'll collect her knives, and the hospital will send over the one that killed Russ. I'd better interview these ladies and let them go."

I followed him into the living room. Nina looked at me questioningly.

I sidled over to her and whispered, "Did you recognize the dead guy?"

"He looked familiar, like I'd seen him somewhere before."

"That's what I thought, but I can't place him. Wolf and Wong knew him right away. It sounds like he might have a criminal record."

Nina waved her phone at me. "How come you're not answering your phone?"

"Really? A man was stabbed to death and that's what's worrying you?"

"It wouldn't be, if people weren't contacting me in an effort to find you."

That didn't sound good. "Who's looking for me?" I pulled out my phone and turned it on. Nina was right. I had half-a-dozen texts.

I started with one from my ex-husband, Mars. He usually got right to the point.

I'm stuck in a meeting. Charlene needs help. Irv is missing.

Chapter 3

Dear Natasha,
My husband and I have demanding jobs and no time to cook! We have three children whom we don't want to raise in restaurants. But if we cook at home, it's bedtime before we eat dinner! What would you do?
Frazzled Mom in Salt Lake City, Utah

Dear Frazzled Mom,
Now that ghost kitchens are cropping up everywhere, it's easy to order a meal that will be delivered right to your door so you can eat at home. You can even accommodate picky eaters!
Natasha

Who on earth was Irv?

When my friend Natasha did a DNA search, hoping to locate her father, Charlene Smith had turned up as Natasha's half sister. As things progressed, Charlene had moved in with Natasha and now lived on the same street as me. I had once helped Charlene locate a kitchen where she could temporarily cook for her clients.

I read Charlene's text next. **I hate to impose, but Irv has disappeared. Do you have time to give me a hand?**

Who was Irv? I looked Charlene up in my contacts and phoned her.

"Sophie! Oh, thank goodness! I'm completely beside myself. Irv went out to deliver food over two hours ago. He should have been back by now. The phone is ringing off the hook because people are asking where their food is. Could you pitch in? Just for a few deliveries? Bernie is loaning me a truck for tonight if Irv doesn't show up, and Mars has agreed to make those deliveries, so that's covered. But I really need someone right now. I've stopped taking orders, but I have a couple that need to go out and replacements for the ones Irv apparently never made. I'm desperate for someone to help. Could you give me a hand? You can take my car. All I need is someone to make the deliveries. I'd do it myself, but I have things on the stove and in the ovens. I can't just step away!"

For years, Charlene had supplied a small group of families with evening meals. She had recently rented a larger commercial kitchen and must have expanded to an online menu. I appreciated her diligence and concern about making the deliveries, but it seemed to me there was a bigger problem. "Irv is your driver?"

"Yes. He makes the deliveries. I can't imagine what happened to him. This isn't like him at all. He's not the youngest guy, so I'm worried that he might have had a heart attack or something. I've phoned the hospitals, but no one fitting his description has checked in."

The man on the floor was named Russ and had been identified by Wolf and Wong. Still, to be sure, I asked, "What does Irv look like?"

"Gray hair, slender. He's in his late seventies. A little on the scrawny side. I usually send leftovers home with him. I don't think he cooks much."

I blew a breath of relief. Irv was definitely not the man who had been murdered. "Have you called the police?"

"Yes, but I would have to go in to file a missing person's report. I can't just leave without anyone here. Besides, it's only been a couple of hours. I keep thinking he'll walk in and tell me some sad story about the van breaking down."

I didn't want to be the voice of doom, but I asked anyway. "Wouldn't he have phoned you if that were the case?"

I heard her draw a ragged breath. "I have called his cell phone, over and over, but all I get is voicemail."

An ugly thought crossed my mind. "Does he carry cash?"

"Not for the business. All transactions are paid for by credit card. Even the tip. That doesn't mean customers don't sometimes tip him more, but it's not usually much."

"Other people might not realize that. Could he have been mugged?"

"I hope not! Would you have an hour or so to help me out? I wouldn't ask, but I'm in such a pinch."

I could hear another line ringing in the background and the clatter of pots being moved.

I didn't have much planned until later in the day. The Association of Ghost Kitchens convention would begin tomorrow. I was meeting with the director, Colleen Stansfield, Gerrie's daughter-in-law, for dinner and I had to check some details at the hotel where it would take place. It probably wouldn't take long to deliver a few meals for Charlene.

"Nina and I will be over as soon as possible."

"I can never thank you enough! See you soon." The line went dead and I imagined she had picked up the other line.

I explained to Nina what we would be doing and the two of us went in search of Wolf. We found him in the kitchen with Gerrie.

"Sorry to interrupt, but Charlene Smith needs a hand. Is it all right if Nina and I leave?"

He nodded. "I know where to find you. But do me a favor and go out through the patio so the others won't see you and give Wong a hard time about it. And don't touch anything. That goes double for you, Nina."

In spite of the sad situation, I chuckled a little at that.

Nina grumbled at Wolf when he opened the latch of the patio gate with a gloved hand.

Relief swept over me as we walked away. I felt for Gerrie, though. She would be dealing with crime scene investigators, and when they left, she would be alone in silence, staring at the spot where Russ had fallen.

Charlene's commercial kitchen was only a few blocks away. Surprisingly, the door that I thought led to it turned out to be the store that belonged to Charlene and Natasha's mothers. Through the glass, I could see Natasha's mother, Wanda Smith, assisting a customer. I pushed the door open.

Wanda looked over at us and smiled. "Bless you for helpin' Charlene. The entrance is around back."

We waved at her and hurried around the side of the red brick building.

"That does make more sense," I said. "Irv would never find a parking spot in the front of the building."

In the alley, an unmarked glass door seemed a likely entrance. A bell rang as I pushed it open.

Two phone lines dueled for attention. Delicious aromas of cooked onions, garlic, and thyme filled the air.

Behind a high counter, Charlene was removing a giant lasagna from an oven. "You're here! I can't believe it!"

Charlene and Natasha had the same father. Their mothers were remarkably alike. Both were into herbs, healing, and natural remedies. Under normal circumstances, Charlene looked a lot like Natasha. They both had beautiful raven hair, but while Natasha was tall and willowy, Charlene was smaller, with softer features. Today, worry etched lines in her face. "Thank you both. None of the deliveries are far away. These folks have been waiting for their food. I've explained the situation and all but one were willing to wait." She placed bags on top of the high counter. "I hope they'll be nice about the delay."

"Any word from Irv yet?" asked Nina.

"Not a thing. Wong has been tied up with something, but I'm hoping she'll come by soon."

"There was a murder at Gerrie Stansfield's house," Nina blurted. "That's what's keeping Wong."

Charlene, who hadn't stopped moving for a second since we entered, finally came to a halt. "A murder?"

I tread carefully in case she knew the victim. "A man named Russ Everett." I watched her for any sign of recognition, but she didn't flinch.

"That's terrible. *Inside* Gerrie's house? What a nightmare! Was he a relative of hers?"

That was a good question. Gerrie had been very concerned and she had known his name. But she hadn't acted like one would toward a relative. Or had she? She hadn't kneeled or held his hand. Wouldn't one do that if it had been a family member? But she did consider pulling out the knife, which would have taken a lot of moxie. "I don't think so. But she knew him."

"Here you go. There aren't too many deliveries. These bags keep the food warm. All you do is ring the doorbell and hand it to whoever answers the door."

"Only adults, right?" asked Nina.

"No. A lot of kids run to the door. And I have some parents who are in their offices and order food for their children who are at home."

She picked up the phone that hadn't stopped ringing. "Dinner at Home! I'm so sorry, but at the moment, we're only taking orders to be delivered after six."

She flicked her hand at me in an urgent motion I took to mean we should be on our way.

We carried the food outside, where a small car bore a sign that read DINNER AT HOME. The hatch had been outfitted with partitions designed to hold food containers steady. I drove while Nina gave me the addresses.

"She even provided a map," Nina exclaimed. "How cute is that? As though we don't know our way around here. There's the first one."

I pulled up in front of the Federal-style house.

Nina grabbed the package of food and darted up the sidewalk. The door opened before she reached it. I could hear their conversation about the delay.

Nina was a pro. "We're very sorry, but we hope you'll love your order and that will make up for it."

Nina hurried back to the car.

"Well done!"

Nina buckled her seatbelt. "I would have been plenty upset. We've become so used to instant everything, haven't we? Email is instantaneous, so are texts. People have their phones on them all the time. You don't have to wait until you go home and realize someone called because they left a message."

Nina directed me to King Street, where we turned left

on a small side street and stopped at a real estate office. I recognized the woman who took the rather large order from Nina.

"You're not Irv!" she said.

"I'm filling in for him," said Nina. "Enjoy your food!"

She returned to the car and directed me across King Street and north several blocks, where we made a number of deliveries.

Back in the car, Nina said, "Only one more stop after this one. That wasn't too bad."

When I parked the car, a middle-aged woman in a bathrobe walked out to take the delivery from Nina.

"I thought this would never arrive. It better be hot! If this is what I can expect, I won't be ordering from you anymore!"

Nina didn't react to the woman's anger in kind. "We had a bad day. That happens to us all, right?"

The woman's face softened. "Just one bad day? I think I've had a month of them. Thanks for delivering this."

Nina returned to the car. "Take a right in two blocks."

Our route took us past Gerrie's house, where crime scene investigators in white jumpsuits were leaving.

"Poor Gerrie," I said.

Just past Gerrie's house, Nina cried, "Stop. Stop!"

"I can't just stop in the middle of the street."

"Then go around the block and park in the alley. We'll never find a spot to park around here."

I took the first possible right, and then another one.

I hit the brakes when I saw a small white van parked there.

"Could that be Charlene's van?" asked Nina.

Sure enough, the DINNER AT HOME logo was printed on the side. It wasn't the newest van. Charlene must have bought it used. But I was pleased to know that her business was growing, and she could afford a delivery van, in addition to the small car Nina and I were driving.

I pulled up behind it and the two of us carefully approached the van. The driver's seat was empty, and nothing appeared to be amiss.

Nina tried the rear door. It opened readily and both of us gasped. A slender man who appeared to be in his seventies lay on the floor in a puddle of blood.

Chapter 4

Dear Sophie,
My son is a zombie in a local play, and I get to fig-
ure out how to make a costume. I can handle the
dirty torn clothes (we have plenty of those), but
how do I make blood? Eww.
        Zombie's Mom in Deadwood, South Dakota

Dear Zombie's Mom,
Blend together corn syrup and red food color, or
for a darker shade, blend chocolate syrup with red
food color.

                                        Sophie

He had to be Irv.

"Nina, call 911."

I crawled into the truck, hoping he was still alive. "Irv? Irv?"

He lay on his stomach with his face turned, so I could see the left side. His eye was closed. I presumed the other one was as well. I gripped his shoulder and gently wiggled it. "Irv? Can you hear me?"

I wedged forward, wondering if he had been knifed like Russ. Blood oozed on the front of his beige T-shirt. "Irv!"

I could hear Nina giving the dispatcher our location and telling her to send an ambulance.

Taking a deep breath, I felt his neck for a pulse. It beat rhythmically under my fingers with unquestionable strength. "Nina, he's alive!"

I was afraid to move him, but I took his left hand into mine and squeezed it. "Irv! Can you hear me?"

His fingers moved and he grunted. He opened his eye and closed it again, groaning.

"It's okay. Help is on the way."

His eye opened again. "It's a lotta blood."

I was so relieved that he was alive that I giggled a little at his remark.

The blood on the floor of the van was a bright red. I'd had no choice but to kneel in it. In my concern for Irv, I hadn't given the blood much thought, but now that he mentioned it, I had to force myself not to think about it on my hands, knees, and dress.

Thankfully, the brief bleat of a police siren sounded as it pulled into the alley. It was followed by the scream of an ambulance.

"They're here to help you. You'll be all right." It dawned on me suddenly that maybe he wasn't Irv. "What's your name?"

A tired eye looked at me. "Irvin Baskin."

I could hear voices behind me.

I squeezed his hand. "I'm Sophie. Charlene is very worried about you. Listen, the emergency squad is here. I'm going to back up so they can come inside and help you."

He tried to raise his head, but winced in pain and gently lowered it again.

I backed up, holding the skirt of my dress down with

one hand so it wouldn't flap up. Hands assisted me out of the van.

"Thanks," I said to all of them. But then I saw their faces. They gazed at me in horror.

"Are you injured?" asked Wong.

The emergency medical technicians gathered around.

I gazed down at my dress. The best dry cleaner in the world wouldn't be able to get that stain out. No wonder they thought I was bleeding. The bright red color scared me, too. "No. I'm fine. It's the man in the truck. He's having difficulty raising his head, but he can talk. His name is Irvin Baskin. He goes by Irv."

They turned their attention to him.

"Good heavens, Sophie. I hope that wasn't your favorite dress." Nina clucked at me. "Bummer."

"As long as Irv will be okay. Small price to pay, huh?" It was icky, though. I gratefully accepted the paper towels that Wong handed to me.

The three of us watched as the rescue squad attended to Irv.

Nina sniffed and wrinkled her nose. "Do you smell garlic?"

I smelled the air. "Maybe it's something Irv was delivering. Garlic bread?"

"It's really strong," said Wong. "Charlene must use a lot of it in her dishes. Have you tried her cooking?"

"Not yet. I knew she planned to expand, but I didn't realize she meant a ghost kitchen. Speaking of which, I have a convention starting tonight." I checked my watch. I still had time to go home and shower.

Two of the emergency medical technicians hopped out of the van and wasted no time in removing Irv on a stretcher. They looked almost as bloodied as I did.

Just then, slimy guts slid off the stretcher.

Nina, Wong, and I backed up and groaned in revulsion. They plopped on the pavement like a mess of worms in blood.

"Why does it smell like garlic?" asked Wong.

I looked down at my dress. Didn't blood get darker when it was exposed to air and started drying? I sniffed my dress, then looked at the blob on the street more closely. "It's spaghetti with sauce."

Nina laughed so hard, tears came to her eyes.

Wong couldn't help laughing, but she discreetly hid it by peering into the van. "Yup. Looks like a Styrofoam clamshell of spaghetti opened and he fell on it." She was still chuckling when she followed the rescue squad to the ambulance. It took off in a matter of minutes, the siren gaining in strength as it drove away.

Wong wasn't laughing anymore. "His chest is fine. They cut open his T-shirt. He's bruised, but it appears the main injury is a blow to the back of his head. They'll probably run a CAT scan to be sure he didn't sustain a concussion and hold him overnight for observation."

"How would he get a blow to the back of his head in the van?" I asked.

Wong looked inside the van. "Irv says the last thing he remembers is opening the back doors to remove the order. There's nothing in here that he could have hit his head on."

"Oh my gosh! The delivery!" Nina squealed and grabbed the final delivery from the hatchback. She hurried along the sidewalk that cut between two houses.

"The cap," I said. "Did you notice the Dinner at Home cap on the floor in Gerrie's dining room?"

Wong grimaced. "That must be how Russ got in the house. He posed as a deliveryman and someone opened the door."

I winced. "But that doesn't make sense. If Gerrie had

opened the door to Russ in a delivery cap, she wouldn't have let him in the house. Besides, she would have known she hadn't ordered anything."

Wong eyed the van with suspicion. "There has to be a connection."

"I think you're right."

Nina returned at a much slower speed than she had departed. It's so hot," she moaned. "We need to return Charlene's car. I'm blasting the air as cold as it can get."

"Want to follow us?" I asked Wong.

"Thanks, but I'll pass. I don't want anyone mucking with the van before we take fingerprints." She raised her eyebrows. "Did Charlene mention anyone driving *with* Irv?"

"I'm sure she would have said something if he was with another person. She was very worried about him. That would have been two people missing."

Wong nodded without saying a word.

"You're thinking of Russ and the hat, aren't you?"

Wong's gaze met mine and she nodded.

Nina sat in the driver's seat with air blowing on her and the door open. "Russ and the hat?"

"We're less than a block away from Gerrie's house. And there's no question that the name on the hat is the same as the name on the door of the van," I explained.

Nina's eyes grew large. "You mean Irv killed Russ?"

"Is there any blood on the ground between here and Gerrie's house?" I asked. "If Irv and Russ tussled, that might explain the injury to his head."

"Whoa! I'm not suggesting that at all." Wong shot us a disapproving look. "Don't you go starting rumors. There must be half-a-dozen possibilities. The good thing is that Irv is alive."

"Hopefully, he'll talk." I wasn't betting on much useful information, though. Not if he was involved with Russ's murder. "Do you know Irv?"

"Nope. But Wolf is going to get to know him pretty well." Wong smiled at us.

Nina and I returned to the Dinner at Home car. She slid into the passenger seat.

I opened the door on the driver's side and looked down at my dress with dismay. "I'm going to get tomato sauce all over Charlene's car and she'll never be able to get it out. Maybe you should drive the car back and I'll walk over there."

"That's probably wise." Nina changed seats and drove away.

I started to exit the alley, when it dawned on me that I was standing directly behind Senator Keswick's house. The very man who had shown up at Gerrie's house after Russ was murdered. I'd found it odd at the time, but so much was going on that I hadn't given it much thought. He had said he was a neighbor and had inquired about Gerrie. There wasn't anything wrong with that. Was there?

His house had a long backyard enclosed by a tall brick fence that provided a lot of privacy. A beautiful wrought iron gate had been backed by frosted glass so no one could peer inside.

Walking back briskly, I couldn't help noticing that people stared at me. Who could blame them? I looked like I'd been shot. There was nothing I could do except avert my gaze and keep going.

I rounded the corner and heard someone shout my name. My ex-husband, Mars Winston, and our friend Bernie Frei raced toward me.

Mars and I had divorced amicably, even if Natasha had moved in on him far too soon. So quickly in fact, I was not alone in suspecting that they were involved before the divorce. If you had asked me a few years ago, I might have snarled about it, but to my surprise, my friendship with Mars had survived his subsequent relationship with Natasha. It was all in our past now. Mars made a living as a political consultant. He'd been quite successful and had some powerful connections. He fit in well with his primped and polished clients, as handsome as any of them and able to be as comfortable in a fancy boardroom as he was on a country porch. He was a decent guy who played on the floor with our dog, Daisy, took care of his mom, and had my back if I was in trouble.

The same could be said for Bernie, who had been the best man at our wedding. Raised in England, Bernie had traveled the globe. No one ever expected him to settle in Old Town, but our friend with hair that always looked like he had just rolled out of bed, and a kink in his nose where it had been broken, turned out to have a knack for the restaurant business. He now owned The Laughing Hound, a popular upscale eatery, though he kept mum about his ownership, allowing people to think he was only managing the place for an absentee owner.

Their voices tumbled over each other. "What happened?"

"How can you walk?"

"I'm calling an ambulance."

"It's tomato sauce!" I shouted.

It took a moment to soak in. Bernie sniffed. "Ahh. I do detect *parfum d'ail.*"

"It's all the rage," I retorted.

People on the sidewalk were stopping to stare. "If you don't mind, I'm supposed to meet Nina at Charlene's." On the way, I explained what had happened, starting with Russ's murder and ending with tomato sauce and the suspicious cap from Dinner at Home.

"Russ Everett," mused Mars. "Do you know him, Bernie?"

"He's not a mate, but I know of him. Not in a good

way. Sometimes he comes into The Laughing Hound and sits around in the bar."

" 'Not in a good way'? What does that mean?" I asked.

"He's a lowlife."

That fit what Wolf had said. But I had trouble imagining what he was doing at Gerrie's. Had he intended to burglarize the house?

"Before I forget," said Bernie. "I'm trying something new at The Laughing Hound tomorrow evening for dinner. Can you fit it in? I'd like your opinion."

"I hope it doesn't involve pasta sauce," joked Mars.

When we reached Dinner at Home, Nina was already inside talking with Charlene, who shrieked when she saw me.

"Relax. It's just your tomato sauce. Irv must have fallen on it. It's all over the floor of the van."

Charlene blew air out of her mouth in relief. "Nina says she thinks Irv will be all right?"

"He probably has a concussion," I said.

"I can't imagine what happened. Why would anyone hit him over the head? He's such a sweet guy."

"Charlene," I said, "did Nina tell you that one of your Dinner at Home baseball caps was inside Gerrie Stansfield's house?"

Chapter 5

Dear Sophie,
My firefighter husband offered to cook a vat of tomato sauce for the firehouse. It's all over his favorite shirt. I know hydrogen peroxide works for bloodstains. Does it also get out tomato sauce stains?
Firefighter's Wife in Burnsville, Minnesota

Dear Firefighter's Wife,
Sadly, hydrogen peroxide doesn't work its magic on tomato sauce. If the garment is important to him, take it to a dry cleaner and let the professionals handle it. Otherwise, run water through the fabric, douse with detergent or stain remover, and rub with an ice cube. Spritz with vinegar, wash, and cross your fingers!

Sophie

Charlene managed a weak smile. "Maybe Irv gave her a hat."

"It was on her dining room floor, the table had been set for a luncheon," I pointed out.

"What are you getting at, Sophie? Are you trying to say that Irv went to Gerrie's house for some reason?" Furrows formed on Charlene's forehead. She tapped on a computer. "Gerrie wasn't on the delivery list."

"Then it's odd that the cap would be there."

She shrugged. "I don't see what difference it makes. So Gerrie had one of our hats. Lots of people have them."

She seemed to be getting irritated.

Mars broke the tension. "I have to get back to my meeting, now that I know Sophie isn't the walking dead. Bernie and I will be here at five forty-five. Does that work for you?"

"That's perfect. I lost a lot of business this afternoon, but I guess that's a fluke. I have someone who can help me out tomorrow and probably the next day."

Her face was flushed, and I wondered why. Of course, the heat in a kitchen could easily do that.

"But if Irv is out for longer, I'll have to find a new delivery person. Do any of you know someone who could use a delivery job?"

I thought I had said enough, and no one came to mind anyway. Besides, I had to hustle home. I hadn't counted on needing a shower before heading over to the convention hotel.

Charlene thanked Nina and me for making her deliveries and I headed for the door in a hurry. "Sorry, I'm in a bit of a rush." I walked home as fast as I could, ignoring the obvious stares at my *bloody* dress.

Daisy, my hound mix, wasn't fooled for one minute. She took a sniff and cocked her head, which made me laugh. "I'm going to change clothes as soon as you come back in."

While Daisy romped outside, Mochie, my ocicat, inspected me. He was supposed to have spots, but had the American shorthair markings of bracelets on his legs, necklaces on his chest, and bullseyes on his sides. He quickly turned his head away in disgust. One thing about cats, they do like cleanliness.

Daisy returned from my fenced yard rather quickly and I wasted no time hitting the shower. I had a very bad feeling that my dress would never recover. I wrapped it up and slid it into a plastic bag to drop off at the dry cleaner's.

After a shower, I dressed in business casual, navy trousers and a sleeveless white silk blouse, with a dropped bow at the neckline, I slid on comfy navy flats, checked to be sure I had everything I needed in my briefcase, and hoped I didn't reek of garlic anymore.

I fed Mochie and Daisy an early dinner because I didn't know exactly how long I would be gone, left a light on in the kitchen, and struck out for the hotel.

It wasn't close to my house, but one of the great things about Old Town was the walkability. I loved strolling along the sidewalks, enjoying the historic homes. I dropped off my dress on the way, assuring the dry-cleaning attendant that the stain was tomato sauce.

The hotel was almost on the outskirts of Old Town proper.

The attendees of the Association of Ghost Kitchens convention would be arriving tonight. At this point, my function was to make sure everything ran smoothly and according to plan.

At the hotel, I was pleased to see a sign directing participants to the registration area. My client, Colleen Stansfield, was already there, seated behind a table stacked with conference information and goodies. With her light-brown toffee-colored hair and burn-in-a-second complexion, she stood out. Two men were asking her questions, and I didn't want to interrupt. I waved to her, just to let her know I had arrived.

She glanced at her watch and called out to me, "Six o'clock at Oats and Ivy?"

I gave her a thumbs-up. I knew exactly what she meant. We could meet at the trendy restaurant across the way where we would be close by if anyone needed us. I guessed someone was filling in for her at that time.

Six o'clock came fast. I had resolved a couple of small problems, but it looked like most things were right on track. I left the hotel and could see Colleen's hair glowing in the sun before I crossed the street.

I joined her at an outdoor table. We ordered quickly and passed on wine with dinner, opting for iced tea instead.

"I presume you heard about Gerrie?" I asked.

"No. What happened? Is she okay?"

I filled her in on Russ's death.

The waitress brought our salads, beautifully topped with strips of grilled red salmon and portobello mushrooms. Black olives, charred red peppers, and rings of grilled onion had been scattered over the top. The dressing arrived in small bowls with miniature ladles.

Colleen stared at me, seemingly oblivious to the arrival of our food. Finally she breathed, "A man was murdered in her house? I can't even imagine going through something like that. I would have fallen apart. But nothing ever unnerves Gerrie. I bet she held her composure, didn't she?"

I thought about Gerrie and how she had offered her guests more to drink. "She was remarkably calm, given the situation, but I think she was shaken underneath."

"She never loses it. One Thanksgiving, a guest dropped a bottle of red wine. Glass flew everywhere. Shards hit two people, who bled, and that deep red liquid splattered all over the floor and an antique rug. You would have thought he did her a favor. She took it in stride. Other guests were making jokes about it happening because one ought to only serve white wine with turkey. But she cleaned it up and went on as though it had never happened."

"The world might be a better place if more people were that way." I added dressing to my salmon.

"Gerrie was a good mother-in-law. I guess I should say *is* because the divorce isn't final yet. I never had any of the problems with her that my friends complain about with their mothers-in-law. She was always very kind to me." Silent for a moment, she stared at her salad without touching it. "Was Todd there?"

I was certain she meant her soon-to-be ex-husband. "I didn't see him."

"I'll give Gerrie a call later." Colleen ate a bite of salmon. "I don't know if I could sleep in my home if someone had been murdered there. Gerrie will grit her teeth and tough it out. I swear she could climb Mount Everest in fake eyelashes and stilettos without blinking an eye and then cook and serve a gourmet dinner at the peak. But I'll ask if she would like to stay at my place for a few days. She loves her house, though. I don't know if even a murder could drag her away from it. A murder at the Stansfields'! It's inconceivable."

I toyed with my salad. "Do you know if Russ was an acquaintance of Gerrie's?"

Colleen speared an olive. "Gerrie knows everyone. No matter how many people you think you know, multiply that by a hundred. She is such a social butterfly. She has a finger dipped in everything. If you have a problem, call Gerrie. She'll make one phone call and everything will be taken care of."

"Sounds like she's more powerful than I thought. I knew she had the kitchen store and was involved with a lot of charities, but I didn't realize she had that kind of clout." I bit into a savory mushroom.

Colleen nodded thoughtfully. "Powerful. That's the right word. I knew her husband, Edwin, had that reputation. But Gerrie surprised me. Gerrie is just as effective as Edwin ever was, but she does it with a voice so soft and sweet, you'd think she was doing *you* a favor. It was a little bit intimidating marrying into the Stansfield family."

"What was Edwin like?"

"Ooof! Very stern. But he had a wicked sense of humor and was hysterically funny with my daughter, Penelope. I hadn't expected that. For some reason, we all left the room one day, leaving Edwin with Penelope, who must have been about two years old. Edwin was quite heavy, you know, but he got down on the floor with her to play. It was adorable. I had never seen that side of him. He was smitten with Penelope. I always felt that he was somewhat indifferent toward me, but he was a great pawpaw. Of course, getting him off the floor was a two-person maneuver. I used to find the two of them upstairs in his home office playing Candy Land or doing a jigsaw puzzle. She was his little shadow and he always had time for her. I have a photo of the two of them. He's in his home office chair, holding Penelope, and gazing out the window. She's fast asleep with her head leaning against his jowl. I'll always remember him that way."

"It's nice to hear that. Sometimes the very stoic types can be a little frosty. Is your husband like his dad?"

"Only when it comes to bourbon and beef, more precisely tomahawk steaks. Unfortunately, Todd didn't get his parents' fortitude. We used to joke about how he must have been swapped with another baby at the hospital."

I stopped eating. "You don't really have reason to believe that?"

"The fact that he looks just like his father pretty much ruins that theory!" she laughed. "His brother, Jim, is more like Edwin when it comes to intellect. He runs the family business, Moss Restaurant Supply. He's slender as a reed. A vegetarian who gardens and runs marathons. His idea of a fun vacation is flying to Africa to rescue baby elephants."

"Wow! Are you serious? He rescues them?"

Colleen nodded. "I don't know details, but I gather they're orphaned. Their mothers died or they were separated for some reason. He says they're very sweet animals."

"That doesn't sound like Gerrie or Edwin at all."

"Except for his job, he's not like anyone else in the family. But Edwin took every opportunity to point out Jim's success to Todd. I don't know why parents cannot comprehend that taunting one child with another child's accomplishments only breeds bitterness."

"Is Todd bitter? He always appears rather jolly to me."

Jolly was a kind word, though I had to admit he always seemed to be smiling. I had met Todd Stansfield socially, and generally tried to avoid the loud, boisterous man at parties.

"Amazing, isn't it? That's his default mode. It's probably the reason I fell in love with him. When Todd arrives, it's a party. He can talk to anyone. Inside of ten minutes, they're best buddies. But that good-natured, happy-go-lucky attitude comes with a downside. He's oblivious to dates, times, appointments, and obligations. He just takes life at his own speed, not dealing with anything until it's a crisis. His calmness and serenity appealed to me when we were dating. But it's difficult and incredibly frustrating to be married to someone like that. All the pressure to get things done landed on me. He grinned and ambled through life without a care, but I was overburdened and seething."

"I can imagine that would be hard," I said soothingly, and then in an attempt to change the subject, I added, "It looks like everything is going smoothly with the check-in at the convention."

"I'm so glad you suggested the meet-and-greet buffet. People who drove all day to get here are tired, and don't want to leave the hotel for a quick dinner. A lot of them came alone, so it's nice for them to find like-minded people to chat with over a light meal and drinks."

I nodded. "They're tired and they don't want to eat alone in a restaurant. This gives them an opportunity to meet other participants without any stress."

"I'm glad to have a moment away from them, though. It's exhausting."

"When only one or two people are running a convention, I like to pull them away for dinner on the day everyone checks into the hotel. It gives them a chance to relax and eat without constant interruptions. And it gives me a chance to go over last minute details with them. Have you seen your speakers for tomorrow?"

"Gack!" Colleen pulled a small notepad out of her purse. "Most of them are local. I should call them tonight to be sure they're all set. What else have I forgotten?"

"Don't worry. I'm sure everything will go smoothly. Before you know it, Sunday will arrive and they'll all be leaving. Relax and try to enjoy it."

Colleen did a double take when her daughter, a mini Colleen with matching toffee hair and freckles, ran up to our table and deposited a canvas bag on her mom's lap before dashing off.

"Penelope! Come back here." Colleen held up the bag on which was hand-painted, *Penelope, you make the world a better place.*

Penelope returned breathless and clearly annoyed. "What?"

"What are you doing here? I thought your father was picking you up."

Penelope sighed dramatically. "He never came. I called him, but he didn't answer, so when Alma's mom asked if I wanted to come with them for dinner, I said yes because there wasn't any point in bothering you. You said you were going to be at the hotel across the street. But this is even better. Now Dad can pick me up here."

Colleen's lips tightened. She wasn't happy about this, but waved at Alma's mother, Mrs. Benfield. "Did you reach him? He knows where to pick you up?"

"Uh-huh. I texted him."

"If he doesn't show by the time you're done eating, then call me and I will come across the street and get you. Do *not* deviate and do something with friends. Do you understand me? You stay here until your father or I come to get you."

She watched Penelope lope away. "She's twelve. It's a terrible age. Half the time, they're irrational, and the other half, they're like sensible adults." She glared at the bag she clutched. "Honestly, I can't count on Todd to do anything. It's his weekend with Penelope. He promised he wouldn't forget. The man thinks nothing has repercussions. He just laughs and schmoozes his way out of every situation, most of which he could have avoided in the first place if he had paid any attention at all."

Colleen held up the bag. "It *is* kind of cute. When you were a kid, did you receive a personalized bag every time you went to a slumber party? I had four brothers and sisters. I can promise you that none of us ever received anything like this." She pulled out contents as she spoke. "Oh great," she groaned. "More glittering green nail polish. Cookies, a book." She waved it at me. "Aww, Nancy Drew! Doesn't that take you back?" She set it on the table. "And a T-shirt and matching mug that say 'I am perfect just the way I am.'"

I heard her, but the cookies had drawn my attention. I picked them up. They looked exactly like the ones that had been on Gerrie's dining room table. Two cookies were packaged in a robin's-egg–blue paper box with a small cellophane window, so the cookies were visible. On the top, in a cursive gold font, were the words *Natasha's Cookies*. Farther down the box, it said, *My promise to you. They're still warm from my oven!*

The box didn't feel warm. I flipped it over and found a link to my Natasha's website, confirming that they weren't from some other Natasha. I handed the box back to Colleen, a little stunned by Natasha's new business venture.

Colleen plunged her fork into her salad as if it were the enemy. "I can't wait until the summer is officially over and they're back in school. My husband will hear about this. I fail to understand why he is unable to be a responsible father."

Chapter 6

Dear Natasha,
So many cookie recipes use "softened" butter. How do I soften it? Does that mean I should melt it?
                    Perplexed in Baker City, Oregon

Dear Perplexed,
Don't melt the butter unless the recipe calls for melted butter. The best way to soften butter is to leave it out on the counter 30 to 45 minutes. Cutting it into smaller cubes can speed it up. Some people place a warm, dry container over the top of it.
                    Natasha

This wasn't the sort of conversation I usually had with my clients. My business lunches were rarely this personal. I tried to brighten her mood. "Penelope looks just like you."

"Incredible, isn't it? The power of genes."

Colleen took a big bite of her salad, and I jumped on the opportunity to bring her back to the subject of our business, the first convention of the Association of Ghost

Kitchens, which was beginning in the morning. I was about to speak when Colleen gasped.

I looked over at her daughter, seated at another table. She seemed okay.

"You know Natasha, don't you?" asked Colleen.

Oh no. What now?

"What if she came to the banquet on Saturday night as a surprise guest star? I didn't know she had a cookie delivery business. That qualifies as a ghost kitchen, doesn't it?"

It probably did. In my wildest imagination, I could not see Natasha baking cookies as orders came in. But being a guest star was right up her alley.

"I can ask her."

Colleen smiled. "Isn't life interesting? If Todd had picked up Penelope, like he was supposed to, we wouldn't have known about Natasha's business in time to get her to make an appearance at the convention!"

I swallowed hard. I hoped Natasha wouldn't have a conflict. She thrived on attention, so maybe she would jump at the chance if I put it to her that way.

After we polished off slices of lemon meringue pie, an end of summer indulgence, I paid the check and left Colleen to deal with her daughter.

I crossed the street to the hotel and checked in with the event manager to be sure there weren't any problems. Before heading home, I peeked in the meet-and-greet room. To my surprise, Colleen's husband, Todd, was there schmoozing with some people.

There was no mistaking him. The best word to describe him was *slob*. I felt guilty for thinking that, but there was something slovenly about him. Maybe it was the unkempt hair that fell onto his forehead. Or the way his sport coat didn't fit right and hung open exposing his ample abdomen. Or the sneakers he wore with suit trousers. I decided it was actually the way he stood and held himself. While the people around him were equally tall and similarly attired, Todd slouched in an easygoing way. He held a drink in one hand and the other hand was in a pocket.

He chatted easily with another man, whose hair was the color of coffee grounds. It tousled on his head. His beard and mustache looked like he hadn't shaved in a couple of days, but maybe that was intentional. It was the trend.

Todd raised his drink to me, then motioned to his friend. Todd ambled toward me in a decidedly casual manner, giving the impression that he was at ease. His friend followed along. "Sophie Winston, party planner extraordinaire, this is Dale Mancini, my girlfriend's brother."

I had rarely been introduced with that kind of flattery. It was so over the top that it sounded phony. I reached out to shake Dale's hand.

"Hi." Dale briefly took my hand into his, then shoved aviator sunglasses up on his head. In that moment, his shirtsleeve pulled back, revealing a Figaro link silver bracelet.

"Everybody is ordering in," said Todd. "I think we're at the beginning of a new way of life. It could be very profitable for people who jump on board now."

I wanted to mention how fortunate he was to have Colleen as a resource, but decided that might be rude in front of his girlfriend's brother. "The conference is timed perfectly, then."

"Actually," said Todd, "I wanted to thank you for being so nice to my mom. She's had a rough time since Dad died. She said you were a big help today."

"Gerrie's a lovely person. We just need to figure out who killed Russ so she can put that behind her."

"What a crazy thing. Mom's pretty shaken up about it. I am, too!"

I longed to ask him more about Russ, but the assistant manager of the hotel interrupted us regarding a minor issue.

I said goodbye to Todd and Dale and followed the assistant manager.

We resolved the issue in short order, but I didn't see Todd anywhere and thought it best to head home, since I would have an early morning.

It was still daylight when I left the hotel. I ambled home, enjoying the quaint Federal-style buildings lining the sidewalks. My own house bore an oval plaque designating it a historic building. I passed it on my way to Natasha's house, which was decidedly Federal on the outside, but she preferred a modern interior.

I knocked on her door.

Natasha swung it open, holding her phone to her ear. She walked away from me. I assumed she meant for me to enter.

I closed the door behind me and followed her into the living room. It had never been more lovely. Natasha's spare modern aesthetic blended beautifully with the antique pieces favored by her mom and her father's second wife, whom she occasionally called her *other mother*.

Natasha's father had left Charlene and her mother in much the same way he had treated Natasha and her mom. Oddly enough, the mothers had found kindred spirits in one another, and the three women had moved in with Natasha. She hadn't been happy about it, but their financial contribution saved Natasha from having to sell her house.

The abrupt departure of her father when we were seven years old had shaped Natasha more than anything else in her life. She strived to be the best at everything and longed to be famous. My mother thought it was to prove to her father that she was worthy. I hoped that wasn't the case because that would be too sad. But maybe Mom was right. She was still looking for her father and hadn't come to terms with his abandonment of them.

We had competed at everything as children. Everything except the beauty pageants she loved. She was tall and willowy, with a slender figure that showed off clothes like a model.

In contrast, I was short and liked to eat, probably too much for my own good. I honestly didn't know how she could pass up pasta and pastries.

Natasha had a local TV show about all things domestic. But nothing was enough for her. She longed to be a star.

Natasha swung around toward me and lowered the phone. "To what do I owe this visit?"

She wore a lime-green sleeveless sheath that looked as if someone had splashed bright yellow and orange slashes of paint on it. Her nails were perfectly manicured, and her shoes matched the orange in her dress. They had heels that could double for daggers in an emergency. Why hadn't *she* been out there making deliveries for her desperate half sister?

"I have a favor to ask of you."

"No."

"You don't know what it is!"

"I don't do favors. They're always a waste of time and never have any benefit for *me*."

How stupid of me. I knew better than to approach her that way. At least she had been honest. I changed my tactic. "That's too bad. I need a local celebrity for a dinner Saturday evening at that new hotel on the west side of town."

I pulled out my phone and looked through my contacts. "I'm sure I can find someone else. Maybe Jack Lapine, that new anchor on Channel Four."

"Ugh. Not *him*! You didn't mention what it was for."

I tried not to grin and moved on to another subject. "Hey, congratulations on your cookie business."

Her mood changed immediately. "You heard about that? You know Mariah Carey has a similar business."

"In Old Town?"

"Hers is all over the country. Mine is only in Old Town so far, but I'm in discussions about expanding."

"Does Charlene bake your cookies?"

She threw me an appalled look and immediately stumbled. She grabbed my arm and regained her balance. "Shh. She doesn't know about it. Our mothers will be furious with me when they find out that I didn't keep the business in the family, but it's much more difficult to deal with family members when it comes to business matters. What if I had to fire her? What if she wasn't getting the cookies there on time or they didn't taste right? I couldn't take that chance."

She was right about that. Not only about the difficulties of doing business with family, but also about their mothers being upset when they found out Natasha had hired someone else to bake her cookies. "Who is baking them?"

"Trade secret."

"Is that the name of the bakery? I've never heard of them."

"It's a trade secret. I wouldn't expect you to understand. You're not involved in the hip new world of ghost kitchens."

She might have a point. I was well acquainted with caterers in our area, but not necessarily the people behind all the new delivery-only kitchens.

"So, what would I have to do?" she asked.

"Oh," I said nonchalantly. "You mean the appearance at the dinner. Never mind. I'll call Wendy Schultz. She loves making public appearances." Natasha had resented Wendy ever since she lost a cooking competition to her.

"Wendy?" Natasha wrinkled her nose. "I'm not usually

available on Saturday nights, but maybe I can shift something around."

I followed her into her home office.

Natasha flipped open an appointment calendar and
quickly snapped it closed. But not before I saw that the
page for Saturday didn't have a single thing on it.

"What time should I be there?"

"I would love for you to attend the dinner. Cocktails are
at six and dinner will be served at seven. In fact, it might
be fun to have packets of your cookies served with
dessert." Now I had her interest. "It's a ghost kitchen conference, so they would love to hear you talk about your
cookie business."

She scowled at me. "I'm not telling them any of my secrets."

"I wouldn't expect you to. You could talk about your
branding, how you selected your packaging, any number
of things. They'll be fascinated."

"All right," she said without any enthusiasm. "I'm in."

I thanked her and headed home. The late dusk of summer had descended on Old Town. Streetlights were flick-
ing on.

Daisy and Mochie greeted me at the kitchen door. I
picked up Mochie and carried him outside in the warm
summer night while Daisy ran around the backyard.
When we went inside, I gave each of them a snack and
checked my phone messages. Several people had phoned
to ask if I was all right. Apparently, word of my "bloody"
dress had gotten around town. I returned the calls and
headed to bed early, anticipating a busy day on Friday.

I relived the discovery of Russ's body in my dreams that
night. I sat up abruptly before dawn, remembering the
knife handle. There was no point in going back to sleep.

At six in the morning, I was dressed in a simple coral sheath, eating oatmeal with brown sugar, when Mars arrived.

He wore shorts and a burgundy Commanders T-shirt. "I heard someone would like to spend the weekend with me."

Daisy waggled her hind end, thrilled to see him. He slid her halter over her head. "My phone rang off the hook last night with people asking about you. Apparently, they thought you were in the hospital or dead."

"Aww. It was nice of them to call."

"I assured them you were not a victim."

"You'd think the fact that I didn't collapse on the sidewalk would have made people realize that I was okay."

His mouth twitched to the side. "I can't really blame them. You *have* been injured before. What is it you're doing today?"

"A ghost kitchen convention. It's just for the weekend. They'll be heading home on Sunday."

"Should I stop in to check on Mochie?"

"Good grief, Mars. I'll be right here at the new hotel on the west side. You make it sound like I'm flying to Italy."

He massaged Daisy's ears. "We'll have a good time, won't we, Daisykins?"

Thankfully, Daisy was eager to get going on a walk. She tugged at her leash and stood before the door impatiently. Mars took her not-so-subtle hint and the two of them were off.

When Mars and I divorced, neither of us could bear to give up Daisy, so we agreed to share her. Our arrangement had turned out to be handy, especially when one of us left town. I had acquired Mochie post divorce, but Mars and Bernie were usually happy to check in on him and feed him.

I poured myself a second cup of tea, fed Mochie a can of shrimp-in-aspic cat food, and got ready to leave.

It was a beautiful summer day. The sun shone in a clear blue sky, holding the promise of a scorcher in the afternoon.

At the hotel, I checked in with the events manager to be sure no issues had arisen during the night. All had gone well. Apparently, ghost kitchen types were not a rowdy bunch.

I headed for the ballroom, where the participants would be listening to experts talk about how to start a ghost kitchen and the various options available. I recognized the first speaker and stopped briefly to greet him. There wasn't any sign of Colleen, though.

I checked the time. She wasn't late yet, but I was surprised that she hadn't arrived early. She had been on the ball with all the arrangements, and this seemed out of character for her. Maybe she and Todd had a last-minute spat about Penelope, and she'd had to drive her daughter somewhere for the day.

Minutes slipped by. I wrote a quick welcome and introduction of the speaker. With only five minutes to go, the room was packed. I walked up to the podium and made sure the microphone was working. I tapped it and asked, "Can you hear me in the back?"

People in the back waved their hands and nodded. Great. But where was Colleen?

Chapter 7

Dear Natasha,
My husband wants me to accompany him to a con-
vention next week. Yawwwn. Would it be wrong to
do some shopping with his credit card?
Wicked Wife in Goldsboro, North Carolina

Dear Wicked Wife,
That's what I would do.

Natasha

I had no choice. At the stroke of nine, I spoke into the microphone. "Welcome to the first convention of the Association of Ghost Kitchens! Thank you for coming. We
have a full and fascinating schedule planned for you. I
hope you enjoy it and get a lot out of the sessions. I'm Sophie Winston, your convention coordinator. If you have
any problems with your accommodations, please let me
know. In the packet you received at registration, you will
have noticed a yellow slip with a lunch menu selection on
it. If you have not done so yet, please fill it out and slip it
into the blue box in the rear." I paused for a moment as

they looked through their registration information. "Don't panic if you left it in your room. There is a stack of additional ones beside the box. I'll be collecting them shortly to make the lunch arrangements, so please be sure you fill them out. And now, I am pleased to present Rick Hafferty, the owner and developer of more than forty ghost kitchens. He's going to explain the basic forms of ghost kitchens and how they differ."

Rick Hafferty must have loved public speaking because he took to the podium with energy and engaged the audience immediately. Not everyone had the talent to do that.

Meanwhile, I hurried back to my box to tally the lunch votes. Colleen had come up with the idea of putting the participants through the experience of being a ghost kitchen customer. I had designed the yellow slips to look like a menu. All the participants had to do was add their names, place check marks, and slide them into the box. I would order the desired lunches from local ghost kitchens to be delivered to the hotel. They would have a chance to see and compare packaging, as well as the presentation of the contents.

I relaxed a little bit. I had fifty minutes before the next speaker. Still, I couldn't help wondering about Colleen. This was her big event. Where was she? I left the conference room, walked through the lobby, and strode out into the sunshine to call her. Her phone rolled over to voicemail. "Hi, Colleen. It's Sophie checking on you. The conference is under way. I'm worried because you haven't arrived yet. Give me a call to let me know you're okay."

I hoped nothing was wrong with Penelope. I went inside, ordered a latte, and sat down to compile the lunch orders. When I had placed all the orders, I explained to the bellman what was going on and handed him a hefty tip. "And this"—I said, giving him more cash—"is to tip the delivery people."

I returned to the conference room, where Rick was explaining that an existing restaurant could boost income by setting up a ghost kitchen business under another name and make the food in their restaurant kitchen. It was a restaurateur's dream come true. It would produce more income, but the overhead costs increased very little because they already had the kitchen and the staff.

He wrapped up with ghost kitchen franchises, which sounded to me like what Natasha was doing. The owner took care of the marketing, but made deals with other ghost kitchens to prepare their food. Companies that handled the details had already sprung up as well.

At that time, I was standing by with the second speaker. As I gazed out over the attendees, it dawned on me that Todd wasn't present, either.

While I introduced the second speaker, Colleen rushed in through a door in the back and Todd sidled in through another. Colleen's pale face was flushed red. She threw a nasty glance at Todd, who grinned at her. His friend Dale motioned to him and picked up his belongings off a seat, as though he had saved it for Todd.

Handing the microphone over to the speaker, I stepped away from the podium and strode toward Colleen. We left the conference room to talk.

"Where have you been?"

Colleen closed her eyes and gently massaged her forehead. "The police took us in for questioning. Guess what? They really don't care if you are supposed to be running a conference." An angry look crossed her face. "They seem to think I know who killed Russ!"

"And do you?"

"Are you kidding? Of course not. I don't know the first thing about it."

But I noted that she spoke without conviction and glanced around as though afraid Todd might overhear.

"Where is Penelope?"

"With my mother. It was awful, Sophie. They treated us like common criminals."

I tried to cheer her up. "Well, the good news here is that everything got off to a splendid start. Lunch has been ordered and should begin to arrive fairly soon."

"Thank goodness I hired you. Can you imagine what would have happened if I hadn't shown up and there was no one to step in? I shudder to imagine."

The bellman, a friendly fellow whose name tag identified him as Gus, rolled a three-tier food service cart toward us. One small bag with the words *Wing It* sat alone on the top.

Colleen peered at the bag. "I guess we know now which is the fastest food joint around here."

Gus laughed. "Hmm, wonder if that speed could have anything to do with the fact that it was prepared right here in the hotel kitchen?"

At that exact moment, no less than five delivery people walked in. Gus accepted the food and I checked them off on my list.

In short order, all except two had arrived. Having foreseen that possibility after Irv's incident the day before, I had ordered extras of the most popular items. We would probably have leftovers.

Attendees emerged from the ballroom and migrated to another room, which had been set up for lunch. They gathered at round tables set with white tablecloths, plates, cutlery, and glasses. Due to the packaging of their meals, which they would likely want to discuss and compare, Colleen had opted to skip centerpieces so there would be more room available on the tabletops.

Colleen called out names and handed each participant the lunch that person had requested. She strolled through the room, with the microphone, as if it were second nature to her, asking each table to vote on the best and worst packaging and presentation.

Breathing a sigh of relief that the unusual luncheon was working out well, I nabbed one of the extra lunches and slipped out of the room to have a bite myself. I had only made it to the middle of the lobby when I saw Gerrie enter the hotel.

"Sophie!" Gerrie hurried toward me. "Just the person I was looking for. I need to speak with you. Can you take a break?"

"Sure. Is something wrong?" I was surprised to see her. I didn't think she would seek me out in the middle of a conference unless something was very, very wrong.

Gerrie didn't hesitate. "Yes."

"Give me a second." I popped back inside and grabbed a couple more of the extra lunches. "Where would you like to eat?"

"Eat?" She gazed at the bags I held. "Someplace private, where we won't be overheard."

Good luck with that. "How about outside?"

We walked toward a dog park where I liked to take Daisy, and found a bench in the cool shade of a tree with a view of the Potomac River.

"Colleen called me last night to check on me. She told me you were handling the conference. I hope you don't mind taking a break to talk to me."

"Perfect timing," I said. When we sat down, I explained Colleen's clever luncheon idea. The participants could learn what they did and didn't want to do from their own experience with a ghost kitchen lunch. "These are extras that I ordered in case one of the companies didn't come through. Burger, mac and cheese, or pulled pork sandwich?"

Gerrie gazed out over the water and sucked in a deep breath of air. "The police think I killed Russ."

I had expected as much. After all, it appeared that she was the only one in her house at the time that he died. Unless she had some wild tale of a home invasion with multiple people involved, the police would have to consider her a prime suspect. "Did they arrest you?"

"Not yet. Alex German says to expect it. He asked Wolf to give me the courtesy of allowing me to turn myself in if we reach that point. I have been saddled with the dreaded moniker *a person of interest*."

I had dated Alex German. He was widely regarded as an ace criminal attorney. If he thought she was going to be arrested, then it was very likely. At least she was in good legal hands.

"Burger," said Gerrie. "And it better be juicy and full of fat. Stuff the stupid cholesterol! Too many burgers are mostly bun and lettuce."

I handed her the bag with the hamburger, extra paper napkins, and an all-natural lemon soda in a bottle. "Do they have an estimate on the time of death yet?"

"I'm told there's a two-hour window, starting two hours before Mindy noticed him. Frankly, I think that's to cover their tails. It's inconceivable to me that he lay there dying for two hours and never uttered a sound. I thought everyone had left the house. I was in and out of the dining room getting things ready. I would have noticed him or tripped over him." She took a big bite of the burger, careful to catch the drips in a napkin. "Not bad," she muttered.

I bit into the pulled pork sandwich, which proved to be surprisingly good.

Gerrie took a sip of the lemon drink and swallowed hard. "This hits the spot. I eat when I'm anxious. Always have. Edwin used to catch me in the kitchen gobbling sweets. 'Gerrie,' he'd say, 'what's wrong?' I never could hide it from him. He always knew when I was upset. Did this come with fries?" She poked in the bag.

I scooted down a bit, spread out two napkins, and laid out all the food I had brought.

She nabbed a couple of French fries and then finished her hamburger. Holding the French fry container in her hand, she nibbled at one, pausing briefly to say, "I need your help, Sophie. I don't know how long I'll be free to amble about. And I'm not sure what to do next."

I had been through this sort of thing before and knew she didn't need my event-planning skills. "I'm not a—"

"Lawyer. No problem there. Alex is taking care of the legalities. I'm sorry if that's uncomfortable for you. I know you dated him and broke up, but Edwin always said he would go to Alex if he was in trouble."

"You're in good hands then."

"I'm sure Alex is great at the legal end of things. Did you know that he recommends you? He says you have an unusual approach to murder. Sophie, you can imagine that I did not invite Russ to my house yesterday. I think Russ came to kill us."

Goose bumps rose on my arms. I tried not to scooch away from her, though she seemed sort of dumbstruck. Gerrie gazed at the river, nibbling French fries like a rabbit with a carrot.

"Why do you think that?" I asked in a gentle voice.

"There has been bad blood between our families for decades. When I was about Penelope's age, I came home from school one day to find my mother very upset. My dad was upstairs in his office with his business partner, Mr. Everett."

It caught my attention that the business partner had the same surname as Russ.

"When Mr. Everett left, he paused in the foyer and stared at me. For a long time, he didn't say a word. Just looked at me with an intense stare. He had eyes like Russ's. And then he said, 'You are not through with me, young lady. This day will return to haunt you.'"

Chapter 8

Dear Sophie,
My husband's mother passed away and left every-thing to my husband. I think we should give her jewelry to our granddaughter, who dearly loved her great-grandmother. My husband thinks we should keep it in case there are more grandchildren. What do you think?
Loving Grannie in Silver City, New Mexico

Dear Loving Grannie,
Compromise. Give your granddaughter a special piece or two, but hold back a few pieces. If there are no more grandchildren, then you can give them to her as gifts on special occasions. If there are more grandchildren, you can decide how you would like to distribute them when they are an appropriate age.
Sophie

Gerrie's chest heaved, and her fingers trembled as she ate another French fry.

"Oh, that's just nonsense," I said.

"My mom was horrified and told me that if I ever saw Mr. Everett again, I was to run away from him as fast as I could. Later that day, I asked Dad why Mom was afraid of Mr. Everett. He said to me, 'Geraldine, no matter who you meet in your life, I want you to assume the best about them. Most of the people in this world are kind. But there will be some who will cheat you. They will take advantage of your good nature. They will have evil in their hearts. Mr. Everett is such a man.' I asked him why Mr. Everett was his partner if he was a terrible person. It turned out that Mr. Everett was skimming money out of the business. Dad gave him a choice. Dad could go to the police or, if Mr. Everett left the business quietly, then Dad wouldn't say a thing. You can imagine which one Everett took. Dad dropped the Everett name from the business and called it Moss Restaurant Supply. Every once in a while, Mr. Everett would show up at our house with some sad tale of woe. Dad never believed his stories, but generally gave him some cash so he would go away. He had a son about my age, Russ's father. We went to the same school and my mom would see him there. Our business was booming, but we were hearing reports of Mr. Everett conducting illegal activities. He landed in jail for defrauding people. No surprise there, I suppose. His son was looking thin and shabby, which troubled my mom, so she arranged for food and clothes to be brought to Mrs. Everett. Mom didn't want her to feel obligated or to have reason to turn it away, so it was all done through the church."

"Wow. Your mother sounds like an amazing person."

"She was so sad. They would have been thriving like we were if Mr. Everett Senior had been an honest man. Unfortunately, that boy wasn't much better. He married a lovely woman, though, who was a wonderful mother to Russ. Unfortunately, Russ's father fell into the footsteps of his grandfather. His mother had a good position at the golf club, which was a blessing for Russ. He had one foot squarely in his mother's world, but the other foot was still firmly in the crooked world of his father. Dad and Jim hired Russ a while back, but after a couple of years, Russ quit."

"Your family has been very kind to them. Why would you think Russ meant to kill you?"

Gerrie looked weary when she said, "You're seeing it from our perspective. Put yourself in their shoes. Compared to them, we have everything. And they want to believe that it's our fault that life has been a struggle for them. The resentment has simmered through three generations, and this is the result. I had such high hopes for little Russ."

"But, Gerrie, if Russ came to kill you, then it was self-defense." No sooner had I spoken than I realized that was wrong. That Gerrie was wrong. Perhaps not completely, there probably was resentment on the part of many Everetts who imagined what their lives might have been like if the original one hadn't tried to steal from the business.

But there was a huge flaw in the self-defense idea. In fact, in the notion that Russ had come with malice in mind. He hadn't brought a weapon. Not unless it had been hidden somewhere.

"It was my chef's knife. It came from my kitchen." Tears rolled down her face. "I have considered turning myself in now, before I'm arrested."

"What? Are you saying that you killed Russ?"

Gerrie faced me, but her gaze darted around like she was confused. "What if I didn't? Then, then it would mean—"

"That one of your sons murdered Russ."

Gerrie whispered, "I couldn't bear that." Her chin trembled. "They have their whole lives ahead of them. Todd has to be there for Penelope. And Jim hasn't even married and started a family yet." Gerrie whispered again, "That's where you come in. We can't let that happen."

"Oh, Gerrie!" How could I put this? "I don't . . . cover things up. I look for the truth."

Gerrie opened her purse and frowned. She pulled out a folded sheet of paper and tissues. She dabbed her tearstained face with a tissue, then unfolded the paper. As she looked at it, she placed trembling fingers over her mouth.

"Gerrie? What's wrong?"

She handed me the long document. It was Edwin's death certificate.

Gerrie sniffled hard. "I did not put that in my purse."

I tried to sound kind. "Maybe you forgot."

"I'm a widow now and I miss my husband terribly, but I haven't lost my mind. They told me to order additional death certificates—"

"Who is they?"

"The funeral home. They said all kinds of places would ask for one and that proved to be true. I keep them in a file in my desk, where I can find them easily. But I did not put this in my purse. Why would I bring it along to meet with you?"

"Habit? Maybe you tucked it in this purse a month ago and forgot about it."

She shook her head ever so slightly. But she wasn't crying anymore. "It's a sign. Someone put it in there."

I doubted that. Her life had been topsy-turvy since her husband's death. In the nicest voice I could muster, I tried to reason with her. "Why would anyone do that?"

"I don't know. To make me think I've lost my mind? To

remind me of Edwin's demise so I'll be upset? I need your help, Sophie. I don't have anyone to turn to for help now. Dad and Edwin were my rocks. They were so much alike. The kind of men people didn't want to disappoint. They unintentionally intimidated people. But the truth was that they were forgiving. They understood the frailties of man. I never knew either of them to hold a grudge or be unfair or unkind. Quite the contrary, they went out of their way to help people. But now they're gone, and it's just me. And this time, I don't know what to do."

"Wolf is a good guy. He'll be looking for the murderer and won't jump to conclusions. I'm not a professional, Gerrie. I'm not even a private investigator."

"Sophie, please! I can't have some stranger tromping through our house trying to trick family members into confessing to murder."

It was natural for her to be a mama bear and want to protect her family. "Gerrie, I'll be here for you. But it will mean considering unpleasant possibilities. Was anyone else at your house that day besides the women you had invited?"

She paused for a few seconds before answering me, as though she was being careful about what she said. "Todd moved in with us when he and Colleen split up. We all agreed that it would be best if Penelope stayed in the home she knew and loved. That way, she would experience less emotional upheaval. I'm sure you understand. Same school, same friends, same neighborhood. There's no question that she misses her father, but keeping everything as stable as possible for Penelope was our priority."

I stared out at the water. Had I understood that correctly? It struck me as curious that Gerrie had been involved in housing decisions for her son's family. Wasn't that something Todd and Colleen would have decided? Of course, I could imagine that Colleen had been delighted about being able to stay in her home.

I gazed at Gerrie. She'd managed to avoid my question. I was more specific. "Was Todd home yesterday morning?"

Gerrie crumpled the empty French fry sleeve and searched the remaining items. "Want to split the mac and cheese?"

"It's all yours."

Gerrie tasted it with a disposable fork. "It's okay. Not as good as mine, but it will do." She took a couple of bites before saying, "Except for Penelope, who was at a slumber party, the whole family was there at some point."

"Even your other son, Jim?"

Gerrie nodded. "I selected some of Edwin's belongings that I thought Jim and Todd would appreciate. Watches, cuff links, mementoes, that sort of thing. Both of them spent the night at the house. Jim lives in Old Town, but I understand they carried on a bit after I went up to bed. I like to encourage that because they haven't been close as adults. When your parents pass, the only people who really understand what you're going through are your siblings. Apparently, it got so late that Jim slept in his old bedroom. Colleen dropped by in the morning because Edwin wanted Penelope to have his mother's wedding ring and"—she flicked her hand—"other pieces of her jewelry. They're a bit too valuable and mature for Penelope now, so I thought it best to give them to Colleen. That way—" Gerrie stopped abruptly. "Yes, we were all there yesterday morning, coming and going."

" 'That way' what?"

Gerrie finished the mac and cheese. "That way, if something happened to me, they would be safely in Colleen's possession."

She didn't trust her sons! Or perhaps, more specifically, she trusted Colleen more than Todd or Jim. I twisted to face her and held out a generously iced cookie. "Gerrie, I've known you for a long time. And that is probably why I think you're holding something back."

She reached for the cookie, but I withdrew my hand.

"Gerrie! Are you concerned that you're in danger? Is that why you said Russ came to kill you? Or do you know something more?"

Chapter 9

Dear Sophie,
My husband is bonkers about our kitchen knives.
No putting them in the dishwasher and they must
hang from a magnetic rack. Now that we have chil-
dren who run through the kitchen at warp speed
with their friends, I don't like the knives on the wall.
Isn't there another way to keep them sharp and out
of sight?
Cautious Mom in Knife River, Montana

Dear Cautious Mom,
Knives can be safely stored away in drawer inserts.
Sophie

Gerrie snatched the cookie before replying, "Russ was murdered in my home with a knife from *my* kitchen! Why was he there? Who stabbed him? Why use my knife? I'm sure he didn't plunge that dagger into his own chest. You better believe I'm worried about my safety. About our safety. I had mixed feelings about Todd moving in, but now I'm glad he's there with me, most nights anyway."

"Oh?" I was trying to be polite.

She waved the remaining three-quarters of the cookie in her hand. "He has a girlfriend. I don't know if she was the cause of the separation. I'm not sure I want to know. Except for whatever is necessary for Penelope's welfare, I'm trying to stay out of it. He's a grown man and it's all the more difficult because I like Colleen so much. She worked for me at one time, you know. We grew quite close. Honestly, it makes me terribly sad for the two of them and especially for darling Penelope." She took a long drag of her lemon soda.

She nibbled at the cookie, then moaned, "I don't know what's happening to us, Sophie. On the day of Edwin's funeral, we had a huge reception. When we went home, I thought it would be my sons and me, Colleen, of course, and Penelope. Just immediate family. But people kept coming by, bringing casseroles and flowers. Total strangers! I'm sure I was supposed to know them. Maybe they were customers of Moss Restaurant Supply or maybe some were Edwin's clients, but the house was teeming with people, just when I longed for the close comfort of my family. If Todd's girlfriend attended the funeral, I don't know about it. I asked him not to include her, as a courtesy to Colleen, and for Penelope's sake. She'll find out soon enough. I think the least we can do is spread out the blows. Losing her grandfather was devastating. At any rate, I thought that day would never end. It felt like the longest day of my life. That evening, after everyone but family departed, we realized some things were awry. It wasn't that items were missing. They just weren't exactly where we'd left them. It was as if someone had been nosing around in our private possessions."

"I don't suppose you called the police?"

Gerrie sighed. "I thought about it. But there were loads of people in the house. And since nothing seemed to be missing, what would we say? Someone moved things? That's hardly a crime."

"You should tell Wolf anyway. It may help narrow down the list of suspects." If Gerrie was right and someone had been looking for something, it had to be an item that person couldn't ask for. And now, there was the possibility that it was an item so important that someone might have killed Russ for it. Maybe that was actually the good news for Gerrie. Maybe the killer had found the item and left with it.

"Did you notice anything missing yesterday?"

Gerrie shook her head. "I don't know what we would have that anyone would want. Watches, jewelry, a few paintings, and collectibles, the same sort of things you'd find in most homes in Old Town. Edwin and I were comfortable, but not the types to buy original Picassos. Edwin liked to call himself low maintenance. He didn't need the latest thing." Gerrie wiped under her eyes with her bare fingers. "I know some people found him to be intimidating and gruff, but he was a wonderful husband and father. And the best grandfather anyone could ask for!"

"Was he ever involved with the restaurant supply business?"

"Edwin worked there summers, when he wasn't in school. That was how I met him. My father and mother put their all into Moss Restaurant Supply. I practically grew up in the warehouses. They expanded it around the Capital Beltway and up toward Baltimore. My dad loved Edwin, who put himself through law school. I worked for Moss for years and then spun off a retail store for home kitchens."

I smiled. "The Sugar Bowl! One of my favorite places to shop."

"I still love it. You'd think I would have grown tired of china, crystal, and cookware, but it's so much fun. I even love tablecloths. I suppose that makes me sadly old-fashioned, but I do enjoy a pretty home."

I'd known Gerrie for years, but most of our dealings centered around charities and events. I hadn't known much about her family and their businesses. "I understand Jim is running the restaurant supply business?"

Gerrie beamed. "Our eldest. He was named after my father. Dad could have retired once Jim took over, but he still went to work every day. The store was my dad's baby. He thrived on being there. Hearing the gossip, greeting old customers, and helping out are what kept him going. He never missed a day. Dad lived a long life. I was a late baby for their time. My parents were in their thirties when they had me."

Gerrie gasped. "Good grief. They were the age of my boys now! We thought Todd was too young to have a child when Colleen became pregnant, but our sweet Penelope brings such joy to our lives. Funny how things work out, isn't it? Edwin was so smart in the way he handled the boys. By the time they came along, we were financially comfortable. They usually had summer jobs in the stores, but when they finished college, Edwin insisted they do something else. Not graduate school, not working at the family business. They could pursue whatever interested them, within reason, of course. It had to pay their expenses, but it could not have anything to do with kitchens or restaurants. The week after Jim graduated from college, he flew to Namibia to help save elephants. He spent two years there before returning to attend law school, just like his dad. But when he graduated, he went into the family business with my father. Jim was a natural at it, just like Dad. Todd, on the other hand, lived at home and specialized in the Washington, DC, nightclub scene until Edwin lost his patience. Then he joined the most dreadful band you can imagine as the drummer and traveled around the country with them. Thankfully, for all of mankind, the band disintegrated somewhere in Arizona and Todd limped home in what was left of their van."

Gerrie laughed at the memory. "That thing smelled like dirty socks and looked like it had been through a few battles. Todd went to work at Moss, like his brother did, but he hated it. There was a big confrontation between Jim and Todd, which resulted in Todd quitting. The two of them are still touchy and working through their issues, but I have no worries about that. They're coming around."

"What is Todd doing now?" I finished the last of my lemon soda.

Gerrie shrugged. "Looking for a new job. My heart goes out to him. Nothing has been a good fit. I was hopeful when he sold life insurance, but that didn't work out. Then he worked at a car dealership. After that, there was . . . Good heavens, I don't even remember them all anymore."

"I hope he'll finally find something he enjoys."

"He was always the kid who made everyone laugh. *With* him, *not* at him. Low-key, relaxed. Never on time, always moseying along at his own pace. It makes for a lousy employee. It would drive me up a wall if I couldn't count on my employees to show up on time. But that's Todd. He says he'll arrive in thirty minutes, and he turns up four hours later. The worst part is that he doesn't appear to see anything wrong with that. I love him to bits, but he has no sense of time and never feels anything is urgent. He told me he was working on a new idea again. I honestly don't know anything about it. What with Edwin's heart attack and subsequent death, I haven't been concentrating on Todd and his issues."

I suspected I knew what Todd was considering. I hoped a ghost kitchen would work out for him.

"You will help me, won't you?"

"Of course. I'll do what I can."

Gerrie whispered, "Thank you, Sophie."

A breeze fluffed her hair into her face. She brushed it back. "I am completely clueless. I thought focusing on A Healthy Meal would get me back in the swing of things. But now this!" She turned and faced me. "If there's one thing I am, it's determined. No one is going to mess with me or my family. You and Nina have to get to the bottom of this."

I smiled at her and nodded reassuringly, but I couldn't help wondering if someone in her family might be involved. And one other thing was bothering me. "Were you home all morning?"

"You sound like the police."

I was going to sound a lot more like them if she evaded my question, like I thought she was doing. "Were you?"

"Of course! It was actually very busy. I made breakfast for my sons. Then Colleen dropped by. I all but threw them out of the kitchen so I could finish my preparations for the luncheon."

"Nina and I saw you racing across the street to your house."

She blinked at me. Her eyes grew large. "I ran out for half-and-half. I've been so upset that I completely forgot. I didn't have enough half-and-half for coffee. I was certain I bought plenty. I baked a strawberry cream roll for dessert, and I guess I confused the half-and-half carton with the heavy cream carton. You know, they're the same size and color. I must have miscounted, and I knew everyone would be arriving any minute, so I dashed out to buy half-and-half."

It was a plausible story. She was right. The two dairy products did come in containers that were the same size and colors. I smiled at her. "You might want to mention that to Wolf."

Gerrie nodded as she stood up. "One favor, please. Between friends."

Uh-oh. That didn't sound good.

Her jaw tightened. "You must promise me that if you find one of my family members is involved, you will let *me* know first. I realize you would feel obligated to notify Wolf. In your shoes, I would do the same. But please promise that you will tell me first so I won't be blindsided."

That seemed reasonable. I would feel the same way about my family. But it made me wonder if she suspected someone in her family had murdered Russ. "I will. Um, Gerrie, is there anything else I should know? About your family's potential involvement?"

"A mother worries. Until her dying breath she will worry." Gerrie thanked me and left, walking briskly.

I tossed our garbage into a trash receptacle and returned to the convention hotel.

Colleen had everything under control. It was early afternoon, and the sessions would end for the day at five o'clock. I'd have liked to speak with Todd, but I didn't want to interrupt if he was really going to open a ghost kitchen. That would have been inconsiderate. I reminded Colleen to phone me if anything developed, but in my experience, there wasn't much for me to do there at this point.

I headed for one of my favorite watering holes, The Laughing Hound. The cool restaurant was a welcome respite in the hot weather. I bought iced tea at the bar and walked up the stairs to Bernie's office.

"Sophie! You're a little early for dinner." Bernie leaned back in his leather chair.

I had forgotten all about it. "I'm glad you reminded me." I slid into the chair on the other side of his desk and gulped icy tea to cool off. "What do you know about Russ

Everett? You said he was a lowlife. Can you tell me more? What was he into?"

"He asked me once to join in a poker game."

"Did you?"

Bernie snorted. "I'm not that stupid. I can smell a con. I don't know what's on his rap sheet, but I was under the impression he jumped from one scam to another."

I frowned at him. "Why would he have been in Gerrie's house?"

Bernie looked me straight in the eyes. "Gerrie's father, Jim Moss, was a pretty savvy businessman. I bought from him, and I always got a good deal. But he was slick. He came across as nice, polite, straightforward. No selling me an oven and then mentioning that the burners weren't included. The thing is that he might have dressed and acted like a gentleman, but he understood the dingy side of business. He never made a deal where he didn't come out on top."

I was a little befuddled. "You make it sound like Gerrie's father was some kind of criminal."

"That's a little bit harsh. But I believe he could play down and dirty when the need arose."

"Do you think his grandson Jim is the same way?"

"Jim likes our ribs and comes in regularly with people whom he's entertaining for business deals. I don't know him as well as I did his grandfather. The two of them worked together for years before the old man passed away. I haven't bought anything major from the younger Jim where haggling might be in order."

"You haggle?" I wrinkled my nose.

He laughed at me. "Everyone hammers out deals, Sophie. There's nothing wrong with that."

"So you negotiated with the older Jim?"

"Why does that bother you? It's how business is done. Gerrie's dad was a decent bloke. But"—he paused, considering his words—"I saw people in his employ whom I would not have hired."

"Maybe he was a kind man who helped people who were down on their luck?" Like Russ, I thought.

Bernie lowered his voice and leaned toward me. "I am the first chap in line to give a person a second chance. I have employees who did dumb things when they were young. Bar fights, that sort of thing. But I won't hire career criminals because they'll turn on you. I don't need that kind of headache."

Chapter 10

Dear Natasha,
I might have accidentally gone out with another girl. Big mistake! My mom says I should send my girlfriend flowers to apologize. They're expensive! What else could I do?
Want Her Back in Bloom City, Wisconsin

Dear Want Her Back,
I recommend roses. Lots of them.
Natasha

I saw the distinction, but found it troubling. Anyone could have a bad moment or make a mistake. But some people, like Russ, had a penchant for crime. "Thanks, Bernie. I'll see you tonight. I'm working a convention this weekend, but how about dinner at my house on Wednesday?"

"Is that the ghost kitchen convention?"

"You heard about it?"

"Ghost kitchens are a hot topic in the restaurant industry at the moment."

"Do you have one here?"

"Not yet. Some of the delivery services pick up from us and deliver. I don't know that I want to start another project under a different name. We stay fairly busy as it is. But it's on my radar."

I thanked Bernie and left quickly. Fridays had to be hectic for restaurateurs.

I ambled home, thinking about Russ. If he was the lowlife that Wolf and Wong had claimed, had he gone to Gerrie's home to steal from them? Maybe he didn't intend to kill anyone. That would account for the lack of a weapon. But surely he hadn't chosen to rob them in broad daylight. That seemed unlikely. Even I knew the cover of darkness was important. And he certainly hadn't known what was happening in the house that day. He would have chosen a day when no one was home. When Todd and Gerrie were out. And definitely not a day when a luncheon was planned.

Even more disturbing, unless Russ was attacked while Gerrie was out getting cream, she had to have been there when he was stabbed. The house was huge. Someone on the third or fourth floor might not have heard another person sneaking around inside the house. But Gerrie had been preparing her luncheon. By her own admission, she had been in and out of the dining room.

As I crossed the street to my block, a delivery guy hopped out of a van and carried a small arrangement of colorful flowers up the stairs to Nina's front door. She opened the door and accepted them. I could see her pointing in the direction of my house.

Sure enough, the driver returned to his van, and just as I opened the gate to my property, he hurried up behind me and handed me a similar flower arrangement. Luckily, I had a few bills stashed in the side of my purse for a tip. He was gone in a flash, but I took the time to admire the bright

sunflowers, bold zinnias, and snapdragons that comple-
mented each other, making the colors seem even more
vivid.

I let myself in the house and set the flowers on the table.
Mochie ran to me as though he was glad to have company.
"Did you miss Daisy today?" I was certain that Mochie
probably spent most of the day snoozing, but I felt Daisy's
absence just walking in the door.

I was still cuddling Mochie and listening to his sweet
purring when Nina knocked and opened the door. "Ah. I
suspected you received the same bouquet. The driver
asked me which house was yours."

"I would think he had the address."

"What can I say? He asked. Are you available?"

"For what?"

Nina plucked the card out of the bouquet and read
aloud. " 'My sincerest apologies for the horrible event at
our last meeting. I am horrified that you were put through
such an alarming experience and the trying aftermath.
Can we try again on Monday? Let me know if you're
available.' Gerrie handwrote these! Can you believe that? I
recognize her handwriting."

"It puts me to shame. How does she find the time to do
everything?"

Nina giggled. "Are we expected to respond via flower
arrangement?"

I burst out laughing. Mochie, however, was not amused
and felt that cuddle time had come to an end. He sprang
from my arms and moseyed to the window, where he
watched birds.

"That's Gerrie. Always thoughtful. I would imagine
quite a few of the ladies who were present aren't eager to
go back to Gerrie's house."

Nina's eyes widened. "I hadn't thought about that.

Some of them might drop out. Maybe you should host the luncheon."

"Don't you think Gerrie would be offended?"

"I think *I'm* going to be upset if we have to find new board members."

I put on the kettle for tea. "Gerrie wants us to find the murderer."

"That's great!" Nina suddenly looked somewhat contrite, and said in a steady, controlled lower tone, "I didn't mean to sound so cheerful about it. We should definitely help her. She must be terrified."

Nina stared at me. "What are you doing? We need to get going."

She was right. "Just one cup while we figure out where to start."

"Okay." She said it reluctantly and hit my refrigerator. "Mmm. Is that coffee cake with berries in it?"

I poured hot tea for us. Even on a steaming day, I liked to mellow out with a mug of tea. "It is. Help yourself." I handed her a plate and fork and carried her tea to the table. "I suppose we should interview Gerrie's sons and Colleen first. Although we just don't know much about Russ."

Nina plopped into a chair and sipped her tea. "I've made a few inquiries. He's a local. Jumps from job to job."

"He was nicely dressed."

"Preppy-ish. He sometimes caddied for golfers."

"That would have brought him into contact with a lot of people."

Nina dabbed her fingertip on crumbs to collect them. "Do we have enough time to hustle over to Moss Restaurant Supply?" She checked her watch.

I quickly Googled them. "I know they have several locations. Okay, great. The Alexandria location appears to be the main one."

Nina rinsed her plate and stashed it in the dishwasher. "Let's go."

I petted Mochie, whose fur was warm from the sunbeams coming through the window. "I'll be back later."

The store was located just beyond the hotel where the convention was taking place. It didn't take us long to walk over.

"Are we going to pretend we're setting up a restaurant?" asked Nina.

"I don't think we need to do that. Let's just ask for Jim."

"So boring. But we could do that. Go straight to the boss."

The cool air in the showroom felt heavenly when we entered. Peaceful strains of familiar pop music played softly. A young woman with faux blond hair, as evidenced by the dark roots sprouting at her part, emerged from a glass office. Bright eyes assessed us over a sharp nose. She was very pretty, even with far too much lipstick in a bloody shade that would be favored by vampires. "Can I help you?"

Nina ran a hand over the spotless stainless steel of a giant eight-burner stove with a griddle. She shot me a hopeful glance.

"We're here to see Mr. Stansfield, please."

She raised an eyebrow. "Like who should I tell him is here?"

A man appeared from the right side of the vast room. "I've got it, Hayley." He strode toward us and held out his hand to shake. "Jim Stansfield."

Even though Colleen had told me Jim was short, I had expected someone bigger. I guessed him to be around five

and a half feet tall. He was casually dressed in jeans and
a crisp white button-down shirt. His cinnamon-brown
hair probably came from Gerrie's side of the family. He
wore it pulled back into a short ponytail. He had her
blue eyes, too.

Nina and I shook his hand and introduced ourselves.

"Mom said you might drop by. We can talk in my office." He led us upstairs, to a room that overlooked the
showroom through panels of glass. A two-foot-high wood
carving of an elephant stood proudly in the middle of a
long sideboard. A charming modern painting of an elephant family graced a wall.

"Gerrie mentioned that you spent some years saving
elephants."

He smiled. "They are such intelligent and kind crea-
tures. We underestimate them. Some of them even remember me when I go back to visit. Could I offer you a soda?
Iced tea?"

He was his mother's son. No question about it. We declined his kind offer.

"I understand you were at your mother's house yesterday morning." I watched his expression.

He looked completely calm. "I was. I live in Old Town,
on South Lee Street. The night before was the first time
Mom, my brother, Todd, and I were together alone after
my dad's death. We had a late dinner out, then went to
Mom's house. We were up until two or so reminiscing
about Dad and our childhood. Mom even brought out the
photo albums. I guess life keeps us kind of busy and we
hadn't had that kind of opportunity, just the three of us, in
a long, long time. I drank more than I should have and
didn't feel like walking home at two-thirty in the morning,
so I just crashed in my old room. Seemed fitting somehow,
you know?"

"It was just the three of you? No one else dropped by?"
I asked.

"That's what made it special. I'm sorry Dad wasn't
there. He'd have enjoyed it."

"Did you eat breakfast at your mom's?" asked Nina.

He thought for a moment. "Coffee, for sure. Yes, I remember making a second pot."

"No food?" Nina tilted her head.

He laughed. "How could I forget that? You know Mom.
She made waffles with maple syrup and fresh berries. And
I distinctly remember her telling us—more Todd than me, I
suppose, since he lives there—that she was hosting a luncheon for her charity that day. In other words, get out of
her way after breakfast."

"Was anyone else there?"

He shook his head. "We open at ten, so I hustled home
for a shower and change of clothes. And then I rode my
bike over here."

"Did you hear anyone else in the house?" Nina asked.

"No."

"Did anything fall or creak?" she asked. "Was there any
sound at all that could have been someone else in the
house?"

"No. Not that I noticed."

And then I had to ask the obvious. "Did you know Russ
Everett?"

Jim nodded. "Russ worked here a few years ago. I'm
sick about the way he died. He didn't deserve that. I can't
imagine the horror of it."

"He parted under amicable circumstances?" I asked.

"He was a driver who delivered our products. It's not
the most exciting job, I guess."

"Did you see Colleen at your mom's house?" asked
Nina.

"No. Mom showed us the jewelry Dad wanted Penelope to have. I was all for it. I'm not married, and even if I were, most of the real value of that stuff is in the sentiment that Penelope has for Dad and his mom. Penelope is a great kid. I'm happy for her to have it."

Jim seemed like a nice guy. "Nothing that morning struck you as unusual?"

"Nope. Just another day at Mom's house."

I was disappointed. Jim was a solid dead end. A brick wall. "Thank you for your time. If you think of anything, even something that seems irrelevant, please let us know."

"Will do. Do you think they'll charge Mom with murder?"

Chapter 11

Dear Sophie,
My boyfriend bought this amazing outdoor grill
that cooks with wood. He just wanders the forest
and collects sticks to cook with. Is that safe?
    Not Willing to Eat in Forest Mill, Tennessee

Dear Not Willing to Eat,
Good decision. Hardwoods like oak and hickory
are excellent for cooking. So are fruitwoods, like
apple. But tell your boyfriend he should not cook
with pine or fir because they contain sap and resin,
which will not taste good and could make you sick.
And as for poison sumac, just no!

                                                    Sophie

Jim looked so worried that my heart went out to him.
"Do you know of any reason they would do that?"

He shrugged. "Russ died in her house. He'd been stabbed
with her kitchen knife. No one else was there."

I stood up to leave, noting the almost imperceptible sound
of someone tiptoeing away from the office door. "It's a

problem. *Someone* murdered him. If there's anything you know or hear, no matter how insignificant, I hope you'll call us."

Proving again that he was Gerrie's son, he thanked us for coming and saw us out the door, as if he had invited us to visit him.

Nina started down the sidewalk toward the center of Old Town.

"Psst! This way." I led her in the opposite direction and we crossed the street.

"What are you doing?"

We ducked into an antiques store. I rushed toward the shop window. "Ha! I thought someone else was there listening! Didn't you notice?"

"What?" Nina peered at Jim's front door.

The glass windows that showed off all the fantastic restaurant gear they had to offer didn't hide much. And they most certainly did not hide a woman talking with Jim.

"Who is that?" asked Nina.

"Good question. I didn't even catch a glimpse of her when we were in the store. Why would she hide? Was she the one who had been eavesdropping or was that Hayley?"

She was petite, with long beach waves cascading over her shoulders. From a distance, if she wore any makeup at all, she didn't appear to use much.

"She could have been working in a back office or something," Nina suggested.

"Possibly. But she made a beeline for Jim as soon as we left."

Hayley approached them, eyeing Jim with unmistakable interest. She cocked her head at him coyly and the other woman walked away.

"Bad Hayley! Bad!" joked Nina. "You are not supposed

to look at your boss that way. That girl has trouble written all over her face."

"While it can be awkward and is certainly inadvisable, there's technically nothing wrong with dating one's boss."

"You sound like you speak from experience," Nina teased.

"They don't seem suited for each other," I said. "She's sort of brassy and he's more earthy, with all his elephant stuff."

"I'm wondering about that. They say opposites attract."

"And for the record, I have never dated a boss of mine," I stated with a chuckle.

"May I help you?"

The two of us swirled around to face a neatly dressed and groomed man. A gentleman, I thought, taking in the perfectly trimmed short beard. Not a thing was out of place. His khakis had been carefully pressed, clean seams running down the pants legs. And his light-blue shirt was impeccable. I took in the antiques quickly. "I don't believe I've been in here before. It's a lovely store."

"We were spying," Nina admitted.

I shot her a look. For all we knew, this guy was Jim's best friend!

He smiled. "Ah. The Hayley-and-Jim show. We watch it quite often. We're taking bets on how long it will take her to seduce him."

"Do you know them?" I asked.

"Not well. I rather suspect that Hayley isn't the antiques type. More a plastic-and-Lucite kind of gal. I'm not at all certain about the other one, but she hasn't been in the shop, either. Pity." He shrugged. "But I'm onto Jim's love of elephants, so I often purchase them on buying trips. You have to know your customers in this business."

"Has Hayley worked there long?" I asked.

"Neither of them has. Before them, there was Betty, who loves antiques."

"Did Betty, um, snuggle up to Jim, too?"

He bellowed with laughter. "Good heavens. The mere image is preposterous. Betty must be late seventies, maybe even early eighties. A most proper woman. I would wager that she never played hanky-panky with a boss. She's a dear and explained to me at great length that she was not an administrative assistant. She was a graduate of some secretarial school that held their students to the highest standards. She was quite proud of it."

"Do you know her last name?" asked Nina.

"Armstrong."

We thanked him and browsed a bit. So as not to be completely rude, I was looking for some little thing to purchase, when I spotted Royal Albert dessert plates in the elaborate, vivid-pink Lady Carlyle pattern. They were really over the top. The quintessential pattern for serving afternoon tea. I didn't need them, but they were so beautiful. I counted them. One dozen in all. They were in pristine condition, as though they'd been sitting in someone's china cabinet for years, unused.

"You might as well buy them, Sophie," said Nina. "You know you want them."

"There aren't any teacups." It was just an excuse.

"Then you'll have something to look for and hunting for beautiful china is half the fun."

"That's why they're marked down," said the man. "It was a stroke of luck that I discovered them. They're very hard to find."

I suspected they weren't as difficult to find as he claimed, but I had always admired the pattern. And the price was quite reasonable. I capitulated and bought them. He very kindly packaged them in four bags to make them easier to carry. On our way home, I decided I could use them when a cold beverage was being served. But in my heart, I knew I would be on the hunt for those matching teacups.

"You could throw a tea instead of Gerrie having another luncheon at her house of horror." Nina shifted her purse to her other shoulder.

I did a quick count in my head. "I could! But I would want the teacups to do that."

"Too bad. It might have cost you, but our outing was worthwhile."

I unlocked the door. "Do you think Francie knows Betty Armstrong?" Francie, my elderly neighbor, had lived in Old Town most of her life and had loads of friends in her age bracket. She was still an active gardener and avid bird-watcher.

"It couldn't hurt to ask."

Mochie stretched in his window seat. I expected him to come for petting, but he turned around and curled in a tight circle, probably annoyed that we had interrupted his snooze.

We set the packages on the table, and I dialed Francie's number.

After the perfunctory greetings, I asked, "Francie, do you know someone named Betty Armstrong?"

Her cackle sounded through the phone. "Of course. I saw her at the garden club meeting a couple of days ago. She's madder than a wet hen about losing her job."

Losing it? So it hadn't been her choice to retire. "Would she mind talking to Nina and me about working at Moss Restaurant Supply?"

"Hah! She'd love it. Are you going to Bernie's for dinner tonight?"

"Yes!"

"I'll see if she's available to join us."

Francie called back in five minutes. "We're on. See you at The Laughing Hound." She disconnected the call.

"We're so spoiled," I said to Nina. "Do you think we take advantage of Bernie because he owns a restaurant?"

"As I recall, we got him off the hook when he was accused of murder."

"Well," I said lightly, "that's just what friends do."

Nina laughed. "I don't have any other friends who would do that. Besides, he asked us to come tonight!"

I ran my hand over Mochie's silky fur. His toes curled under, indicating he'd felt my touch.

Nina headed home and I went upstairs to change into a sleeveless cotton shirtdress in an ivory-and-black print.

I puttered around the house, watering plants and straightening papers in my office. Mochie joined me, purring loudly, and sitting on papers so I couldn't file them. I stroked his fur and thought about the Stansfields.

They had clearly known Russ. But why had he been there? I believed Gerrie when she claimed she wouldn't have invited him that day. She was busy with the luncheon.

It crossed my mind that someone might have invited him intentionally when guests were coming as an alibi. But that would take some split-second timing.

Russ didn't break in, which meant one of the Stansfields had let him in the house or someone had left a door unlocked. I'd heard stories of people with bad intentions walking along a street and trying the front doors until they found one that was open. A scary thought! But in the middle of the day? I hated to think it, but it was more likely that one of them was in cahoots with Russ and let him in. But which one? And why murder him?

I fed Mochie a new ground-turkey can of cat food that he appeared to like. I grabbed my purse and prepared to go out to dinner. I left a light on in the kitchen, as well as outdoor lights, even though it wasn't dark yet. Nina met me on the sidewalk in front of her house. The stroll to The Laughing Hound was brief but lovely, cooler evening air had begun to set in. Potted plants and window boxes over-flowed with bright flowers. A stranger walking through town would never guess that someone had recently been knifed to death in one of the beautiful homes.

On arrival, we walked past the line of people waiting for a table. I couldn't help feeling a little guilty. But the host quashed my concerns when he said, "Bernie is wait-ing for you on the terrace."

We walked through the large dining room to the stone terrace. As I expected, the tables were full of diners. All ex-cept for one in the back, at which Mars and Bernie sat. Be-hind them, wood logs blazed in a stainless-steel and brick hearth. The scent of apple wood perfumed the air.

They greeted us enthusiastically.

"What's this?" I asked.

"Wood-burning cooking is all the rage." Bernie escorted me for a closer view. "I need your opinion on some of our new dishes."

"It smells delicious!"

"I think you're smelling the pork with grilled pineapple."

My mouth watered at the thought. Francie arrived with another lady. Francie's face reflected the time she had spent out in the sun gardening. She made no effort to hide her wrinkles. But she still colored her hair straw yellow.

She introduced her friend as Betty Armstrong. Betty was surely about the same age, but she had let her hair go a beautiful silver gray. She wore it short in soft waves. I knew I shouldn't judge anyone on their appearance, but I liked her immediately. There was something slightly melan-choly about her, though. She peered through round black glasses at us and smiled wanly. "Thank you for including me at your tasting dinner."

A server with red hair pulled back in a ponytail took our drink orders and served them promptly. A chef manned the wood-burning grill and the server delivered small portions of several dishes to each of us. There was pork with pineapple, crisp grilled whole fish, spiced lamb, brined chicken with sweet corn, smoky pork belly mac and cheese, grilled zucchini, and salad, as though anyone had room for that! The server also roamed the terrace offering samples to other diners, who appeared delighted to have a taste.

Conversation came to a halt while we ate, but it soon started again with all of us weighing in on our favorites. I was in love with the pork and pineapple, though I had to admit the mac and cheese with smoky pork belly was delicious. It all was!

"Will you be able to serve everyone?" I asked. "Is the grill big enough to handle a lot of orders?"

"There's room to expand if necessary. We'll see how it goes." Bernie looked about as happy as I had ever seen him. He called the chef and the server to join us at our table and try the dishes.

As much as I loved sweets, I didn't think anyone could possibly entice me to eat dessert after all that food, but when chocolate ice cream, topped with French chocolate liqueur and lightly charred marshmallows, appeared, there was no way I was turning it down.

Done eating, the server resumed her work, offering us after-dinner drinks, decaf coffee, and tea. As we ate our dessert, the conversation swung over to the dead man in Gerrie Stansfield's house.

Chapter 12

Dear Sophie,
Everyone knows Amaretto tastes like almonds. My idiot boyfriend insists there are no almonds in it! It's my favorite liqueur and a bottle of it is riding on your answer.
Amaretto Lover in Almond Valley, Maryland

Dear Amaretto Lover,
Your Amaretto might or might not have almonds in it. It is commonly made with almonds or apricot pits!

Sophie

"I understand you know Gerrie Stansfield very well?" Nina directed her question to Betty.

"I know the Stansfields better than my own brothers and sister." Betty savored her Amaretto coffee topped with a mound of slowly melting whipped cream.

"Francie says you worked at Moss Restaurant Supply," I said.

"Almost my whole working life." Betty's silver hair caught

the gleam from the fire. "Well"—her smile faded—"up until Edwin's death anyway. Then they threw me out like dirty bathwater." She lifted her forefinger. "You just wait. They'll come calling."

"I'm so sorry, Betty," said Francie. "That place must be falling apart without you."

Bernie smiled at her kindly. "I'm sure that's true. You were the backbone of that business. I can't imagine it running smoothly without you."

"Gerrie's father, Jim the senior, and I were a team," Betty said proudly. "He handled the business, and I took care of the office. The billing, the paperwork, the phone, placing ads, running off paychecks. You name it and I did it. He was a wonderful man. Up until I got canned, I thought highly of Jim the lesser, too." She sighed noisily. "I used to call him Jim the younger, but he's not the man I thought. I saw who he brought in for interviews. My job went to a gum-smacking fake blonde in a tacky short skirt and halter top. Doesn't she know how to dress in a business? She won't last past Christmas. If that long. She doesn't know the first thing about restaurants, or cooking, as far as I could tell. Didn't know the difference between cast iron and stainless steel!"

"Gee, Betty. Don't hide your feelings about her," laughed Francie.

"She's not a proper secretary, Francie. I shudder to think what she'll do to my files. I am a graduate of Miss Brigg's School for Professional Secretaries. My goodness, we had a grand time. Mind you, the training was tough. We had to be perfect. There wasn't a delete key on typewriters when I was in school. To be a Brigg's girl, you had to type fast with no errors. We did *not* get things wrong." She gasped and began to chuckle. "I wish I could see her when she encounters something I wrote in shorthand!"

Francie joined in the laughter and the two of them

couldn't stop. It was contagious. We all chuckled along with them. I couldn't read shorthand, either.

When she caught her breath, Betty became serious. "I am angry with them now. Jim the senior was a good man. He started a retirement account for me long ago. It wasn't necessary, but he insisted on it and deposited money in it each payday. Because of him, I am financially independent and comfortable. I don't need to work, except to keep myself busy. I'm not one to lounge around at home. But I *am* having difficulty getting over Jim the lesser's treatment of me. I've known him since he was born! And I worked with him many years. It's audacious of me, I'm sure, but I was like part of the family. First he tried to demote me to an ordinary shopgirl! He knew I would never accept that. To be summarily discarded was simply hurtful and came as such a blow."

"I'm surprised that Gerrie didn't stop him from firing you," said Bernie. "Doesn't she own the business?"

"I'm not sure she knows that I was dismissed."

Francie spoke up. "We think Jim the lesser timed it so Gerrie wouldn't notice."

"He was waiting for his father to die?" asked Mars.

"Probably not that exact scenario," said Betty. "The heart attack was very sudden. But I think he was waiting for a time when they would all be absorbed by something else and wouldn't know what was happening at Moss."

"Have you seen Gerrie?" I asked.

"Not since the funeral and the wake. He sacked me two days later."

I wondered how her computer skills were. Wasn't everything done on them these days? Billing, payroll, and many of the other tasks she had handled for Gerrie's father were routinely done on computer now. But it seemed entirely too rude to inquire. She might be defensive about her lack of computer savvy.

"We paid Jim a visit today." Nina toyed with her napkin. "He and Hayley were *very* friendly."

"Hayley received one day of training from me." Betty's tone was harsh. "That young woman didn't know how to use a copy machine," she sneered. "Oh! 'Very friendly'! Is that a euphemism for *sleeping with the boss?*"

"I don't know about sleeping," said Nina, "but she was looking at him like he was special."

"There was another woman, too. A petite blonde?" I said.

"That's the computer woman. She's very nice. But I find Hayley's behavior disgusting and so inappropriate." Betty scowled at her coffee. "Has she no shame? That's not what one does at work. Of course, Jim is ripe for the picking."

Bernie narrowed his eyes. "What do you mean?"

"Even though I am angry with him, I have to admit that Jim the lesser is a very hard worker. He puts in long hours. The store is open six days a week and available for emergencies around the clock, every day of the year. If Bernie's burners or ovens go out at four in the morning on New Year's Day, Jim will send in someone to repair them, and most times, he'll be there, too, to make sure it gets done. Clearly, he doesn't have a lot of time for romance. He, um, well, his brother married Jim's childhood sweetheart and—"

"Colleen?" I blurted.

"Yes. Do you know her? Lovely woman. They have an adorable daughter. But Todd bungled it badly. You can imagine that it put a burr between the two brothers. Oh my, what a mess that was. To make matters worse, Todd is not an ideal employee. At Gerrie's insistence, he went to work for Moss Restaurant Supply. He ambled in late, left early"—she closed her eyes briefly—"and drank on the job. Jim made an effort to accommodate Todd. He really did. He moved Todd around and let him try different positions, but I think Todd just wasn't interested in restaurant supply."

Betty sipped her Amaretto coffee. "You see, restaurateurs depend on a working kitchen. So they like to form a bond with their suppliers. They need to know they can depend on them. Quite often when they require a replacement, they need it as soon as possible. You can imagine the chaos in a restaurant when a stove or refrigerator isn't working. I think it's the reason Jim the senior was so successful. Everyone knew he was dependable. Jim the lesser understood that, too. So when Todd lost a major account by bungling an order in every way possible, Jim fired him. You can imagine the uproar in the family. Gerrie tried to protect Todd. Edwin sided with Jim the lesser. There was a major family implosion. Naturally, Todd claimed Jim fired him out of jealousy because Colleen had married him. Fortunately, Jim the senior was still alive and he backed Jim the younger. Todd had to go."

"I had no idea. Did any of you know about this?" I asked.

Only Bernie spoke up. "I knew about Todd mismanaging an order for The Black Olive."

"I love their pizza!" Nina tapped her finger on the table. "They were closed for several days a few years ago."

Bernie nodded. "It was a mess. I'd guess Moss lost more than one account as a result."

"Todd is what they call an empty suit," said Betty. "He talks a great game, but that appears to be his sole strength. He simply cannot follow through on anything. Unfortunately, after he was fired, he used his connections and the Moss reputation to talk his way into an enormous loan so he could open his own competing restaurant supply company. He had some nerve. Think about it. It's called Moss Restaurant Supply, even though everyone knows

the family as the Stansfields. Well, that snake called his
new business Stansfield Restaurant Supply, which confused everyone."

"I have a vague recollection of that," said Bernie. "He
had the worst reputation in town."

"The family was furious, but there was nothing they
could do to stop him," said Betty. "It flopped in no time.
You actually have to be there to run a business! That was
the end of Todd's career, such as it was, in restaurant supply. It left him with a hefty debt, too. He expected his dad
to pay it off for him, but Edwin told Todd in no uncertain
terms that *he* had signed for the money, *he* had squan-
dered it, and *he* could figure out how to pay it back."

A few things were beginning to fit in place for me. I now
understood why Jim had said the evening with his mom
and brother had been special. And why Gerrie had been
pleased that her two sons got along that night. Even if they
were on speaking terms, that kind of chicanery within the
family would leave deep wounds that would be hard to
heal.

But as interesting as it was, it still didn't explain what
Russ Everett was doing at Gerrie's house. "Betty, do you
know a man named Russ Everett?"

"Oh sure. I saw his name every time I printed his pay-
check."

I blinked hard. "You knew him when he worked at
Moss?"

"Sure. He was a delivery driver for them a few years
back. Russell G. Everett. I remember him well. But his departure was a little odd. One day, Jim the lesser asked me
to place an ad for a new driver. When I inquired about Russ,
Jim simply said he was no longer in our employ. I don't
know what happened, but I always thought that odd."

Nina and I exchanged a look.

Chapter 13

Dear Natasha,
My husband left me for another woman. Even
though he was a lousy husband, I miss the big lug.
How do I get him back?
                    Lonely in Old Town, Alexandria

Dear Lonely,
My boyfriend ended our relationship, too. I know
how you're feeling. I still believe the way to a
man's heart is through his stomach. Bake for him.
And if you don't have the time, you can send him
my Natasha's Cookies!
                                        Natasha

Why would Jim be cagey about Russ's departure from the store?

"Betty, can you tell us anything about Russ?" I asked.

"He was a friendly fellow. Always polite to me. He took a lot of guff from the other guys."

Nina frowned. "Why was that?"

"He was always bragging about people for whom he

had caddied. Dropping names, that sort of thing. 'Last week when I was talking to the mayor, he told me blah, blah, blah.' And he dressed like he was caddying. The delivery drivers are supposed to wear T-shirts or jackets that say 'Moss Restaurant Supply.' These days, you want to know to whom you're opening your door, especially if you're alone in a closed restaurant, waiting for your equipment to be repaired or replaced so you can open the next day. You have to remember that a lot of our customers have small operations. When the drivers and repair people are in transit, our employees text the customers. Many of them have told me how much they appreciate that. It's a small thing, but those little courtesies can make a difference. Anyway, Russ talked Jim into getting golf shirts with the name of the business because he didn't like wearing T-shirts. Oh my word, did they make fun of him for that!"

"But I thought he was trouble. Wolf and Wong were familiar with him."

Betty nodded. "Where I grew up, they used to say that you can't make a silk purse out of a sow's ear. My personal opinion is that he wanted to be part of that golfing crowd. He picked up on some of their habits, but in his eagerness, he didn't always use good judgment. Most of his troubles with the law were misdemeanors, like petit larceny. Both Jims were big on second chances. They must have thought those days were behind him, or we would not have kept him in our employ."

That was interesting. Russ was trying to improve himself. One could hardly fault him for that. I was almost sorry I had asked. Now I felt very sad that he had come to such a horrible end.

But what was he doing in Gerrie's house? Had Russ been summarily dismissed like Betty? Why? Was Jim al-

ways so inconsiderate when he let employees go? Maybe
Gerrie was on the right track when she said Russ wanted
to kill them. Even if that wasn't the objective, he might
have gone there to collect what he felt the Stansfields owed
him. Or for revenge.

I was glad to walk home after pigging out on dinner. But
it was all so delicious! It wasn't far, but it felt right to walk
in the cool night air with stars sparkling in a velvety sky.
Betty had gone in a different direction. Francie and Nina
chattered as they walked in front of Mars and me.

"I miss Daisy. It doesn't feel right not to have her there
when I come home."

"No. No, no, no. This is my weekend with her. You'll
be out all day tomorrow. The deal was that I get her until
Sunday."

I turned my head away so he wouldn't see me smile. We
had adopted Daisy when we moved into the house in
which I now lived. As much as I missed her, it was actually
pretty terrific that someone else loved her as much as I did
and was taking good care of her.

"All right. At least I have Mochie to snuggle with." I
changed the topic. "Did you know Russ?"

"Perhaps you have noticed that I don't own a restaurant."

"You have been known to golf."

"It's entirely possible that he caddied for someone, and
I don't remember. But his name doesn't ring any bells
for me."

"What do you know about the Stansfields?"

"Not much. Nice folks. I knew Edwin better than the
others. He was brainy and analytical. He'd make a very
good point in kind of a deadpan voice. And then, just
when you thought he was a bore, he'd say something
wildly funny."

"Sounds like a nice guy."

"Not terribly talkative, but when he spoke, it was worth listening."

We said good night as Mars peeled off to his house. Nina waved as she trotted up her steps. I walked Francie to her front door in spite of her protests. It was right next door to mine, but I would feel better if I knew she'd made it inside safely. Not because someone might harm her, but at her age, she might take a fall and that would be awful.

Mochie complained when I opened the door. He circled my legs once, but when I bent to pick him up, he shot for the small counter where he ate, leaped up, and sat next to his empty bowl. He couldn't have made his thoughts more clear. *I'm glad you're home. Now serve another dinner, please.*

I set my purse down and spooned chicken cat food into his bowl. He purred as he ate.

I checked to be sure the door was locked and trudged up the stairs to read in bed.

I took my time on Saturday morning and ambled into the hotel half an hour before the day's program was scheduled to start. Happily, Colleen was present and busy working. I checked around to see if there had been any problems overnight. Apparently, the ghost kitchen people were a well-behaved bunch. That wasn't always the case at conventions.

Todd ambled over to me, one hand in his pants pocket and holding a tall latte in the other. Dale, the man he sat with the day before, came with him. "Hi, Sophie!"

"Good morning."

Todd stood with an odd bent. It was very casual, very comfortable.

"Are you planning to open a ghost kitchen?" I asked, mostly just making polite conversation.

Dale swiped a hand along his beard. "It's very tempting. Your speakers are great. They make it sound so easy. Hey, where'd you get that coffee, Todd?"

Todd pointed. "There's a barista just around the corner."

"I'm parched. Need my morning java!" Dale hurried off.

I could relate. We all needed our morning coffee or tea.

Todd grinned at me. "Mom said I might see you here. Listen, I wasn't home when that guy was stabbed, so there's nothing I can tell you about it. Mom is freaked out, though, so I hope you can calm her nerves."

"It doesn't worry you that a man entered your mother's house and was murdered?"

"Yeah, not much. I'm just glad Penelope didn't see him."

I gave him kudos for worrying about his daughter, but what kind of person wouldn't be worried about a murder in his home?

My shock must have shown on my face because he kept talking. "People get far too upset about things like that. It happened. Time to move on."

"I guess Russ wasn't a friend of yours?" I studied the careless lock of hair that flopped onto the left side of his forehead. The easy smile and trendy barely-there beard were neat and orderly, but his posture screamed carefree and breezy. I hardly knew him, but he exuded confidence.

"No. I mean, I knew who he was. Tough way to go, though. Poor guy."

"You do realize that your mother is the suspect?"

He laughed. "Oh sure. Like she would kill someone."

I stared at him. "She was the only person there. What would you think if you were the police?"

"That there must have been someone else in the house because she could never have done that."

"Do you recall what time you left the house?" I asked.

"Not really. Mom wanted everyone out of there because of her luncheon."

"Did you see Russ?"

"Don't think so."

He was so casual it made me want to scream at him. "Your mother could go to jail for his murder."

He laughed. "No, she won't."

I was aghast and changed the subject, hoping to get more out of him.

"I guess you're planning to open a ghost kitchen?"

Todd bobbed his head. "Thinking about it."

"Do you have any restaurant experience?" I asked, mainly to put him at ease.

"Not a bit. But one of the speakers didn't have any, either. He said he hired some good cooks. You don't even need a pricy chef. His background is marketing, so it looks like restaurant experience isn't an absolute necessity." He grinned at me. "But I'm sure that's not what you want to talk about."

I moved on. "Tell me what happened on Thursday morning."

"At breakfast, Mom reminded us that she was having lady friends over for a luncheon, and that we had to scram. Except I believe her exact instructions were to 'vacate the premises.'"

"Then what?"

"Oh, I don't know. Colleen was coming by to pick up some stuff and I wanted to see her. I guess we left about ten or ten-thirty."

That would be easy enough to confirm. "You left together?"

"Yes. Would you excuse me? It looks like they're about to start." He turned to walk away.

"Just one more thing, Todd. Where did you go when you left?"

He paused just long enough for me to wonder if he was busy thinking up an answer. "I had a business meeting at The Laughing Hound."

I watched as he sauntered to the ballroom. He had no idea how easy it would be for me to confirm that. I would have to get more information from him. He might have left with Colleen, but he could easily have doubled back to the house. I felt guilty for not liking Gerrie's son. It was as though I was betraying her. And there really wasn't any reason for it, I supposed. There was just something about him that made me wary. Why was he so certain his mother wouldn't go to jail for Russ's murder? Was that his care-free personality, or did he know something?

I opened my laptop and checked my list of things to do before the grand banquet tonight, which would wrap up the weekend for them. *Remind Natasha* was at the very top. I texted her and made a note to phone her if she didn't respond. And then I ordered a couple hundred of Natasha's Cookies for the banquet. There would still be a real dessert, but attendees could take the cookies with them and eat them whenever they liked. Even as a midnight snack in their rooms.

As I finished taking care of a few more odds and ends, Colleen slid into the seat next to me.

"Todd has dumped Penelope on his new girlfriend."

I snapped the laptop closed. Colleen hadn't sounded like she wanted to reconcile with Todd. Still, when an ex, or soon-to-be ex, dated someone else, it could be rough. "I'm sorry, Colleen. For you and for Penelope." I wasn't sure if I should mention having met the new woman's brother, Dale. Colleen probably met him at the conference, though if Todd were wise, he probably wouldn't have said Dale was his new girlfriend's brother, so she might not know that.

She held up her phone and wiggled it. "One Nicci, with

very long blond hair, huge sunglasses, a diamond-encrusted watch, probably faux, and wearing a white halter top barely tucked into the waistband of her denim shorts, she picked up my daughter for her swim class this morning."

"Oh."

"I thought Penelope would be safe from that kind of thing, since she stays over at Gerrie's house when Todd has visitation," she huffed. "But today he allowed this total stranger to pick her up!"

"Where is she now?" I dared to ask.

"Nicci is taking her for a mani-pedi and then they're going to lunch."

"Maybe Nicci isn't so bad. I love mani-pedis. I bet Penelope will have fun."

Colleen shot me a miserable look. "I don't like her in the hands of a stranger."

"I'm sure she's had babysitters before. Would it help if you thought of Nicci as a babysitter?"

Her mouth drew tight and her nostrils flared. "When I was dating Todd, it never occurred to me that I would end up in this kind of mess. To make matters worse, he's two months behind in child support."

I didn't want to be rude. But the more I knew about Todd, the better. I phrased my question carefully so it wouldn't sound critical. "He's not working?"

"Apparently not. It's a lucky thing that I got this job. I actually liked working for Gerrie at The Sugar Bowl, but this pays much better. And there he is now." She held up her hand and crooked her finger for him to join us.

"Hello, ladies. That was a fantastic session. I'm learning so much." Todd slid into a chair. "How about joining me for lunch?"

Colleen ignored his question. In a tone that could have frozen boiling water, she asked, "Who is Nicci?"

Todd smiled, probably not the best reaction, given Colleen's state of mind. "Just a friend."

Her face turned a hot red. "And you left our child with her?"

"Relax, Colleen, they're having a great time." He leaned toward her. "I think you're jealous!"

"We are going to have a long talk about this. You can't go leaving her with just any woman you picked up in a bar."

"You'll love Nicci once you meet her. Everyone does."

Colleen collected her purse and stood up. "I seriously doubt that." She stalked away.

Chapter 14

Dear Natasha,
I have a neighbor who always drops by exactly when I'm eating my breakfast. He often helps himself to some toast or oatmeal. I no longer think this is a coincidence. How do I stop this behavior?
Always Out of Jam in Egg Harbor, Wisconsin

Dear Always Out of Jam,
Stop feeding him! He'll find another place to sniff around for his breakfast.
Natasha

"I'm sorry you had to see that." Todd grinned at me as though Colleen's distress didn't bother him a bit. "Colleen is kind of high strung."

"Most mothers are like that about their children."

"Nah, I think it's just Colleen. She always has to be in charge. She hates handing Penelope over to me. But it's not Penelope that she's so upset about. What's really killing her is that she can't control *me* anymore." He rose from his seat. "Hey, great convention. I'm off to get some lunch before the next session begins." With a wave, he ambled away, seemingly without a care in the world.

I checked my messages, relieved to see a reply from Natasha. **See you tonight.**

To be on the safe side, I texted her with the name and address of the hotel, as well as the time she needed to show up. I padded the time a little, something I had picked up over the years. Not everyone interpreted times the same way. It was far better if they arrived too early. Plus, it gave them a little extra time in case they were lost or went to the wrong place. It had happened to me too many times.

Just before the sessions recommenced, Colleen arrived with Penelope in tow. Penelope continually admired her sparkling magenta fingernails, so I assumed the mani-pedi had been a success.

I verified that cocktail hour would be on track, then headed home to change into a simple black sheath dress. I carried heels in a tote so I could change into them when I arrived at the hotel.

On my return, I checked details on the dinner being prepared, tipped the bellman for receiving the cookies, then monitored the cocktail hour as it got under way. While I wasn't really eavesdropping, I couldn't help hearing bits of conversation. Todd, with one hand in his pocket and a drink in the other, said, "There's no limit to this business. Once you get a good kitchen going, you can duplicate it across the country. Or franchise it!" He wasn't the only one who was eager. I heard several comments along those lines. Everyone was excited to get their new ghost kitchens going.

Colleen showed up looking frazzled. She wore a becoming fit and flare dress in a sunrise orange shade, but her hair was falling out of a French twist, and she must have rubbed her left eye because her liner was smeared.

"Can you believe this? Penelope's friend can't spend the

night with her at Gerrie's house because her mother is afraid someone else will be murdered. How ridiculous is that? Like Gerrie is running around the house brandishing daggers? Really? And you know the other problem?" Colleen stashed something in her purse. "Even though it is my husband's weekend to take care of our daughter, I was the one she called in tears when her friend couldn't come over. And it became my problem. And worse, I bet anything that he's hanging around here somewhere guzzling booze, not paying a bit of attention to his daughter's anguish."

I whispered to her, "Take a minute to catch your breath in the ladies' room." I pointed at my hair.

She raised a hand to her own hair. "Oh great. That figures." She bustled off.

The bellman found me to let me know my order of Natasha's Cookies had arrived. I let myself into the ballroom, which had magically been changed over to an elegant dining hall. White tablecloths hung on round tables. Low clusters of yellow and orange flowers were surrounded by white votive candles. Silverware gleamed under the large chandeliers. I moved swiftly, placing one package of Natasha's cookies at the top of each place setting. The robin's-egg–blue color blended nicely with the bright shades of the flowers.

As I moved around the silent room, I couldn't help overhearing someone's phone conversation. I couldn't see him and only heard half of his conversation.

"No kidding?

"Yeah. I'll take care of that.

"Pretty good. I'm glad I came. I didn't know about all this stuff.

"It's going great. Don't worry about a thing."

I looked around for the person, but he must have been in a back hallway somewhere.

I took care to set my phone to vibrate so it wouldn't be going off during the dinner, distracting everyone.

Two hours later, Natasha walked up on the dais with grace and dignity. All those beauty pageants had certainly paid off. Her dress, not coincidentally, I was sure, matched the color of the packages of Natasha's Cookies. She told the story of her involvement with ghost kitchens. As far as I could tell, everyone was fascinated.

When the dinner ended and everyone was leaving, I nabbed Natasha. "Thank you for telling your story. You were great!"

"You say that as though you're surprised."

Oops. "I know you're good at public speaking and events."

"Maybe I can do more of these. Raise the reputation of your little business."

Why did she always do that? She managed to turn everything into a put-down. "It's nice to know you're available if the occasion should arise." Of course, I meant "fat chance," but she wouldn't perceive it that way.

"When are you going home? We really should walk together. Did you hear about that dreadful man who broke into Gerrie's house? I heard she had to stab him!"

I blinked at her for a moment. So that was the rumor around town. "I'll be another half hour, if you don't mind waiting."

The hotel staff had already moved in to clear the tables and break them down. Attendees sidled up to the bar, including Todd and Colleen, though I noticed they kept a good distance apart.

I joined Colleen to thank her for her business and wrap up my part of the event. But as she walked away, I noted that she was very good at her job, winding through the attendees and making sure they knew about the organization she worked for and how it would benefit them.

Natasha was busy flirting with a man who had loosened his tie and unbuttoned the collar of his shirt. I could hear her saying, "It was Edwin who had the brains in that family. Gerrie will be lost without him."

I swapped my heels for sneakers and slid my phone into a side pocket of the tote bag, then sidled up to Natasha. "I'm ready to go when you are."

She used the opportunity to make a gracious exit. We walked out into the sultry summer night. It was nearing ten o'clock and the streets teemed with people enjoying a fun Saturday night.

"You have opened my eyes," said Natasha. "I have spent my life focusing on gracious living and aspirational lifestyles. I can't believe that I have overlooked my innate talent for business. They were fascinated by my cookies and how I did everything, from marketing to baking. They just couldn't get enough information. I never realized that I should be a business expert."

Uh-oh. She had a tendency to jump to conclusions. "You did something with your cookies that they aspire to."

"And I spoke well."

"Yes, you did."

"I was a star. Do you do a lot of these conferences?"

"Not on this particular topic. It's fairly new," I explained.

"I would like to do more of them. I'll phone my publicist. Thank you, Sophie."

I said good night and turned off to my house.

I slept late on Sunday. Mochie snuggled in bed with me, in no hurry to go anywhere. I looked forward to retrieving Daisy and having a leisurely day before Monday arrived with all the bells and whistles of work again.

Eventually I pulled on skorts and a favorite old sleeveless button-down shirt that had been washed so many times it was soft and comfy. Mochie and I made our way down-stairs just as I heard crazed knocking on my kitchen door.

I hurried down the stairs to find Gerrie looking in the window.

"Good morning!" I said cheerily when I opened the door.

Gerrie dashed inside and peered out the window. "I don't think anyone followed me."

"Someone's following you?"

"I don't know." She sounded breathless.

I put on the kettle for tea. She might have preferred cof-fee, but I didn't think she needed more caffeine. Tea would help calm her. "Did you see someone? Why do you think someone is following you?"

I tried to sound placid and low-key. Her back was to me. She was still looking out the window. I wished I had cups that matched the plates I had bought. Gerrie would have appreciated them. Instead, I pulled out two sets of the Villeroy & Boch Mariefleur oversize breakfast cups and matching plates.

She'd been stress eating the other day. I suspected she would be again and popped sourdough bread into the toaster. It was really closer to time for brunch than break-fast, so I arranged a quick platter of sliced ham and smoked salmon.

"Someone's coming. She's running!"

I looked out the window. "That's just Nina. You poor thing. What happened?"

"Are you sure it's Nina?"

Nina opened the door, which evoked a wretched scream of terror from Gerrie.

I took her by the arm and steered her into the banquette so she would be looking inward.

"Gosh," said Nina. "I know I'm not wearing makeup, but I didn't think I was *that* scary."

The barest hint of a smile crossed Gerrie's face. "You look fine. I'm just on edge. Has anyone ever shot through this bay window?"

Nina gasped. "Someone shot at you?"

"Is that what you heard?" asked Gerrie.

Oh no! This was how rumors got started. I tried to distract them. "Nina, could you get a cup and plate out of the cupboard, please? Gerrie, Nina loves bacon. Maybe you could cook some while I make a fruit salad?"

It worked like a charm. In no time at all, Gerrie was busy glazing bacon with maple syrup and Nina had set a place for herself at the table. I fried eggs, then spooned blackberry jam into a jam jar and set it on the table with butter. Then I cut up a cantaloupe and placed the bite-size pieces in a large bowl. I added halved strawberries, raspberries, blueberries, and blackberries, and sprinkled them with sugar. A squeeze of lemon sparked up the flavors. I tossed it and brought it to the table just about the time that Gerrie added a platter of bacon to the tabletop.

Nina snitched a slice immediately.

We sat down to our impromptu brunch. "Okay, Gerrie, tell us what happened."

"Where's Daisy? I didn't hear her barking." Gerrie slathered toast with butter and jam.

"She stayed with Mars this weekend."

"Oh. I may get a dog. The biggest, barkiest one I can find!" Gerrie sipped her tea. "When I stepped outside for the newspaper this morning, I found this." She pulled up a photo on her phone and showed it to us.

The photograph was of a peculiar statuette resembling a gargoyle. It had wings, a square face, and was resting its head in one hand.

"What is it?" asked Nina. "It's vaguely reminiscent of a bulldog."

"The statue is called *Grumblethorpe*. Don't ask me why. Edwin thought it resembled him. You know, chubby and sort of grumpy. This morning, I found it outside my house positioned as though it was looking into my kitchen."

"Where was it before?" I bit into a slice of the sweet-and-salty bacon.

"In Edwin's home office."

Nina and I shared a look.

Nina helped herself to the fruit salad. "A member of your family must have taken it outside for some reason."

Gerrie shook her head. "I think it's a message. Just like Edwin's death certificate in my purse."

Chapter 15

Dear Sophie,
I have heard that you always have something ready
to serve people when they drop by. How do you do
that? If someone came to my house unexpectedly,
they'd be lucky to get a saltine.
                    Empty Fridge in Soda Springs, Idaho

Dear Empty Fridge,
Many baked goods freeze very well. I stash them in
my freezer. That way, I don't gobble them all, and
when friends drop by, cupcakes or cookies need
only be thawed.
                                              Sophie

"Was there a note on the statue?" I asked Gerrie.
"No. Nothing that obvious. I think the person
who killed Russ placed it there to scare me."

He'd done a good job of that. "Did you call Wolf?"

"I did. I used to like Wolf. He came over right away, but
when he saw the gargoyle statue, he dismissed my concerns. And then, making matters worse, my son Todd, my

flesh and blood, a man to whom I gave birth, told Wolf," she shifted her voice into a whiny tone, " 'Mom has been very anxious since Dad died. She probably took it outside and forgot about it!' He's a traitor to his own mother. Now, Wolf will assume I can't think clearly and he won't believe anything I say."

"I believe you," I said softly. I had read about people being confused when they lost a spouse. But nothing Gerrie had done or said indicated anything of the sort to me. In fact, I was more concerned about Todd. Could he be trying to mislead Wolf? Surely, he didn't want Wolf to think Gerrie had murdered Russ! Or did he?

"Thank you, Sophie." She reached out and clutched my hand for a moment. "I knew *you* would understand. I'm telling you, I am on the verge of throwing Todd out of my house. Maybe that will be the kick in the pants he needs to lose Nicci and go back to Colleen, where he belongs."

I couldn't blame her for being angry, but I didn't think Colleen was eager to take Todd back. "When I dated Wolf, one of his most frustrating characteristics was his poker face. It drove me bananas. I'm sure it's useful for a cop, but I hated that I couldn't tell what he was thinking. So don't give up on Wolf. He may not have bought into Todd's story."

Gerrie's face brightened. "I hope you're right!"

"When did the gargoyle go missing?" I asked.

"That's part of the problem. I can't really say. I didn't notice that it was gone. If the killer didn't take it, then it means someone has been in my house!" she screeched. "The police took a lot of pictures. I don't know if they took any of Edwin's office, though. This is a nightmare."

"Do you have an alarm system?" asked Nina.

Chewing on a piece of toast, Gerrie nodded. "I turn it on every night before I go to bed. Well, not so much since Todd has been living there. He often comes in late and forgets to turn it off. There's nothing like waking to the wail of the alarm. Then I'm wide awake and Todd ambles off to bed to sleep. So I haven't been using the alarm unless he's already home for the night."

"Not during the day?" Nina reached for the jam.

"I never thought it was necessary before now. I still don't understand why Russ was in my house. Although Todd seems willing to throw *me* under the bus, I will not reciprocate. I *know* my sons did not kill him."

"That means there had to be an intruder," I said. "There's no way around that. If it wasn't you, your children, or Colleen, then someone else had to be in the house." It was a possibility, but I hadn't really considered it. I hadn't been as magnanimous as Gerrie. I hadn't ruled out one of her sons as the killer. "When you go home, I'd like you to take photos of your house. Walk through every room. Photograph bookshelves and objects similar to the gargoyle. If this happens again, we'll know if an object was taken on the day of Russ's murder, or if someone is getting into your house."

Nina waved her toast in the air. "And if you don't have them, put cameras on the front and back doors."

Gerrie appeared to relax a little bit and I could tell she felt better when she left with Nina to pay a visit to the animal shelter.

But I was even more worried than before. That Russ's murder took place in her house had been odd. And finding Edwin's death certificate in her purse could easily have been something she forgot having stashed there. But having the gargoyle statue show up was very strange. Why would anyone do that? Had someone meant to frighten her, or was that some kind of threat?

In the afternoon, I headed to the local grocery store in search of something interesting to serve for dinner on Wednesday. I passed by my usual purchases of shrimp and hamburger, and was contemplating beef, when someone whispered in my ear, "Don't turn around or acknowledge me."

I sucked air in a little gasp before I realized that the voice sounded familiar.

In fact, it sounded just like Wong. "I need to talk with you. Meet me in your backyard tonight at eleven. I'll be coming through the alley."

Her voice stopped, and I felt her presence leave. What was going on?

"Sophie? Sophie?"

I snapped my head up.

The butcher grinned at me. "Some nice pork shoulder just came in."

"That would be terrific, thanks." Pork shoulder made excellent pulled pork. I took the package, thanked him again, and strolled through the store, adding staples like eggs to my cart, as well as a dozen fresh peaches.

I was pulling my little grocery cart along the sidewalk, when I heard a yelp. I stopped and turned to find Daisy waggling her entire body in joy. She pranced in circles and panted.

Mars laughed at her. "Gee, I don't think she missed you at all!"

"The house feels so empty without her."

"I'd love to keep her longer, but I won't be home much this week. She might as well hang out with you."

"Thanks, Mars. I appreciate that and so does Daisy."

I took her leash from him and she walked home beside me.

At eleven o'clock, I turned out the lights, as if going to bed. Only my bedside lamp was on. I carried a flashlight, but didn't use it in case someone was watching my house. It was a little bit too cloak and dagger, which wasn't at all like Wong.

I loaded a tray with her favorite chocolate cupcakes and

iced raspberry peach tea, which wouldn't keep us from sleeping. I considered alcohol, but the fact that she'd set up our meeting in such a clandestine way led me to believe she needed to keep her wits about her.

I decided to let Daisy roam in the yard. She wasn't very barky, but if she noticed anyone hanging around in the dark, she might bark to let me know.

We were a little bit early. I placed the tray on the outdoor dining table and waited in the dark.

My eyes had adjusted to the light of the moon, and I watched the gate in the back of my yard. It looked a lot like Gerrie's gate, constructed of wood, the slats ending in an upward curve too tall to see over.

It opened with a slight creak and I could see Daisy loping toward the gate.

Wong patted Daisy and took care to latch the gate quietly behind her. She stood still for a moment, only her head moving as she checked out the yard. She finally walked over to me.

"Wouldn't it be better to meet inside?" I asked in a low voice.

"The houses are too close to the street. Back here, someone driving through the alley won't see us. And if someone should open the gate, we can slip away through the gate to Francie's house."

When I put that gate in a few years ago, I had only thought of Francie. It never dawned on me that it would provide an escape route from my yard.

"Who are you afraid of?"

She peeled the paper from a cupcake. "My ex-husband is back in town."

I hadn't expected that. Wong had never said much about him except that he was the wrong man for her by a mile. "Was he violent toward you?"

"Mmm, these are my favorite. Chocolate cupcakes with

chocolate frosting. Yum!" She finished the last bite. "Just what I needed. I've been worried sick since I heard Eddie was in town. Eddie is a narcissist. He comes across as a gentleman toward women. But he's always trying to manipulate people. He will twist your words and make you believe that he's right."

"Then he was violent toward you."

Wong ducked her head. "Yes. And I have the photos to remind myself if I ever get lost that way again. You never know about a guy like Eddie. He's a class-A con artist and I do not want to get involved in whatever he's up to. I'm afraid of being swept up into his vortex. I've notified my boss at the Alexandria Police about his presence."

"Notified them? Why?"

Wong snorted. "The timing is entirely too suspicious. Russ was one of his delinquent accomplices. One of his associates in crime. The last I heard, Eddie was laying low in Florida. His reappearance at this particular time can't be a coincidence."

"You don't trust him at all. Why did you marry him?"

"Oh, Sophie. I was young and naïve. Wait until you meet him. He's a charmer. Don't let him suck you in."

Wong was one of the smartest women I knew. I found it difficult to imagine that she would have succumbed to some scammer.

"My whole family bought into him. When he would pick me up for a date, he would bring flowers for my mother. My dad is a statistician for the government. He's no pushover, but Eddie impressed him right away. My parents thought the world of him. He said he went to Columbia and then to Oxford. All lies. You can't imagine their disappointment when I ditched Eddie." She stopped talking for a moment and guzzled the cold tea. "I nearly lost my job because of him. When I found out about his scam, I turned him in."

"That's why you're afraid of him."

"A sharp lawyer got him off for time served. But by then, I had packed up and moved out of the house. He doesn't know where I live, at least I don't think so. But I'm pretty sure he didn't come back here because of me. He smells an opportunity."

"I don't understand. Russ is dead. How can that be an opportunity?"

"I haven't figured that out yet. But I know Eddie. There's a reason he came back now. He's up to no good. That's why I'm here. If Eddie thinks he can get something from you, he'll be your new best friend. I'm warning you, Sophie. He'll tell you all about a new business venture. Trust me, there isn't one." She sat silently for a moment. "I figure he needs money to live on. If he thinks you have information that he can broker, like about Russ's death, he'll be on you like a tick."

"That's crazy. He doesn't know me." I wondered if she was overreacting.

"To him, you are a ripe peach, just waiting to be plucked. Did you know that narcissists are attracted to clever, confident women?"

"I'm more concerned about you, Wong. If you turned him in, doesn't he hold a grudge against you?"

"Probably. But I could be worth more to him for whatever slimy swindle he has in mind. He'll anticipate being able to con me again. But you, Sophie, are going to be on his radar because everyone knows you're well-connected and you will be snooping around Russ's murder."

"I'm surprised he was able to fool you the first time around."

"Me too. But it won't ever happen again." She picked up another cupcake. "I know I shouldn't eat this, but I figure my stress is burning calories like crazy."

"If you haven't seen Eddie, then how do you know he's in town?"

"People have been calling to warn me. He's been visiting some of our old haunts. And my dad is pretty sure he saw Eddie drive by my parents' house."

"He's looking for you."

She took a deep breath. "I'm ready for him."

"How will I know him when I meet him? What does he look like?"

She stood up and ruffled Daisy's fur. "You'll know. He'll stand out from the crowd. He always does. Be careful, Sophie." She slipped away to the gate, peered around before she stepped into the alley, and then pulled the gate closed.

Daisy romped around, following fireflies. It was such a beautiful night. The temperature was perfect for sitting outside, but Wong's concerns had left me uneasy. There wasn't anything I could do about her ex-husband. I hoped she was exaggerating, though that wasn't like her at all.

Chapter 16

Dear Sophie,
The staircase in my house leaves an overhang of
sorts underneath it. I have no idea what to do with
it. Any suggestions?
                        Renovating in Pine Bluff, Wisconsin

Dear Renovating,
That kind of niche can be very attractive. Depend-
ing on the location of your stairs, it's a super place
for a Christmas tree! You can also build in book-
shelves. One of my perennial favorites is a com-
fortable chair with a lamp for reading.

                                        Sophie

Wong and Eddie were the first things I thought of on
Monday morning. I longed for a cup of coffee, but
when I let Daisy out in the backyard, I could feel another
scorcher coming. It would be too hot to walk her later on.
I slid her halter over her head, attached the leash, locked
the door, and the two of us set off. Our walk took us by

Gerrie's house. Senator Keswick's home stood across the street.

It was silent and stately. The kind of house that surely protected its inhabitants from tragedy. But life wasn't like that. No matter how strong and impressive the outer trappings were, nothing could shield any of us from adversity. A sleek black Audi sedan idled in front of it. The driver stood on the sidewalk, near the open rear door, holding a file and a to-go cup that probably contained coffee. When the senator emerged from his home, the driver waited until he was seated, handed him the coffee and the file, then closed the door, and hurried around the car to get into the driver's seat. The car merged slowly into traffic.

I gazed at his elegant home. Nothing moved in the windows.

Gerrie's luncheon had been on a weekday. Yet Senator Keswick had shown up very promptly, just after the rescue squad. Why hadn't he been at work? There were loads of possibilities. He came home for lunch. He had the day off. He wasn't well. Whatever the reason, he might have heard or seen something. I needed to pay him a visit.

Daisy and I strolled home. I fed Daisy and Mochie, then noshed on a croissant that I had bought the day before. I spent the morning in my office, making calls and sending emails with contracts.

Nina stopped by around noon. "Did Gerrie's flowers convince everyone to try another luncheon date?"

"I haven't heard anything more. I guess we should find out. We need to get on the ball with A Healthy Meal. We could stop by The Sugar Bowl to see if Gerrie is there. And I was hoping to pay a visit to Senator Keswick."

"And to Mindy and Jenna. Did you get the impression that there was something suspicious about the way Jenna ran out?"

"I'd like to think she was hysterical about seeing Russ with that knife jutting from his chest. But maybe there was more to it."

Leaving Daisy and Mochie to enjoy the comforts of air-conditioning, Nina and I walked over to Gerrie's store, The Sugar Bowl. The cool air and classical music in the store were soothing. And the merchandise was so tempting. One entire wall offered china, both high-end, special-occasion dishes and less expensive, everyday dinnerware. A young woman stared at the selection with an iPad in hand. She appeared to be choosing items for a wedding registry. I tore myself away and wandered into the kitchen area. A professional oven and stovetop were arranged so several people could cluster around them during the classes the store offered. I eyed a rondeau, a multipurpose pan with a broad base, straight sides, and two handles. I had a smaller one that I used for everything from cooking rice to frying and searing, but it would be nice to have a larger one, like this.

I heard Nina's voice. "I knew it. She's shopping!"

I turned around to see Nina with Gerrie in tow.

Gerrie smiled at me. "Sophie is one of my best customers."

"I guess Nina told you we're actually here about A Healthy Meal?"

"She did." Gerrie took a deep breath. "Everyone was lovely about it, except for Jenna, who isn't taking my calls!"

"Finding a dead person is never easy. And that knife! It was—" I winced at the memory "—especially gory. Do you think she knew Russ?"

"If that was the case, why wouldn't she have wanted to comfort him or try to help in some way?" Gerrie shook her head. "I don't think so."

There were other possibilities. "Maybe it brought back bad memories."

"Good heavens! I certainly hope she hasn't encountered anyone else with a knife stuck in his abdomen," said Gerrie.

"Maybe she's very sensitive," suggested Nina. "But you'd think she could have waited for Wolf, like everyone else."

Gerrie huffed. "Maybe she thinks I'm a murderer and she doesn't want anything to do with me."

That thought had crossed my mind. I hoped she would talk to Nina and me.

"With or without Jenna," said Gerrie, "we need to move forward with our plans. We can't delay any longer. I would hate to replace Jenna, but maybe that would be best for her if she's uncomfortable with me now. I've known Jenna since she played in sandboxes with Jim. Mindy says Jenna is furious with her for telling Wolf she ran out on him."

"I see. So we have some built-in animosity." I groaned.

"Honey, I think I'm going to have to resign. I can't see how else we're going to get anything done," said Gerrie.

"Don't do that! We need you on board. And everyone loves your luncheons! I'll touch base with the two of them and see what we can work out. We're on our way to Jenna's now. Hopefully, we can get her to come around." I waved goodbye and left with Nina.

Jenna's home wasn't far away. Like Gerrie's house, it had no front yard and abutted the sidewalk, but it was much smaller. Like Gerrie, Jenna had placed planters on each side of the front door, except hers were filled with boxwoods.

I banged the door knocker, which was shaped like a dragonfly.

Jenna opened the door, her sandy hair perfectly coiffed in a classic bob. She gasped and slammed the door shut.

Nina and I exchanged a look. I hadn't expected *that*!

I knocked on the door softly. "Jenna, what's wrong?"

"I don't want to talk about it!" she said from the other side of the door.

"Are you afraid of something?" I asked.

"I can't be involved."

"With A Healthy Meal?" asked Nina. "Do you want to leave the group?"

"No." The door opened a crack. Jenna peered outside. "Is it just the two of you?"

We nodded.

"Okay." She opened the door wide enough for us to edge inside. We watched as she locked and bolted the door.

The front door opened directly into the living room, which had been nicely decorated with white wainscoting and pale-yellow walls. A sofa and chair were upholstered in a buttery color. We could see into the dining room, where the white wainscoting continued, but the walls picked up the buttery shade of the furniture.

Jenna observed us with a worried expression. "Iced tea?"

"Please!" said Nina. "I'm parched."

"Maybe we should talk in the kitchen."

She led us through the dining room, where a narrow white staircase led upward. She'd done a great job of making the most of the resulting niche it created under the staircase by placing a chair and small table there with a lamp.

The kitchen was the third and final room on the main floor of the house. I had to guess that a door led to a tiny powder room. The kitchen was a good size and must have been recently renovated because it was loaded with the latest appliances. The cabinets and walls were white, and at the very end was a brick fireplace that had seen quite a bit of use.

"Is that original to the house?" I asked.

Jenna beamed. "My husband wanted to tear it out, but I think it adds character."

"I do, too. It's charming."

Nina and I sat at a white table, set with blue place mats adorned with sunflower-yellow piping, while Jenna poured three iced teas.

When she sat down, I got right to the point before she could get upset. It was a matter of business for the organization. "This is so refreshing. Thank you, Jenna. We need to know whether you want to leave A Healthy Meal. We would be sorry to see you go, but if that's what you'd prefer, please tell us."

Jenna stared at the table. "I was engaged to Russ!" she blurted, then covered her mouth with her hands, seemingly shocked by what she'd said.

For a long moment, Nina and I drank in the implications. "Why didn't you tell us?" asked Nina. "Oh, Jenna! It must have been horrible for you, seeing him dead like that."

"I'm so sorry," I added.

Jenna whispered, "I can't believe I told you. I think the pressure was just building up and I couldn't hold it in anymore. Now what have I done?" She looked from Nina to me. "Please! My husband cannot know."

Chapter 17

Dear Sophie,
I love my friends. Really, I do. But I went to a lot of trouble to bake a beautiful cake for a dinner party dessert. Well! One of them was on a diet. Another one no longer eats butter. Yet another one won't eat real sugar. Now I'm stuck with an entire cake that took me half a day to bake and decorate! What's a hostess to do?

Fed Up in Baker, Ohio

Dear Fed Up,
If they are dear friends, you might ask what they can eat for dessert. It can be fun to present a platter of miniature pastries to choose from. Maybe some of them will suit their dietary restrictions. Or meet with those friends for movies or concerts and find different dinner party companions.

Sophie

"Oh? Was there a jealous tiff between your husband and Russ? Did they fight over you?" Nina teased.

Jenna was not amused. "I knew I shouldn't tell you. Promise me you won't breathe a word to anyone. Especially you, Nina!"

"Hey, I can keep a secret," she protested.

All the while, I was thinking that we now had another suspect. At least as far as motive went. "I'm a little confused. You were engaged to marry Russ, but you broke off your engagement to marry your current husband?"

"Yes. But my husband, Eli, doesn't know. There wasn't a confrontation or anything because I never told Eli about Russ. Eli is, well, sort of a snob. He would have thought less of me if he knew I was involved with Russ." She winced and wailed, "I can't have Wolf show up at Eli's fancy law firm asking him about Russ. Eli will never forgive me for putting him in that position."

"You're going to have to come clean to Wolf, you know," I warned. "Otherwise, it will look worse. Like you're hiding something."

"She *is* hiding something!" said Nina.

"I mean about the murder."

Jenna grasped her iced tea glass that was wet with condensation and ran it across her forehead. "I don't know what to do. Russ showed up here a couple of days before he was . . . killed. He needed money and threatened to ask Eli for it if I didn't cough it up. It was a lot of money! I had to sell some jewelry to keep him from going to Eli. He clearly didn't realize that I never told Eli about him. And now," she moaned, "now Wolf will think I murdered Russ so he wouldn't be able to blackmail me."

Jenna was correct about that. I was beginning to think she could be the killer, too. Except for two things. Unless Jenna stabbed Russ an hour or two before we arrived, there was no way she could have gotten blood spatter off her dress and hands without any of us noticing. And Gerrie surely would have known that Jenna was in her house.

Tears streamed down Jenna's cheeks. "Who would have ever expected this? I thought Russ and the people with whom he associated were all behind me. A closed chapter of my life. I never imagined that anything like this could happen. Russ hadn't been in touch since my engagement to Eli. I admit that when I gave Russ money, I worried about him coming back for more. I was afraid he would blackmail me. How do you ever stop that? But then to have him show up at Gerrie's house, dead in the dining room? Everyone else was talking about who could have done it and all I could think was that Wolf would arrest me. I haven't slept. I've been eating everything in sight. I lie awake at night, waiting for Wolf to knock on my door. I'm just sick about the whole thing. My life has come to an end."

"That's not true," I tried to speak in a soothing voice. "You just have to get over the hurdles of telling Wolf and Eli. You can go to Wolf first and explain the situation. Maybe he won't think it's necessary to interview Eli!"

"Fat chance," muttered Nina.

I kicked her gently under the table. No matter what, Jenna *had* to tell Wolf. There was simply no way to avoid that.

Jenna perked up. "Maybe I wouldn't have to tell Wolf if you two would figure out who killed Russ! I could help you."

"How can you help us?" asked Nina.

"Well, I can tell you about Russ and the people he hangs out with." Jenna dabbed at her eyes with a paper towel. "Um, like after me, he had this girlfriend named Lucky. I don't think that's her real name, but it's what they call her. She won big at a poker game one night and the name stuck. She's, um, you know, a sexy dresser, heavy on the makeup, and I've heard she has a tiny butterfly tattoo on the back of her ankle. Russ was against her getting a tattoo, so she went with a really small one."

"Did she have any reason to kill Russ?" I asked.

"Not anything that I know about, but he hangs with some shady people. He grew up in that crowd. He walks the walk, talks the talk. But then he became the contact for people who wanted to buy drugs. They were people who were well-off. You know, the types who drive Beemers and Hummers. He met them at the golf club where his mom worked. That was where I met him. Not because of drugs, but because he liked to hang around there. I didn't realize he was a dealer. He had become friends with my friends at the golf club and seemed like a nice guy. He was a chameleon, going back and forth between the two groups. He quit selling drugs, but you know, it was kind of hard for him because he had dropped out of high school, and without an education, it was hard for him to find work. The drug sales had kept him flush and popular. Some of the people at the golf club hired him to do odd jobs. I don't think they knew anything about his drug connections, but maybe they did. Everybody wants connections to people who can do things for them, right?"

I didn't like this at all. It meant there were two different groups of people Russ might have ticked off. He might have found out something about one of the golfing guys and tried to blackmail him. Or he could have cheated one of his old friends. This opened a whole new set of possibilities! But I would bet that Wolf knew that by now.

"Who would know more about what was going on in his life?" I downed the remaining tea in my glass.

She winced. "I'll make a call."

"I'm starving," said Nina. "Can we meet this person in a restaurant?"

Jenna looked uncomfortable.

"Maybe I can get Bernie to give us a private room." I made a quick call to him and reported back. "He has a couple of rooms available right now, if your contact can come."

Jenna dialed a number and walked into the dining room. We heard her voice, but it was more of a murmur than anything else.

She returned to the kitchen. "We're on in thirty minutes. Nothing personal, but I'll meet you there. I think it's best if I'm not seen hanging with you."

I wasn't sure I could trust her. I liked Jenna, but I didn't know if she was being truthful about anything. "No problem. We'll meet you there in half an hour."

"Would you mind going out the back way?" she asked. "Fewer prying eyes."

Nina and I left through her gorgeous backyard. The center had been bricked and the branches of two giant trees hung over a table and chairs, as if they were sheltering her outdoor dining area.

"This is bigger than her kitchen and dining room combined," Nina observed.

"It's charming. I bet they spend a lot of time out here."

We were on the sidewalk, heading to The Laughing Hound, when Nina said, "She's getting a divorce. Pity. It will be hard on her."

"How do you know that?"

"Are you kidding? There is no possible way that she will be able to keep her previous engagement to Russ a secret from her husband. And when he finds out, he will never trust her again. *Ever.* He will always wonder what else she's hiding from him."

"That would be a shame." I feared that Nina was correct, though. Trust had to be one of the most important cornerstones of marriage. And once Eli found out that she had neglected to mention her previous engagement, even if it wasn't important, he would always wonder what other secrets she had.

Both of us were wiping our brows by the time we entered the cool restaurant. Bernie spotted us and showed us to a small, charming room upstairs that overlooked the street below.

"Thanks for accommodating us, Bernie." I gave him a peck on the cheek.

"Anything for my two most favorite ladies."

"Hey, Bernie, did you see Todd Stansfield in here the day Russ was killed? He claims he had a business meeting."

"It's possible that I didn't notice him, but I don't think he was here. I haven't seen Todd in a month."

Bernie was about to exit, when Jenna walked in with a man I had never met.

Nina let out a double sigh.

He was gorgeous, with a perfectly oval face, high cheekbones, a light tan, velvety brown eyes, and luscious lips that curled into a dangerously enticing smile. Wong had been right. I knew him as soon as I saw him.

I reached out my hand to shake his.

"Hi. I'm—"

"Eddie Wong," I said.

Nina gasped. "You're Wong's ex-husband?"

He smiled. "None other. How is my darling ex-wife?"

Bernie withdrew quietly, but I caught the look of surprise on his face.

"She's well. I'll tell her you asked about her." I accepted a menu from a server who had quietly slipped in.

Eddie laughed. "I dare say she won't be happy to know I'm in town."

I supposed it would be rude to ask why she wouldn't be happy about it, although I was itching to know what he would say, even if it didn't match Wong's explanation. But we needed him to tell us about Russ first. I couldn't afford to alienate him. Not yet anyway.

I watched Jenna carefully when she ordered. Why would

she think that Eddie Wong, who had recently returned to Old Town, would know anything about Russ's life in recent years?

I ordered a mango chicken salad, but the other three went with The Laughing Hound's famous sandwiches.

We chatted a few minutes about Wong and where Eddie had been living.

Eddie gazed at Nina, who could hardly take her eyes off him. "I understand you ladies would like to know about Russ and who killed him?"

"Do you know?" I asked.

He didn't respond for what felt like an inordinately long time. Either he was carefully considering his response, or he liked an air of drama. When he turned his attention to me, he smiled and met my gaze. If Wong hadn't warned me about him, I might have thought he was being seductive. "I knew Russ very well. Better than most. But I must ask, how well do you know the Stansfields?"

Nina flashed me a look.

The tension in the room was oppressive. I reminded myself that he was trying to intimidate us. There wasn't a good reason for him to be acting like the Godfather. No wonder Wong had suffered through her marriage to him. What had she said? He could twist your words? I was willing to wager that he could do exactly that. "I have known Gerrie for many years."

There. Let him try to flip that back at me.

He stared at me and gently touched his lips with his forefinger. "You are dealing with the most dangerous family in town."

He paused and watched silently as the server brought our food. I caught the sly wink he shot her.

When she closed the door, he ate half his sandwich and acted as though he hadn't told us anything astonishing. I wondered if he'd eaten recently.

Nina, Jenna, and I exchanged horrified looks.

Eddie guzzled his beer. "Everyone knows better than to go up against a Stansfield because no matter what they do, the stink slides off them. Really?" he asked, looking around at us. "It never occurred to you that Gerrie Stansfield knocked off her husband?"

I choked on my chicken salad and hastily sipped tea.

"Oh sure. It goes way back. A couple of years ago, one of her sons stabbed a guy at a bar just outside of Old Town."

I nearly spewed my tea.

"Exactly which bar was this?" asked Nina. "I don't remember anything like that."

"It was called Ruby's. I'm told it has closed down. There was a big fight. Both the Stansfield brothers were present when Russ was stabbed."

"Were you there, too?" asked Nina. "Or are you telling us what you heard?"

He gave her a sly smile. "I have issues with self-incrimination. I believe I'll decline to answer that question."

Nina looked at me with shock in her eyes.

"It was brutal. You know why you didn't hear about it? Because money talks. The Stansfields hire the best attorney in town and *whoosh*! All is erased."

Nina dropped her sandwich, which, fortunately, landed on her plate. "Do you mean there was a cover-up?"

I thought I saw some satisfaction in Eddie's eyes when he said, "They probably paid off somebody." He continued to eat his sandwich.

Jenna, Nina, and I stared at him.

I was trying to cope with that news and thought they probably were, too.

"And now she has murdered her husband," said Eddie.

Jenna clapped a hand over her mouth.

Nina gasped.

"Are you sure?" I asked. "He died of a heart attack."

Eddie wiped a crumb from the corner of his mouth. "How convenient. I think we all know what happened there. A guy that tubby? He had to be on meds. Who do you think was administering his meds?"

"You're just speculating," I said. "You could say the same thing about anyone who died that way."

"Once again, a Stansfield gets away with murder. And no one even questions it." He smiled at me and bit into the remainder of his sandwich.

I tried to be cool, but inside I was reeling. Was it possible? Could Gerrie be the one who stabbed Russ?

"And now," Eddie said, finishing his sandwich, "the queen of the clan has killed Russ. True, he was a little worm. He cleaned up well, but he fed off women with money."

Jenna cried out, "He did not. Say that's not so."

"Sorry, Jenna." Eddie did not look remorseful. "I told him more than once that was going to end badly. You know what they say about women scorned. I may not have been an ideal husband, but Russ was nothing more than a leech, making promises he never intended to keep and draining them dry."

Jenna let out a strangled laugh. "Then my engagement was nothing but a sham. What have I done?" She leaped to her feet and ran out the door.

Eddie shook his head. "Pity. But he's gone now. It's all over for everyone who was involved with Russ. Gerrie did them a favor when she knocked him off."

I stared at him. "Let me get this straight. The Stansfield brothers were at a bar when a fight broke out. How do you know one of them stabbed a guy?"

"Maybe I was there."

"How do I know it wasn't you who stabbed him?"

"It wasn't."

He didn't have very convincing answers. "How do you know that Gerrie killed Russ? It could just as easily have been one of her sons."

"It wasn't. Very clever of her to hire you. Took everyone's eyes off her, didn't it? I bet you haven't ever really considered her as a suspect. Tell me, did she hire the best lawyer in town?"

He was right about that, but I wasn't going to admit it. Countless other people had done the same, some of whom were innocent, surely. Hiring a smart lawyer wasn't just something guilty people did.

"Ah. Your silence speaks volumes. The police must consider her the primary suspect. They're way ahead of you. The only question remaining is whether her lawyer can get her out of this fine mess."

"When did you arrive in town?" I asked.

"Oh, no you don't. My name does not come into this. I did you fine ladies a favor, and now I shall disappear. I'd better not hear my name being mentioned in connection with Russ or the Stansfields." He placed his napkin neatly by his plate. "Thank you for lunch."

He stood and walked to the door, where he turned and gave us a slight bow before he left.

Chapter 18

Dear Natasha,
I called the number to have some of your cookies delivered to me. They never came! Not only did you charge me for the cookies, but you also charged me $899 for designer jogging pants and a T-shirt! What gives?
Ripped Off in Cheat Lake, West Virginia

Dear Ripped Off,
That wasn't me. I don't jog and I never wear T-shirts. I can't help it if scammers use my name.
Natasha

"Well! If that wasn't the weirdest thing I've ever seen!" Nina let out a noisy breath. "I can see how Wong fell for him, though. He's dreamy!"

"He is that."

Bernie whipped the door open. He carried a tray with dessert dishes, which he set in front of us. He added one for himself and sat down. "Are you okay?"

"I'm fine now," Nina sipped ice water. "What is this? Looks like a mini mocha éclair, a raspberry tartlet, and a lemon square?"

Bernie nodded. "This is our dessert trio for people who can't make up their minds. How is it that you don't work in a restaurant, Nina?"

"I can't. I would eat all the food."

I made quick work of the mini éclair. The tiny pastry was only a couple of delicious bites.

"He's quite a character," I said. "Do you know Eddie Wong?"

"Not really. I used to see him in the restaurant. But that was a few years back. I understand he left town. Wonder what he was running from?"

"Trouble," I said. "Definitely trouble."

The rest of the day passed quietly after I returned home, but our meeting with Eddie Wong left me on edge. I baked a berry galette, but I jumped at every sound and repeatedly made certain my doors were locked. I didn't have a reason in the world to imagine anyone would threaten me, but I remained uneasy.

I thought I knew Gerrie fairly well. She wasn't my best friend, but we had worked on a number of charitable projects together. Eddie's depiction of her as Ma Barker shook me to the core.

He was wrong. He had to be. And I was determined to prove it.

I didn't sleep well that night. I was up before the sun on Tuesday, sitting in my kitchen drinking a strong cup of tea with milk and a breeze of sugar, when Nina arrived with her sweet dog, Muppet, whose name suited the little floofball perfectly.

Nina wore a baby-blue silk robe over her nightgown. "I didn't sleep a wink. No wonder Wong divorced Eddie. Do you think he's like that all the time?"

I poured her a cup of tea and brought it to the table. "Probably. Did you see him winking at our server?"

"Ugh. Do you think he likes anyone?"

"Probably people he can con. I got the impression that he thinks most people are idiots to be taken advantage of."

"Me too! He's very self-impressed, isn't he?"

I nodded. "I wonder how Jenna is."

"Poor thing! Will it be easier or harder for her to tell her husband about her relationship with Russ now?"

"We should probably check on her today. I also want to stop by the Keswicks'. Their house looks directly at Gerrie's place. And Senator Keswick showed up awfully fast the day Russ was murdered. I'd like to know if they saw anything."

"Guess I'll go home and get dressed. Are you available around eleven?"

"Sounds good."

Nina left and I went upstairs to shower.

I dressed in a white skirt and a sleeveless yellow blouse, which I thought looked like the essence of summer. I let my hair air dry, and I didn't bother with makeup, other than sunscreen.

Intending to walk with Daisy, I retrieved my phone and realized that the battery was dead. I plugged it in on my dresser to charge while Daisy and I went for a lovely morning walk to beat the heat that would arrive all too soon. On our return, we shared oatmeal for breakfast, but Mochie preferred a salmon-and-chicken combo. Armed with a mug of steaming tea, I retreated to my home office and settled in to work. Half an hour later, I heard banging. Mochie and Daisy scampered ahead of me and disappeared into the kitchen. I opened the door to Mars.

"Where have you been?" he demanded.

"Right here."

"I've been calling and texting you."

I glanced around for my phone. "You could have called my landline."

"I did! You never picked up."

Mars seized the landline phone and examined it. "The ringer is off. I'm turning it back on."

I couldn't imagine how that happened. I must have hit a button and not realized it. "Is something wrong?"

"Apparently so. Natasha and Wolf have called to ask where you are."

"That can't be good." I retrieved my phone from the charger in my bedroom. I immediately saw there were texts and missed calls from Natasha and Wolf.

"Wolf just pulled up," said Mars.

I waited at the door and smiled at Wolf as he walked in. "What's going on?"

"Why aren't you answering your phone? I thought you were dead."

"It was in my bag, and I forgot to charge it. I have a landline, you know."

"Maybe you should check your messages."

I ignored his sarcasm. "What's so important? Did you identify Russ's killer?"

He heaved a sigh. "Your buddy Gerrie is going down for that one."

"That's not funny."

Nina rushed in with Muppet on her heels. She closed the door behind her. "What's going on?"

"I'm not joking, Sophie. It appears that Gerrie was the only person in the house and the knife came from her kitchen."

I sank into a chair at the kitchen table next to Nina. "Then it must have been self-defense."

"Possibly. But I'm not here about Gerrie." Wolf shoved a robin's-egg–blue flyer in front of me. "What can you tell me about this?"

It was an ad for Natasha's cookies. She had outdone herself. *Natasha's Cookies* looped across the top in a handwritten font. The front side contained a photograph of a scrumptious chocolate chip cookie next to a tall glass of milk and a phone number. The reverse side showed a beautiful photograph of cookies in four flavors, and a phone number to order them.

"Great photos!" I said. "Now I'm hungry for cookies."

"Me too!" Nina pulled out her phone and started to tap in the number.

"Nina, don't!" Wolf snatched her phone away and canceled the call.

"Well, that was rude," said Nina.

"Just bear with me," Wolf grumbled, still clutching Nina's cell phone. "Sophie, what do you know about this?"

"Natasha started a cookie line. She doesn't bake them herself. They're made in ghost kitchens."

"Natasha says you gave away her cookies at a banquet on Saturday?"

"That's right. She came as a speaker, and I thought it would be a nice promotional giveaway for the guests."

"Did you make up these flyers?" asked Wolf.

"No. I don't work for Natasha. I ordered the cookies because they fit the theme of the conference. She must have made the flyers."

"She denies any association with the flyers."

I was confused. "She didn't have these printed?"

"She says she didn't."

My kitchen door flew open. Natasha wasn't nearly as attractive when she was angry. Her eyes had reduced to slits. Her lips mashed together, and two serious creases formed between her eyebrows. "What have *you* done?"

Mars scooted around the banquette, as far away as he could get from Natasha. I had to suppress my amusement. I rose to close the door behind her and spoke as calmly as I could. "I don't know what you're talking about."

She shrieked, "How can you lie straight to my face? I did not do this! It's all your fault. You have ruined me!"

I still had no clue what was going on. I moseyed over to the stove. "Iced tea or should I put on some coffee?"

Natasha's eyes grew large. "No wonder Mars left you! You're impossible!" I winced a little, mostly because she was screaming. I pondered retaliating with some accusations of my own about her behavior toward Mars before the end of my marriage to him, but Wolf broke in.

"There's no need to shout, Natasha. We can all hear you just fine. Soph, do you have any coffee?" asked Wolf.

I put the kettle on.

"Easy for you to say. You're not watching a lifetime of hard work crumble before your eyes," Natasha snarled.

"'Crumble,'" snickered Mars. "Cute, like your cookies are crumbling."

"How can you joke around? I want the money, Sophie." Natasha spoke fiercely.

"What money?" I asked in a soft voice so she would have to listen.

"Aargh! Wolf! You're useless. Why haven't you arrested her?" Natasha glared at him.

This was the woman who called *me* her *bestie*?

I poured scalding water over fresh coffee grounds in my French press. While the coffee steeped, I brought cream and sugar to the table, along with napkins that matched the tablecloth's cream-and-rose colors.

Natasha huffed when I added dessert plates and forks to the table. I retrieved the blueberry and raspberry galette I had made and set it in the center of the table with a little pot of sweetened whipped cream, then poured coffee for everyone. "Look, Natasha. I have no idea what's going on or why you would blame it on me. I thought I was doing you a favor and that it would be cute to give your cookies to the participants of the conference." It was low of me, and I realized that, but I said it anyway, "It was probably the biggest order of cookies you've ever gotten."

Natasha was still fuming when I sat down, sliced the galette, and handed each of them a piece.

Natasha glared at me with a look that could kill. "A galette is not going to make this any better for you, Sophie."

"You don't have to make that face, Natasha," I said. "Whatever it is, I had nothing to do with it."

Wolf had already eaten half his piece of the galette. He waved the flyer at me. "Did you pass these out?"

"The first time I ever saw them was when you showed them to me a few minutes ago."

He studied me.

"What's the problem?" I asked.

Through gritted teeth, Natasha said, "The problem is that you have ruined me. Everything I have worked for. My name is mud!"

"Did you *pay* someone to distribute these? Or leave them at the conference hotel somewhere?" asked Wolf.

"No. I just told you, I never even saw them before you walked through my door. I don't get it. Does this have something to do with Russ's murder?"

"Probably not," Wolf grumbled.

Having finished his slice of galette, Mars reached over to cut another piece. "What's the big deal about the flyers?"

"They're fraudulent," said Wolf. "When you call to order cookies, they take your credit card number and place the charge. Then they make a much larger purchase elsewhere using the credit card information that you gave them. Usually, something for several hundred or thousands of dollars that they turn around and sell. But you never get any cookies. You do, however, get the bill for the other things they bought."

Chapter 19

Dear Sophie,
I have so many beautiful furnishings and acces-
sories, but none of them go together well. It just
looks crowded and cluttered. I don't want to get
rid of these lovely memories. How do I incorporate
them in my décor?
Mishmash in Treasure Lake, Pennsylvania

Dear Mishmash,
Look for similar colors or patterns among your
treasures and use them as groups. Vary the sizes
and number of items and place groups of them
apart so the eye has a moment of rest. Use throw
carpets to define the distinct areas for large items
and trays to corral smaller ones. As long as you feel
comfortable and love it, that's all that matters.
Sophie

"That's terrible!" Nina said. "I order lots of things."
"Just make sure you're buying from a legitimate company," warned Wolf.

"I *am* a legitimate company," Natasha griped.

I examined the flyer again. "It certainly looks convincing. They used your colors and—" I stopped abruptly. "Take another look." I handed it to Wolf. "It says 'Nataska's Cookies'! But in that particular font, the lower case *k* is easily mistaken for an *h*."

Wolf examined the flyer. "That was intentional. They're tricking people, to rip them off."

"And using my good name." Natasha groaned. "Why me? Why did they pick on me? I can't go and change my name. Natasha is my brand and now they're destroying everything I have worked for. *Everything!*"

"Maybe it's not as bad as you think." I said, mainly to give Natasha some hope. "A lot of the people who visit Old Town don't live here. Many of the people attending the conference were from other towns. They'll think you don't deliver that far away."

"So far, we have eighteen complaints of nondeliveries." Natasha bit her upper lip as though she was trying to stop herself from crying. "Eighteen!"

"On the bright side, everyone liked your cookies," I pointed out.

She shot a look of daggers at me. "They're not even using my recipes. They refused to carry my signature cookies!"

Mars choked on his coffee. "Agh!"

But he was grinning. Natasha had tried to serve him those cookies too many times.

"Who is *they?*" I asked.

She flapped a hand at me. "It's all very complicated. A corporation sets it up with various kitchens that bake the cookies. They provide the boxes, which I designed, and they give the bakers the recipes."

"But they wouldn't use your recipes?" I asked.

"Apparently, someone there didn't like my recipes. There's

no accounting for taste. He had the nerve to say people wouldn't buy them!"

"What is your signature cookie?" asked Wolf.

Oh no! He was stepping into dangerous territory. Natasha dragged those cookies out every chance she got. On occasion, they'd been so spicy that I'd had to hide them. I knew for a fact I wasn't the only one who told her they'd all been eaten, when they'd actually been hidden away. In retrospect, that might not have been such a good idea because she kept baking them!

"Chocolate chip with jalapeño peppers." Natasha gazed at him proudly. "I'll have to bake some for you."

He waved her off. "I think I may have eaten one before. But please don't bake anything for me. I'm, uh, not eating anything hot or spicy."

"That's too bad. They're delicious."

Natasha had never listened to me, or anyone else that I knew of, about her overly liberal use of jalapeños in sweets. I wondered who was advising her. "Natasha, who told you not to feature your signature cookies?"

"The company that sets it all up and manages everything. They have bakers in cities all over the country. That way, I'm not wasting my time looking for people to bake the cookies."

"So your name is on them, but they're not your recipe and you don't actually bake them?" asked Mars. "What a business!"

"Right." Natasha sat up straighter and fluffed her hair. "I'm a brand."

"Does that company know about the fraud yet?" I asked.

She didn't have a chance to respond before Wolf said, "I'll need to contact them. Can you give me names and phone numbers?"

Mars rose and made more coffee.

As Wolf jotted down the information, I wondered why he was involved. "Wait a minute. You're usually assigned to homicide. Why are you following up on fraud?"

His face flushed red. "Because I know Natasha. Great galette, Sophie."

"It would have been better with jalapeños," muttered Natasha, who hadn't even tried it.

He had blown off my question. I couldn't help being suspicious.

"So, how are you going to track this guy down? Do you need a volunteer to charge something? I could do that for you." Mars poured more coffee for everyone.

"Thanks, that's a very kind offer, but it won't do us any good. He's using a fake phone number. These guys are pretty tech savvy. They know all the tricks."

"What do you mean by 'fake phone number'?" I asked.

"He uses a number that rolls over to his real number, which is probably assigned to a burner phone," Wolf explained.

"That doesn't help me," whined Natasha. "What am I supposed to do? Tell the world not to order my cookies? That's not fair."

"I'm not an expert on that, Natasha. You should probably contact a public relations firm for guidance. Our job is to find the creep and stop him."

"Couldn't he be anywhere?" Mars asked. "Even overseas? I thought these types of crimes were impossible to stop."

Natasha screeched, "Nooo!"

"In many circumstances, that's true. But someone delivered these flyers around town. That suggests it's a hometown job."

When they left, Nina and I made quick work of cleaning up, then headed for the Keswicks'. I felt Natasha's frustration. Even though she could be a pain, and everything was a huge drama with her, this time there wasn't much she could do.

"It's good to know that no one is unsuspectingly ordering those wretched jalapeño cookies, but I can't believe how quickly a scammer jumped onto that. It's scary. I order all kinds of things. Now I'll always wonder if it's a scammer or for real."

We reached the beautiful home with the Juliette balcony over the front door. I banged the eagle-shaped knocker twice.

Henrietta Keswick answered the door dressed in a shapeless shift dress that had seen better days. Although it was almost noon, she had a bed head, and appeared unprepared for the day. Three dogs sniffed us and wagged their tails.

"Sophie. Nina. Do come in. I was just going to have a latte and a bite of breakfast. Oof! It's hot out there again."

She closed the door behind us, and we followed her into an elegantly appointed kitchen, with white marble countertops. She picked up the wall phone and dialed. "Stevie, darling, I have guests. Would you send up two more lattes and something to serve them?"

Nina squatted to pet the dogs. "You're a woman after my own heart, Henrietta."

"Oh?"

"I cook with my phone, too."

The two of them roared.

"And why not?" asked Henrietta. "I appreciate good food and I don't see the point of getting the kitchen dirty when I haven't a clue how to cook."

"I know what you mean." Nina stroked the wall phone like it was her pet. "All that chopping and slicing! Who do you order from?"

Henrietta led us into the living room. A giant red Oriental rug covered the hardwood floor. Smaller Oriental rugs lay atop it in a scattered pattern around the room. The walls had been painted a deep coral shade. A portrait, nearly life-size, of Henrietta around age twenty hung over the fireplace. Bookshelves filled an entire long wall, interrupted only by window seats with dark teal cushions that looked extremely comfortable for curling up with one of the thousands of books.

Henrietta dropped onto a worn beige sofa. "I use Dinner at Home five days a week."

"I love their food. And I'm fond of ordering from The Laughing Hound."

"Oh yes. Bernie's place! You can't beat their barbecue."

As they chatted, I was intrigued by Henrietta's style. Everything seemed to be a hodgepodge, with no coordination. And yet, it was charming, warm, and inviting. One felt immediately at home, even though nothing matched, and an old carousel horse oddly dominated a corner.

The dogs lounged comfortably. The largest appeared to be a sweet Staffordshire terrier, whose face was half black and half white. Next was a dog whose mix I couldn't identify. His body shape reminded me of a Chihuahua, except he was bigger. He had a white face and body, with crooked black ears that were too large for him and stuck out sideways. The third looked to be a three-legged Pomeranian, who had no problem getting around despite her missing hind leg.

The doorbell rang and a chorus of barking commenced.

"That must be our lattes." Henrietta jumped up to get them. She returned right away and set them on the coffee table. She reached for a large silver platter, unfolded a napkin on it, and set triangular sandwiches on it. "I'm starved. I hope you like grilled cheese."

She helped herself to one. "So, what brings you two by? The commotion across the street at Gerrie's house?"

Commotion was certainly soft-selling it.

"Were you home that day?"

"Oh gosh, yes. I'm a late sleeper. I rarely leave the house before one, if at all. My husband ran over there to make sure his girlfriend was okay."

" 'His girlfriend'?" asked Nina.

"It's that Gerrie Stansfield. I can't stand the woman. I truly don't know what he sees in her."

"Are you joking, or are they—"

Henrietta interrupted me. "Having an affair? I honestly don't know. I certainly hope not. Although"—she licked cheese off her pinkie finger—"it would be scads better than her son marrying my daughter. I would have had to see her all the time. On holidays and such, you know."

I was a little taken aback. She had just suggested so many things. "Was one of her sons engaged to your daughter?"

"Thankfully, I managed to break that off. Trust me when I say it wasn't easy. They didn't actually make it to an official engagement with a ring and all, but they would have if it weren't for me."

"What did you do?" Nina helped herself to another sandwich.

"Oh, nothing terrible. I just planted ideas in their sweet young heads, and made sure my daughter, Emily, saw another girl leaving Jim's apartment."

"That would do it," said Nina in a disapproving tone.

"They weren't right for each other. I didn't want my baby stuck in an apathetic marriage like mine."

"Oh, Henrietta," I said softly, "I had no idea."

"I'm not the only one. It happens to a lot of couples. But to be truthful, at this point, only inertia is keeping us together. I have tired of his never-ending political dinners, and he has grown weary of me completely. If only it weren't Gerrie. I do loathe her." Henrietta shook her finger. "Never trust anyone who tries so hard to be perfect.

Like Natasha. I think she's your friend, but you should beware. Gerrie's house is always impeccable. I have yet to see her in any outfit that didn't match perfectly head to toe. Never a spot or a wrinkle anywhere. She runs that kitchen store. I suppose she's still involved with her father's business, too, and I see her name connected to charities all the time. How can anyone do all that and throw parties and cook and bake, too?"

Nina frowned at her. "Good question."

"She acts like she's some kind of princess because her father started that business. Well, I've got news for her. My roots go back in Old Town for generations. But you don't hear me talking endlessly about that." She giggled. "Of course, some of my ancestors weren't exactly upstanding citizens. I just don't care for her."

I couldn't help wondering if the real reason for her dislike of Gerrie was her husband's alleged interest in Gerrie.

"Does your daughter live in Old Town?" Nina sipped her latte.

"I'm relieved to say that she now resides in New York City. That suits me just fine. It's a short train ride, but far enough to discourage her from seeing Jim Stansfield. You know how they say long-distance relationships never work. I think that's true."

I tried to move her off that subject. Besides, I wanted to return to the subject of Russ's murder. "Did you happen to see anyone going in or out of Gerrie's house on Thursday?"

"You mean the day she murdered that man?"

Chapter 20

Dear Sophie,
My sister wants a rondeau for her birthday. What on earth is that?
                    Clueless in Cooks Corner, South Carolina

Dear Clueless,
A rondeau is a wonderfully versatile cooking pan. Imagine a stockpot that is only four or five inches tall. The rondeau has handles on both sides and a lid. It can be used to fry, poach, braise, roast, simmer, and boil!
                    Sophie

"They were up late the night before. My bedroom windows overlook the front of her house, so I really can't help noticing things and I'm a night owl, so I knew they were up. You would think my biggest dog, Oscar, would be the barky one, but it's Elmo who is always looking out the window and announces arrivals and departures at the Stansfield house. Peanut, our Pomeranian, uses any excuse to join in, but half the time I don't think she knows what she's barking about."

"Anything that moves, huh?" Nina held her hand out to Elmo. "I love these crazy ears!"

"He's a sweetheart. But he has a little bit of Jack Russell in him. People say they're not good guard dogs, but they let you know if anyone is around. Gosh, it wasn't that long ago. As I understand it, Gerrie was having a luncheon. When my morning latte was being delivered, there was a big cluster of women in front of her house."

"Did you see anyone before that? Members of the family arriving or leaving?"

"You'd have to ask my husband. He's the one who can't take his eyes off that house, and he's up much earlier than I am. I'll see what I can arrange."

Henrietta yawned and stood up. All three dogs focused on her to see what she would do. "We so rarely get visitors, unless Emily is home from New York. I look forward to it, even if you are trying to help Gerrie."

She and the dogs saw us to the door. While Nina thanked her and said goodbye, I studied Gerrie's house. It seemed so tranquil and beautiful. Henrietta and her husband certainly had a perfect view of comings and goings. In fact, I could see Gerrie through an upstairs window with her back to me.

Henrietta closed the door behind us.

"Let's check on Gerrie and see if Jenna ever got back to her about another try at a luncheon for A Healthy Meal," I suggested, thinking it might be interesting to pop in unexpectedly. Especially now that two people thought she had murdered Russ.

"We may never have to buy food again. We could just go door-to-door asking people questions. Do you think everyone feeds Wolf?"

"Probably not. He's usually there on official business."

We crossed the street and rang the bell. A cleaning woman holding a mop answered the door.

"We just stopped by to see Gerrie," I said.

"Come on in. She's upstairs on the second floor."

At that moment, something large crashed upstairs.

"Gerrie?" I cried, running up the stairs. I'd seen her through the window, so I headed that way at the stair landing. "Gerrie!"

I stopped in the doorway so abruptly that Nina ran into me. Silently, we took in the situation.

The paneled room was larger than I would have expected. An antique partners desk, with a leather top, stood in front of the window. A hefty chair was overturned behind it. Gerrie stood a few feet from the desk, staring at it in horror.

Slightly crumpled newspaper lay on the desk. In the middle of it was a knife, the blade encrusted with something dark reddish and black.

Nina screeched.

Gerrie's chest heaved with each breath. Her eyes met mine. "I don't know." She spoke with fear in her voice. "I don't know anything about it."

"Where did you find it?"

"In the safe. I've never seen it before. Well, I had probably seen the newspaper in there. I know I saw it after Edwin passed and assumed something must be wrapped up in it, but with the funeral and everything, all I wanted were the will and trust. Just the things I needed right then. I had a few minutes today and thought I should see what else was in there."

The three of us stood motionless, stupefied.

I moved closer. Something had dried on the wooden handle, as well as on the blade. Although it was dark, a deep reddish tinge remained, suggesting it was blood. "It looks like a pocketknife."

"My dad has one just like it," said Nina. "The blade folds into the handle. That way, you don't jab yourself or grab the blade by mistake."

This wasn't Nina's dad's knife, but I sure wished it were. I suspected I knew the dreaded answer, but I asked anyway. "Who has access to the safe?"

"The boys and Edwin. Just family. We don't keep much in there. Important papers, the deed to the house, that sort of thing."

A door opened downstairs. "Cookie, I'm here! Where are you?" The voice was young and sweet.

"Is it one-thirty already? Oh my! I don't want Penelope to see this." Gerrie hastily wrapped the newspaper around the knife and bent to slide it into the safe. She closed the door, gave the combination lock a twirl, and slid a wood panel across it. I would never have guessed a safe was behind it.

Standing straight, Gerrie took a deep breath and called, "I'm coming, Penelope!" Then she looked at Nina and me. "This must stay between us until I can get a handle on it. I don't know what it is or where it came from. It could belong to one of Edwin's clients. Agreed?"

The sound of feet on the stairs neared us.

"Hi, Cookie! What are you all doing up here?"

"*Cookie?*" teased Nina. "What happened to *Granny* and *Nana*?"

Gerrie forced a smile. "Hello, angel. When Penelope was learning to talk, she started calling me Cookie, and it stuck. Frankly, I like it better than some of the alternatives. Cookie sounds so young and appealing. Everyone loves cookies! Right, Penelope?"

"I don't suppose we have any cookies in the kitchen?"

Her cute manner broke the tension in the room. Gerrie chuckled a little bit too hard. But Nina and I smiled, too.

We begged off the cookies, but true to form, Nina snagged an oatmeal cherry chocolate chip cookie before we walked out the back door.

"What do you think?" Nina asked between bites.

"A bloody knife in the safe and a stranger shows up at the house and ends up knifed to death? There has to be a connection."

"We know it's not the knife that killed Russ. Has anyone else been knifed that you know of?" asked Nina.

I nearly choked at the thought. "Only the incident at Ruby's when Russ was attacked."

"One of Gerrie's sons!" Nina exclaimed.

I hated to imagine that could be the case. Gerrie had clearly been worried about their possible involvement. Had their father hidden the weapon the first time one of them attacked Russ?

"Maybe it's tomato sauce," Nina teased. "Henrietta was right about one thing. Gerrie's outfit looked almost as comfortable as Henrietta's, but she didn't look like she had just crawled out of bed."

"Apparently, someone was not focusing on the elephant in the room." I was so distracted by the knife that I didn't even notice Gerrie's attire.

"She wore a black-and-white short-sleeved dress with a black belt and black sandals. Easy, cool, and simple. But what made it was the belt." She looked down at her own attire and then her watch. "Good grief! Look at the time. I have to drop my husband off at the airport. I'm heading home. Are you going that way?"

Nina's husband, a forensic pathologist, traveled constantly and was often out of town for weeks on end. "Not yet. I'd like to stop in at Alex German's office, but it's a little awkward."

Alex and I had run into each other on the street, but it was still uncomfortable. I really needed to find a new source of legal information.

"Good luck. I hate to miss that. It could be quite amusing, but I'd better hurry. Dinner later?"

"Sounds good."

Nina picked up her pace and crossed the street, while I headed toward the courthouse, where many of the law firms had their offices. As I walked, I wondered what happened when lawyers died. How did it impact their clients? What happened to evidence? Could that knife in Gerrie's safe belong to one of her husband's clients? I hoped so!

I stopped walking and leaned against a brick wall while I looked up Edwin's law firm on my phone. At least I hadn't dated anyone there. That I knew of, anyway. I readily found the listing for Peters, Stansfield & Grant on North Union Street. It wasn't far from where I stood. I walked on slowly. The name of the firm was engraved on a brass plaque next to the door.

The office wasn't quite what I had expected. The walls had been painted a deep burgundy that gave the reception area a warm cocoon feel. The chair rails were white, as were built-in bookshelves and the receptionist's desk. A large brass Colonial chandelier gave it an additional touch of elegance.

In a stroke of luck, I knew the woman at the reception desk from various local projects. Leigh Ann Kenney decorated cakes like a pro. She insisted she'd learned by trial and error.

"Leigh Ann?"

"Sophie! What brings you here?"

"I'm so sorry about Edwin's passing."

"Thank you." Leigh Ann pushed short, curly hair out of her face. "Edwin's death took a toll on me. I was his assistant for twenty-nine years. You know, they joke about work husbands and such, but I feel like a widow. It's so quiet and empty in our offices now. This is actually my last week here. A new lawyer has been hired and I've decided it's time to retire. Edwin's death made me realize it can happen anytime. There's so much I would like to do. I don't want them to walk in one day and find me dead on the floor."

"Is that how it happened?"

"You mean Edwin's death? Something like that, except it was at his home. Gerrie found him."

"Poor Gerrie. On a brighter note, I think you've made the right decision. I guess congratulations are in order!"

"Yes. I'm excited about moving on. I've spent the last couple of months closing down Edwin's work life."

She removed a large photo from the wall. "Do you suppose Gerrie would want this?"

It showed Edwin with Senator Keswick in a truly authentic moment. Neither was posing. The two of them were laughing heartily about something. "I bet she would love it. Would you like me to give it to her?"

She thrust it at me. "Would you, please? I have so many things to take care of."

I took the photo. "No problem at all. Leigh Ann, I could use some information on what happens when a lawyer dies. Where do his clients go?"

"Wherever they want. Some of them are staying here with other attorneys. Some are going elsewhere."

"I see. And what about evidence?"

She blinked at me. "What do you mean?"

"Say if someone brought in a murder weapon or illegal drugs?"

"We don't keep anything like that. It has to be turned over to the police."

I was confused. "I thought lawyers had a duty of confidentiality. Wouldn't it defeat the confidentiality if lawyers turned in murder weapons that would convict their clients?"

"I think you need to see one of our lawyers, Sophie."

"That's not necessary."

"Let me get you an appointment. How's Friday morning?"

"Leigh Ann! I haven't got a legal problem. I didn't murder anyone. I was just curious."

At that moment, Sam Peters walked into the reception area, carrying a stash of papers.

I held out my hand to him. "Sam, how nice to see you." Thanks to my job, I knew a lot of people. Maybe not well, but enough to say hello and ask some questions.

"Sophie!" He lowered his voice. "Thanks for helping Gerrie. She has been a rock through everything. She needs friends like you to stand by her now."

"I presume you would have told Wolf if Russ Everett was a client?"

"Wasn't that the weirdest thing? No, Russ was never a client. Seems like a lot of people knew him, though."

"Sophie was just asking about confidentiality and murder weapons," whispered Leigh Ann.

Sam's eyebrows rose. "Perhaps we should speak privately."

Chapter 21

Dear Sophie,
I am painting my house inside and switching things up. I would love to have several different color rooms, but some of my rooms can be seen from other rooms. How do I handle that?
    In Love with Color in Red Oak, Pennsylvania

Dear In Love with Color,
The key to a smooth transition is to use a dominant color from one room as a secondary color in the next room. If your living room is a sky blue with white accents, then use sky blue as the accent color in the next room. Or you can paint the next room a color three levels darker or lighter than the sky blue. Be sure you stay in the same tonal family.
    Sophie

I laughed aloud. "I'm sorry to disappoint you, but I'm not going to be a client. I just thought it odd that you would have to turn the weapon over to the police. How does that work with confidentiality? Seems like it would sew everything up for the prosecution and condemn your client."

"I see." Sam grinned at me. "I'm glad to know you haven't got a murder weapon on you. I'll be honest, it's a problem. Definitely a conflict. In this firm, we have selected some lawyer friends to whom we can turn over a weapon. They would take it to the police so there would be no connection to us or to our client. Of course, we can't be responsible for what the weapon might reveal. That's out of our hands. But at least the police wouldn't know the source of the weapon."

"Wouldn't it make more sense then *not* to turn it in? You could, for instance, keep it in a desk drawer? Or a safe?"

Sam didn't pause for a moment. "A lawyer would be disbarred for that."

"Wow. So it's far better all around for a villain to dispose of a knife or a gun and hope it's never found."

He laughed. "That's not the advice I would give, but I imagine some people would feel that way if they knew."

I thanked both of them for their assistance and left, wondering why Edwin, who was known for being on the straight and narrow, would have risked disbarment by hiding a weapon in his home safe.

The afternoon had become miserably hot and humid. I was hurrying home to get out of the heat when my phone rang.

Mars asked, "Are you available for dinner tonight?"

His question caught me by surprise. Once upon a time in my life, when I was married to Mars, that kind of phone call was the norm. But not these days. Instead of being gracious, I blurted, "What's up?"

"We're invited to the Keswicks' for dinner. It's short notice, though. I told them I wasn't sure you could make it.

They've invited Nina, too. Her husband's out of town, so she's bringing a mystery date."

I stopped walking. It smacked too much of being coupled again. But I did want to speak with the senator, and this might be my only opportunity. "Are you friends with the senator?"

"We're not close. I've worked with him before, if that's what you're asking. He's a fair guy. A little pompous and opinionated, but that's to be expected."

I'd better take the opportunity. Besides, Nina was bringing a mystery date! That should be amusing. "Sure. What time?"

We arranged a time to walk over together and ended the call. I pushed away my uneasy feelings about being coupled with Mars. The Keswicks were probably used to entertaining couples. I didn't need to make something out of nothing.

Daisy was thrilled to see me, but when I let her out, she didn't linger. Bernie phoned me as I was contemplating what to cook for tomorrow night's dinner.

"Hey, Soph! Remember the dinner we talked about? I'd like to provide all the dishes."

"That's very nice of you, but you don't have to do that."

"I want to. It's sort of an experiment."

More taste testing, I suspected. "All right. I'll make a dessert."

"Nope. I'll take care of everything. Soup to nuts. But you and Nina could whip up some nice cool drinks."

"Wow. I feel so spoiled. It sounds good to me!"

"Great. I'll phone Francie and Betty. By the way, I invited Wong and Humphrey, too. Hope that's okay. You'll remind Nina?"

Our old friend Humphrey would be delighted to be included. Very lean with blond hair that was almost white, he had the palest complexion I had ever seen. In fact, he looked like he'd never spent a minute in the sun, which sort of suited his profession as a mortician.

"I will tell Nina that we're on and it's better than okay to include Wong and Humphrey."

I hung up and decided to bake a peach cobbler anyway. As I peeled peaches, I thought about Gerrie and the knife. Maybe we were jumping to conclusions. The red on the knife could simply be rust or paint. But then why place it in a safe? To keep it out of Penelope's hands? Doubtful.

That would mean one of the Stansfields had stashed it there. Heart attacks came on suddenly, so I didn't think Edwin had tried to save a client by placing it there in expectation of his imminent demise.

Gerrie could have been putting on an act, but she had seemed genuinely shocked. Had she known about the knife, wouldn't she have quickly stashed it in a drawer or back in the vault when she heard us running up the stairs? And she wouldn't have screamed. Or would she? I had dismissed Eddie's claim that Gerrie had murdered Russ. It seemed so preposterous. Surely she hadn't put on a show for Nina and me about the knife if she had used it to attack someone. Or if her sons had used it in the stabbing at Ruby's. What would be the point of that when she could simply keep it safely tucked away in the safe and no one would be the wiser?

That left Jim and Todd. I wished I knew more about them. They had grown up in Old Town. There had to be loads of people who knew them well.

As my cobbler baked, my thoughts went back to A Healthy Meal. I phoned Jenna.

To my surprise, she answered her phone. "Jenna, it's Sophie."

"I've been meaning to call you. I apologize for running out on you like that yesterday."

"It's all right. You were clearly distressed."

"That's no excuse. When Eddie told us about Russ and how he used women, it turned everything upside down for me. All this time, I worried about my husband's shock and disapproval. I can't tell you how many sleepless nights I've had over this. But Eddie changed everything. I realized that Russ had taken advantage of me. All his sweet talk and attention were only to manipulate me. I feel like such a fool! I knew I had to deal with the situation. I had to face it, no matter what happened. Last night, I told my husband about Russ, and how I was a stupid dupe."

"Are you still married?" I held my breath.

"I love Eli more than ever. He was so kind. He didn't put me down for being a clueless idiot at all. If anything, I think it made our relationship even stronger."

"Jenna, that's wonderful."

"I wish I had done it sooner."

"No more worries about Wolf going to his office to interview him?"

"Nope. Wolf came to the house today and talked with both of us. So that's all behind me now."

"I'm very glad for you. Now, what about A Healthy Meal?"

"I'm still mad at Mindy, but I'll phone Gerrie and let her know I'm in."

Relieved to have that behind me, I hurried upstairs and changed into a flowing white dress with a pattern of flowers in shades of blue. It was long and casual, but dressy enough in case the Keswicks were being formal. I pinned my hair up in a loose French twist and added dangling earrings. As I looked in the mirror, I thought once again that it was all too reminiscent of the days when Mars and I were married.

I worked at shaking off that feeling as I went downstairs to feed Daisy and Mochie. When they were settled, I walked outside in the vain hope that meeting Mars on the sidewalk wouldn't seem quite so much like a date.

Mars looked dashingly handsome, as usual. He kissed me on the cheek and then asked, "What's going on with you, Nina, and the Keswicks?"

We began to walk toward their street. "On the day Russ was murdered," I said, "I went to the front door of Gerrie's house, looking for the EMTs. They had just arrived. But Senator Keswick was out on the sidewalk."

Mars shrugged. "He lives across the street. The sirens probably drew his attention."

"Could be. It just seemed to me that he was there awfully fast. Can you keep something under your hat?"

Mars laughed. "If you knew how many things are under my hat . . ."

Of course. Anyone who dealt with politicians surely knew a lot of secrets. "Henrietta thinks he's having an affair with Gerrie. She referred to Gerrie as *his girlfriend*."

"Ouch! I hadn't heard any rumors to that effect. Do you think they were seeing each other before Edwin died?"

"I honestly don't know."

"Around the time of a loss, I have seen sympathy and support of the bereaved confused for a different kind of emotion. Maybe that's what's going on?"

"Possibly. Their marital woes aren't any of our business, unless they tie him to Russ. Tonight I'd like to find out what he saw and heard the day of Russ's murder."

"Good to know. I'll try to steer the conversation that way."

While Mars banged the knocker on the Keswicks' door, I observed Gerrie's house. I didn't see any movement in the windows. It was quiet and peaceful.

The Henrietta who opened the door at eight in the evening looked amazingly different than she had in the morning. She wore a colorful gauzy dress of the type I imagined glamorous movie stars lounged in at their beach homes. Multiple gold bangles adorned her wrists. Her hair had been swept up in a messy bun, and her makeup, while considerable, looked as though a professional had applied it. She was actually very attractive. Not that she hadn't looked fine without makeup, but now that she no longer appeared to have just crawled out of bed, I was struck by her beauty and felt quite plain in my dress.

"Please come in. Do you think it's too hot to be outside? I was hoping we could make use of the garden tonight."

I agreed enthusiastically. "It will be cooling off soon."

The dogs underfoot, Henrietta led us outside and down a gently curving staircase to a remarkable garden. Heavy cast-iron furniture with plush white cushions offered loads of seating, easily enough to accommodate a large party or barbecue. A pool set the garden off from the patio. Beyond it, there was a fountain that looked like it belonged in an Italian villa. It served to transition from the house to brick raised gardens overflowing with sunflowers, tomato plants, an array of peppers from hot to not, bean stalks on wire pyramids, rosy flowers on sprawling begonias, tall gladiolas, and fuchsia crape myrtles. Blue and pink hydrangeas lined the brick walls on the sides of the yard.

"Is that corn in the back?" I asked.

A familiar male voice responded, "You bet it is! We look forward to it all winter." Senator Albert Keswick joined us. He clapped Mars on his upper arm with an air of confident familiarity. Then he held out his hand to me to shake. "Good to see you."

Chapter 22

Dear Natasha,
I can never remember names! It's a terrible afflic-
tion. How do I handle those awkward moments
when I don't know someone's name?
　　　　　　　Blank in No Name, Colorado

Dear Blank,
Don't worry about it. Ask how they are and move
on. If they don't remember your name, they're
probably not important anyway.
　　　　　　　　　　　　　Natasha

I felt like Senator Keswick had gone into auto mode, as he probably did when he met people at political events. He was tall and in good shape, with engaging blue eyes. They made a very handsome couple, which undoubtedly drew cameras their way at political functions.

"I know we've met before," he said to me. "Where would I know you from? I'm afraid I can't quite place you."

"Oh, Albert," said Henrietta in a teasing tone, "Sophie

is the event planner for the annual opera gala. You've met many times. She was Mars's wife."

I saw a spark of recognition in his expression. I shook his hand. "You must meet hundreds of people. You can't possibly remember them all. And if you've seen me at the opera gala, it was probably in passing. I'm always on the run, making sure it goes smoothly."

He shot me a grateful look when he said softly, "Thank you."

It turned out that Nina's secret "date" for the evening was Humphrey. It was easy to be intimidated by powerful people, but he seemed perfectly at home with the Keswicks, which reminded me that he had an arrogant mother who considered herself to be above just about everyone in the world. I had felt sorry for him on occasion because his mother put on airs, but now it occurred to me that her constant social climbing had prepared Humphrey to be comfortable with all sorts of people, even senators.

Humphrey was slender, though not as bone thin as he'd been. But his hair was as white-blond as ever and his complexion still very pale. Apparently, Humphrey had a crush on me when we were in school. I knew nothing about it at the time. I'd been so immersed in my own childhood and teen issues, I hadn't even noticed him. My younger sister, however, remembered him as the boy who rode his bike past our house all the time.

I had balked when my mother tried to set me up with him after my divorce. But over the years, we had become friends and I was always glad to see him.

The senator now beamed at Humphrey and gave him the same sort of arm clap that Mars had received. Since Humphrey was an undertaker, I assumed he might have handled a funeral for the senator's family.

Henrietta showed us to the table, set with a soft green

tablecloth and rustic, yet elegant, scalloped white plates in the French provincial style.

"You went to so much trouble for us," I said.

"It's nothing. Table setting is my superpower."

Nina and I gazed at her in surprise.

"It's all about the table. You must recognize that, Sophie. It doesn't take a genius to throw a tablecloth on a table. Add some candles and flowers and the entire ambience changes. It's easy! People always think it's about the food, but it's not. It's about the feeling you get when you walk into a room with a beautifully dressed table. I love a chance to use these dishes. I bought them at The Sugar Bowl."

At the mention of Gerrie's store, I glanced at Henrietta's husband. He was nodding approvingly.

We mingled for a while, admiring the garden and noshing on hors d'oeuvres of salmon on cucumber rounds, bowls of kalamata olives, and mushrooms stuffed with crabmeat.

"Honestly, Henrietta, I don't know how you put this dinner together so fast."

Henrietta beamed. "Sophie, I can throw together a sit-down formal meal for fifty on two hours' notice. Maybe less, these days. Used to be that I had to have a caterer at the ready, but now that I can have anything delivered here almost instantly, it's not a big deal at all. I'll tell you the secret. It's the table."

Nina and I exchanged a look.

"Darlin's, I am the queen of table setting. I don't cook, but I set a beautiful table in no time. We eat with our eyes, they say, and the table sets the scene. Rustic French with touches of elegant crystal, like we're doing tonight, or gold-rimmed super formal, or rodeo roundup, I can do them all. Oh, it's time we sat down and ate."

"Can we give you a hand?" I asked.

"You're so sweet. I'd love that."

Nina and I followed her to the kitchen. Garlic and rosemary filled the air.

"I'll bring in the leg of lamb. Sophie, could you carry the vegetable platters, and, Nina, maybe you could grab the potatoes?"

In a matter of minutes, we gathered at the table and sat down to eat. The conversation revolved around the fantastic leg of lamb and local restaurants we liked.

Henrietta served tiramisu and decaf coffee for dessert. The sun had disappeared, but the candles on her lovely table arrangement provided a warm glow and the moon shone like a light in the sky.

Her husband poured brandy into Grasmere cut-crystal brandy snifters.

"These look familiar," said Nina. "They're beautiful!"

"The snifters are the brand of crystal used in *Downton Abbey*," said Henrietta. "They were a gift from Albert. We laugh about being plain old Americans, but we can pretend we have elegant British style."

I understood what she meant. Brits always sounded so clever with their wonderful accents. And they looked stylish, too. But part of me wondered if that was the Keswicks' life. Did they try to play parts to present an elegant image?

We chatted about local matters and their stunning garden as we ate the tiramisu, which had been ordered from a local Italian restaurant. It was delicious, but I was eagerly awaiting the right moment in the conversation to ask about Russ's death.

It didn't emerge until Albert, who had informed us that he loathed being called Al, mentioned how very much he missed Edwin. "Such a fine man. We had the same issue with our names, you know. We used to laugh about it. He was no more an *Ed* than I am an *Al*. When someone called us Ed or Al, it was a dead giveaway that the person did not know us. We found it humorous because they used the common nicknames in an attempt to establish familiarity."

"Poor Gerrie," I said. "Such a shock to find a murdered man in her house."

Albert choked and spilled brandy. His eyes met mine, and in that moment, I knew he had remembered where he last saw me—at Gerrie's house the day Russ was murdered.

Henrietta jumped to her feet and dabbed at his shirt with a napkin. "Albert! It's not at all like you to spill your drink. Are you feeling ill?"

Albert said calmly, "That's enough, Henrietta."

He regained his composure swiftly, but I couldn't bring myself to meet his gaze.

I didn't know of a reason in the world that I should be afraid of Albert. And yet, there was something in that glance of recognition that had provoked a deep inner caution in me. More than anything, I longed to jump up from my seat and run from him. But I couldn't do that. He would think I knew something, when I hadn't a clue.

Albert looked straight at me. His jaw tight.

Mars, clearly oblivious to my reaction, steered the conversation back to the Stansfields. "I understand you know their sons very well."

"Todd is like his father, even looks like him," said the senator. "A fine young man. Alas, our daughter had eyes for the elder brother. The elephant-obsessed tree hugger. He went to law school, for pity's sake. He could have walked straight into his father's firm. Not everyone has that kind of opportunity handed to them. And yet he blew it off for restaurant supply."

"Do you think one of them killed Russ?" asked Humphrey.

The moment of silence probably seemed longer than it actually was.

"It's certainly possible."

"Albert!" Henrietta appeared horrified.

"Well, do you think Gerrie did it?" asked her husband.

"Of course not! It had to be an intruder. You know none of the Stansfields would have done anything like that."

"*Russ* was the intruder, Henrietta. Then again, perhaps he wasn't. Maybe the Stansfield boys knew him and invited him into their home before they stabbed him to death."

"You can be so vicious, Albert." Henrietta turned to Nina and me. "Honestly, I can't imagine what went on in there."

"I think it's quite simple," said Albert. "Russ broke into their house, probably intending to rob them. When he was discovered, one of the Stansfields drove a knife into him and now they're covering it up."

"The boys, young men now, are far too genteel to do anything like that," said Henrietta. "Todd does like to drink, though. He's such a dear. Always the life of any party. His father was more formal, like Albert. The serious type."

"Are you inferring that I am a bore?" asked her husband, a bit too tersely for my taste.

"You're an intellectual, Albert. Not a bore."

"You live so close to them. Did you hear anything in the morning? Unusual sounds or angry voices?" I asked.

Henrietta looked at her husband, waiting for him to respond.

"It seemed to me there were quite a few people in and out of the Stansfield house that morning. I had an afternoon meeting scheduled, so I happened to be home in the morning to get a little work done. Elmo"—he pointed a long finger at the dog with the unusual black ears—"was in my office with me. He sat on a window seat to look out and barked several times. I'm quite certain I saw Colleen, the daughter-in-law, arrive. Hmm, has anyone considered that she might be the killer?"

"Albert!" scolded his wife.

"I'm only being honest. She was definitely there. And I recall Jim leaving the house. Now, he may well have doubled back and gone in the rear door. We can't see what goes on around the back."

"Any screaming?" I asked.

He paused to think. "Yes. Quite a bit of it. Oh, but that was shortly before the ambulance arrived." He looked at the dog. "There must have been a scream. I can't fathom anyone being stabbed without screaming. Elmo probably heard it."

"Have you noticed anyone hanging around on the sidewalk? Or sitting in a car?" I asked.

Henrietta gasped. "Do you think someone was watching their house?"

"Henrietta! Presumably the victim didn't barge into their house with the whole family there." He looked over at me. "Then again, I suppose that's a possibility. Did they know him?"

I dodged the question a little. "Some of them may have. I'm told he often caddied for golfers."

"Good heavens!" Henrietta gazed at her husband. "You golf all the time. Did you know him?"

"I may have run into him once or twice. I see so many people. I can't remember them all."

Deftly avoided! Given Russ's reputation, I suspected he would have made a point of caddying for a senator. Power, money, prestige. They were synonymous with holding a high office.

"I had never heard of him before," said Humphrey.

"On the morning he was killed, did you see anyone running from the Stansfields' house?" I asked the senator.

"No. Of course, I showered and ate breakfast. The kitchen windows overlook the garden. I could have missed it."

Or the senator could have killed Russ and run home from the Stansfields' to his house in no time at all. I longed to see their laundry room, though he would surely have washed his blood-spattered clothes by now.

We wound up our evening with chitchat. Nina told them about A Healthy Meal and Henrietta expressed an interest in participating.

On our way out, Nina paused at a framed photograph. "Is this your daughter? She's beautiful!"

She was, at that. In the photo, Elmo was kissing her chin. She was laughing, with her head thrown back. I stared at her familiar face. Where had I seen her?

"I miss Emily," said the senator. "She brightens up our lives. Henrietta, why don't we take the train up to see her this weekend?"

"Honey, she's in Chicago. Remember? She had to go there for work."

"What does she do?" asked Mars.

Henrietta blushed. "I'm such a computer doofus. I can barely work my phone. Our Emily is a technical whiz. She does something with programs that businesses use to keep track of everything. At least that's how she explained it to her old, befuddled mom."

Nina laughed. "*Befuddled* is a wonderful word for how I feel around technology. As soon as I think I understand something, they go and change it!"

We thanked them profusely for a lovely evening and left on a high note.

The air had cooled to a balmy temperature. We weren't the only ones enjoying a stroll along the charming street. Several people were taking advantage of the cooler temperatures to walk their dogs or get in an evening run. We had gone about three blocks when, ahead of us, a woman walked alone, her head down.

As we neared her, I recognized Gerrie.

Chapter 23

Dear Natasha,
I just love your show! What's the trending must-have decorating color for next year?
                    Big Fan in Blue Bell, South Dakota

Dear Big Fan,
It's sage! It's a very subtle green, with tones of black and brown mixed in. It's the new neutral.
                                        Natasha

Gerrie wiped under her eyes and sniffled. Nina elbowed me.

"Gerrie?" I said.

She looked up. "Sophie, Nina, Mars, Humphrey!" She sniffled again and swiped her fingers under her eyes. "Where are you headed?" she asked with fake cheeriness.

"Are you all right?" I asked.

Gerrie forced a smile. "Yes, of course. Must be allergies."

Allergies, my foot.

"What happened?" demanded Mars.

"Nothing! Really, nothing to worry about. I just miss Edwin."

"Of course, you do," said Humphrey. "It's completely natural. It wouldn't be right if you didn't sense his loss."

"I feel so foolish. A family friend invited me to dinner. He lost his wife last year. I thought he would understand better than anyone else how I feel, you know? But when we were leaving, he tried to kiss me. And I don't mean a polite kiss on the cheek. And then he said he would like to go home with me! I was horrified and pushed him away. Ugh!" She shuddered. "It has only been a few months. For heaven's sake. He, of all people, should realize that. Edwin was my love. I don't know that I will ever meet anyone who could fill the void he left in my heart and my life. That stupid man! I can't imagine what he was thinking. I'm not through mourning Edwin. I might not *ever* be."

"That's a shame, Gerrie," I said.

Nina nodded. "People can be so thoughtless."

"We'll walk you home," said Mars.

The four of us clustered around her as we walked.

"What a blockhead I was to think we would have a nice dinner lamenting our lost spouses."

"I don't think you're a blockhead," said Nina. "In your shoes, I would have expected the same thing. He was the one who got it all wrong."

Gerrie sighed. "I guess there's a lot I have to learn about my new life as a widow. I never imagined anything like this would happen. Edwin was such a gentleman. I suppose not all men can be as gracious and smart. You know what I miss the most? Talking with him. Just the two of us. We have a little den upstairs where we read or watched TV at night. With spiked hot chocolate in the winter. And we would talk. About our days, our boys, about politics and the law. He had such depth of knowledge. Edwin was very special."

We stopped at her front door.

"I wish I had known him better," I said.

"Me too. Would you like to come in?" asked Gerrie.

Nina declined. "Thanks, but I'm beat. Maybe another time?"

Gerrie nodded. "Just as well. The boys and I are scheduled to see Edwin's partner in the morning. I want to be sure we straighten out our plans in case anything happens to me."

"Are you afraid of something?" Mars asked.

"A little bit. I should have gotten a dog when Nina went to the shelter with me the other day."

"It's all right, Gerrie," said Nina. "The dog for you wasn't there that day, but, unfortunately, they're always getting new ones."

Just then, Todd walked up with a woman I didn't know, and the man he'd introduced to me as Dale at the conference.

"Hi, Mom! Looks like a party here! Hello, Sophie." Todd nodded at me. "You remember Dale. And this is my girlfriend, Nicci."

I introduced everyone to them.

Todd and Dale disappeared into the house.

Nicci lagged behind. "Don't worry, Ger. I'll clean up the kitchen real good after they raid the fridge."

When Nicci closed the door behind her, Gerrie sighed. "It's like having a teenager in the house again. Don't they have jobs? Don't they need to be at work in the morning?" She shook her head. "Good night. I hope all of you get some sleep."

We walked away.

"At least she doesn't need to be scared now," said Mars. "She's not alone in that big house."

"I'm not sure she'll get much sleep, though," said Humphrey.

"You must have met her sons when you handled Edwin's funeral arrangements, Humphrey. What were they like?" I asked.

"People are rarely at their normal best when a loved one has passed. It's probably not the best time to judge them. Some don't want to talk, and others yell at each other, but they're not angry, they're stressed. And they fight over minor things."

"And how did Gerrie's sons react?" Nina nudged Humphrey for an answer.

"The larger one, Todd, mostly stood around, shaking hands and patting his mom on the back. She consulted more with her other son, Jim. And when she was unable to make a decision about something, he would make it for her. She appeared fine with that. I must say, all three of them were well-mannered and lovely to work with. There was no hysteria or family argument."

"Do people really do that?" asked Mars.

Humphrey chuckled. "Everyone reacts differently. You have to learn to deal with it. Dale and Nicci made quite a scene when an uncle died. Let's just say they're a very vocal bunch. Are there any leads on who murdered Russ?"

"It had to be one of her sons," I said. "Nina and I saw Gerrie running back to her house."

"She could have killed Russ earlier, changed clothes, and then gone out to mislead everyone," said Mars.

"Or someone else killed Russ while she was gone," said Humphrey.

"How long do you think she was out? Fifteen minutes?" asked Mars.

"Had to be longer," I said. "Let's test it tomorrow morning."

"Oh no! I don't run," Nina protested.

"Do you honestly think Gerrie runs?"

Nina snorted and giggled. "No."

"So we're actually the right people to find out how long it might have taken her."

"Why do I think this will require me to get up early?" Nina groaned.

"It's your choice. We can test it around eight, when it's cool, or around noon, when it's not."

"I'll see you at eight." Nina gave Humphrey a hug and headed up the stairs to her front door.

Humphrey hugged me, too, promising to be at Bernie's dinner the next night. He stepped into his chili-red Mini Cooper and waved at us before driving away.

Mars crossed the street to my house with me. I unlocked the door and Daisy bounded out to see him. After telling her she was the best dog in the world, which she clearly believed from the way she leaned against his legs, Mars looked at me. "Seems like old times."

"Are you going to sing?"

He leaned toward me and gently kissed me full on the lips. I didn't push him away.

He wrapped his arms around me and kissed me again.

And then he stepped back, bent over to Daisy, and whispered loudly, "Don't worry. You're still my best girl." He strode off into the night whistling "Seems Like Old Times."

I called Daisy inside and locked the door. I wasn't at all certain how I felt about this development. After feeding Daisy and Mochie midnight snacks, I went up to bed.

I tossed and turned for hours. When I finally fell asleep, I woke with a start far too early on Wednesday morning because I knew why I had recognized the Keswicks' daughter. And I knew where to find her. She wasn't in Chicago.

I didn't know if I would gain any useful information from Emily Keswick, but it was worth a shot.

Nina arrived at my kitchen door at eight o'clock, wearing a yellow-and-white floral chiffon maxidress.

I opened the door. "Good morning! Have you changed your mind about our little test?"

"Not at all. I see you're not properly dressed."

I looked down at my baggy T-shirt and shorts. "We're running, right?"

"Gerrie was wearing a dress and heels."

I studied her shoes. "Those look like sneakers."

"I have no intention of breaking my ankles, but I thought we ought to dress like Gerrie did. As much as possible anyway."

"I agree about the sneakers. We may be a little faster, but probably not much." I slid Daisy's harness over her head. "Ready?"

Nina, Daisy, and I walked over to Gerrie's house. Todd's friend Dale Mancini sat in a car outside, wearing his aviator sunglasses. We waved at him.

"Do you think he spent the night?" asked Nina.

I shrugged. "Maybe he's picking up his sister or Todd." Changing the subject, I said, "I'm assuming Gerrie went to Garfield's."

"Probably. It's closest."

We turned on the stopwatches on our phones, and the three of us set off as though we were in a rush. Daisy strutted beautifully, wagging her tail, and having a grand time.

Nina and I eased off after one block. By the time we were on the second block, we had slowed to a semi-brisk walk.

Panting, Nina said, "I think this is very accurate."

"Me too. We're probably faster, if anything." We reached Garfield's, huffing and puffing. Outside of the store, I bent over, trying to catch my breath.

Nina leaned against the glass door of the store.

Daisy waggled her tail at passersby.

I straightened up and handed her leash to Nina. "I'm going in to buy half-and-half."

Still breathing hard, Nina simply gave me a thumbs-up. I found the dairy section, selected half-and-half and vanilla ice cream, and took them to the cashier. "Hi, Tom."

"Morning, Sophie. Out for a run?"

I nodded. "Hey, were you working last Thursday?"

"Sure was."

"Do you remember Gerrie Stansfield coming in? She would have been in a rush."

"Sure. She had on that colorful dress. Said she had ladies coming to lunch and thought she had enough half-and-half for coffee, but it was gone."

"Sounds about right. Thanks, Tom."

I was out of the door in a flash. "Ready, Nina?"

"Noooo. Let's just double the time it took up to now." She handed me Daisy's leash.

"But it might take us longer to run back."

"No running."

"C'mon." I tried to walk briskly.

"Sophie, I'm sweating! Why do people torture themselves this way?"

"They say you get a runner's high."

One block later, we had slowed to a fast stagger.

"High?" Nina croaked. "I think I'll stick with walking."

When we reached Gerrie's house, I checked the time. "Almost half an hour."

"Certainly long enough for someone to stab Russ. How long would that take? Mere minutes!"

Chapter 24

Dear Sophie,
My husband and I are hosting a dinner party for his work colleagues. My mother-in-law has suggested we serve panna cotta. She's simply vicious and thrives on embarrassing me. What's the difference between pudding and panna cotta? Is it appropriate for a formal dinner?
Suspicious Second Wife in Puddin' Swamp, South Carolina

Dear Suspicious Second Wife,
This time, perhaps she has her son's success at heart. Panna cotta can be a very lovely and elegant dessert. Both panna cotta and pudding are made with dairy milk and cream. However, cornstarch is most often used to stiffen pudding, while gelatin gives panna cotta its firm consistency. Serve it with a berry sauce and a sprinkling of grated chocolate on top.

Sophie

"Tom at Garfield's remembered Gerrie coming in that day. He even described her dress. So it's not like she stabbed Russ and then pretended to be away from home. She really went there."

"Hey! Are you two Hot Girls Walking?" Wong approached us.

"I have no idea what that is, but I'm hot," said Nina.

Wong chuckled. "It's a new trend. You walk while appreciating your life and thinking about how hot you are."

"Even Daisy is hot," I joked.

"Not that kind of hot. *Hot* as in how *beautiful* you are," said Wong.

"You're joking," I said. "That's not really a thing?"

"Yes, it is! Nina is clearly with it in that dress."

Nina explained to Wong what we were doing.

Wong shook her head. "I don't think she killed Russ, either. Imagine what a cold person you'd have to be to pull that off. Gerrie is smart and emotionally strong. She doesn't have the uncaring brutality you'd need to stab Russ like that."

Wong's radio crackled. "Gotta go. I'll see you tonight for dinner."

Nina, Daisy, and I walked home.

At my house, Nina picked up a magazine and fanned herself with it. "I am so glad I didn't live in the time before air-conditioning. What's for breakfast? Do you have anything cold?"

I opened the refrigerator. "How about peach cobbler with vanilla ice cream?"

Nina laughed. "I have never seen that on a breakfast menu, but it sounds about perfect to me."

While Nina put on coffee, I fed Daisy and Mochie.

I wasn't sure about our breakfast. Nevertheless, I ladled the cold peach cobbler into white bowls, microwaved them just long enough to take the chill off, and topped them with vanilla ice cream.

I handed one to Nina, who had poured coffee for both of us.

"Now, this is the life. Why don't people eat this for breakfast on a regular basis? Mmm."

"Maybe it's because people are avoiding sugar," I said.

"Fie on such heathens! This is delicious. Besides, there's an oatmeal crumble on top. Dairy, fruit, and oatmeal. It's a perfect breakfast!"

I had to admit that it was good, even if it was unconventional.

As things turned out, I was glad Bernie was bringing dinner. I liked to cook and bake, but it was a nice break to have someone else do the cooking. He was probably bringing food from The Laughing Hound, which was always delicious.

Still, I felt compelled to contribute in some way. After Nina left, I checked the fridge for berries and heavy cream. Perfect! Panna cotta was quick and easy to prepare and would be a delicious dessert, no matter what foods Bernie might bring for dinner.

I sprinkled gelatin over water and let it sit for a few minutes as I set out the ramekins. I poured the milk, cream, and sugar into a pot and heated it until it boiled. I removed it from the heat, and stirred in the gelatin and vanilla. After filling the ramekins, I set them on a tray and slid it into the refrigerator for the panna cotta to set.

I took a long shower and tried to steer my thoughts away from Mars and back to Russ's murder. If I was right about Emily Keswick, she was a low-key type of person. She may have grown up with a senator for a father, but I had a hunch she wasn't a prima donna and that she liked dogs. I dressed in a khaki skirt, with a brown belt, and a white cotton shirt without sleeves. I added a station necklace with polished beads in blues and greens to add a little interest. A pair of white sandals completed my simple earth-tone outfit.

With apologies to Mochie for leaving him alone, I suited Daisy up in her halter and leash and walked her out to the car. I would have liked to walk, but it might be too hot for her to walk home. I honestly wasn't sure how long our little outing would take.

I parked close to Moss Restaurant Supply. Daisy and I staked out the business from a corner. I saw no sign of Jim Stansfield.

"Okay, Daisy. Turn on your charm, sweetie."

She wagged her tail. I was hopeful that she understood. We crossed the street and entered the store. I gazed around for Jim or the other employee, Hayley, but neither was readily apparent.

"Good morning!" The woman I thought was Emily Keswick walked toward me. She resembled her mother, Henrietta. And as I had guessed, she stretched her hand out and cooed at Daisy.

"Hi! This is Daisy and I'm Sophie."

"Aren't you a pretty girl? And so friendly! Would Daisy like a dog treat?"

"She would love one!" We followed her over to a bowl with itty-bitty dog treats in it.

"She's a sweet dog! How can I help you?" Emily handed Daisy a treat.

I wasn't quite sure where to start. But I thought she would be angry, and rightly so, if I wasn't up front with her. "I think I was at your parents' home last night."

Her smile vanished. "Why would you think that? You don't even know me."

"Emily Keswick?"

"People mistake me for her all the time."

I bet they did. Because she *was* Emily! "Look, I'm not here to give your secret away. I'm trying to help Jim's mom. She's a suspect in the murder of Russ Everett."

"Oh." A big wrinkle formed between her eyes when she frowned at me.

"You must love Jim very much to move back here and keep it a secret from your parents. I have no need to tell them. I'm just trying to figure some things out."

"Jim didn't kill Russ."

"But he knew him."

"The whole family knew Russ."

I heard Eddie Wong in my head telling me that Gerrie was some kind of Ma Barker type. "How did they know him?"

"From the golf club, I think."

The golf club. How many times had I heard that? Russ had met a lot of people there.

"If you don't mind my asking, why are you hiding from your parents?"

Emily tried to laugh, but the sound she made was bitter. "Mom went to ridiculous lengths to break us up. I just want to have a peaceful relationship. My parents think I love the wrong brother. I grew up with the Stansfield boys. Todd was in my class in school and Jim was the older, cool one. My parents rave about Todd. 'He's so friendly. Everyone loves him.' I know the real Todd. We were in the same crowd at school. You know why my parents like him? Because he walks into their house and is instantly at home. He does that everywhere. He's one of those people who has never met a stranger. He embraces everyone. In truth, Todd is a lazy lush. And he's *married*! I like Colleen and, believe me, she hasn't had an easy life with him. My parents have it backward. They think Jim is the lazy one who walked into his family business and took the easy path. They make fun of him for rescuing elephants."

I stopped her. "That's hard to believe. I've met your mother's dogs. Aren't they rescues?"

"Exactly! If she actually met an elephant, Mom would be the first one out there saving them. She'd give up the garden and build an elephant shelter in the backyard! They don't like that he went to law school, but isn't practicing law. How ridiculous is that?"

"I'm sure they mean well."

She nodded. "Maybe. But they make it impossible for me to be with Jim, so for now, please keep my secret?"

It was her life, and as far as I could tell, her presence in town and her relationship with Jim had nothing to do with Russ's murder. It wasn't my concern, nor was it my place to butt in.

"I promise. By the way, I met Betty Armstrong."

Emily winced. "How is Betty?"

"She's angry and very hurt."

"She didn't understand. I think we should bring her back. If she'll come. Hayley is no help at all. Seriously. She can't even make a copy without help."

"What happened with Betty?" It wasn't really my business, but she was a nice woman and I felt sorry for her.

"Offices have changed so much. It made no sense anymore to have her filing papers and taking notes in shorthand, which no one else could read. Jim wanted to switch over to a computer system, which makes things easier. Everything is automated. When Jim first converted to computers, it was an adequate system. Pretty simple. But it had a major problem. It was easy to hack. Jim received a hacker threat that freaked him out. Someone threatened to put his customers' credit cards on the dark web unless Jim paid thousands of dollars."

"That's happening everywhere. To a lot of big companies."

"Exactly. Computerized systems were fabulous, but they had loopholes that made them easy targets. Jim called me to ask what to do because that's my line of work. At that time, I still had my job in New York. I was able to help him, but he needed to move to a newer system, and Betty just couldn't handle it. I tried to explain to her how to transfer all the business records to digital. But it was just beyond her. Don't get me wrong, it wasn't her age. It was as though I was speaking a foreign language to her. She's not the only one. It's something you have to learn. It was a massive job, so I agreed to move down here to help him. But Betty interpreted me as her replacement. She was out of her element and didn't like me in *her* office."

"I see." Betty was so proud of her office skills. "It must have come as a big blow to her."

"She just couldn't handle it. She thought Jim didn't have the guts to fire her, so she marched into his office and confronted him. He wanted her to stay, but she couldn't deal with what she perceived as a demotion. Answering the phones and helping customers were things she had always done. But she interpreted it as being forced out of her job. It broke Jim's heart. She was like a grandmother to him."

I understood what had happened. She had been the boss when it came to paperwork, and suddenly someone else was doing all that. Betty had been amused by the fact that they couldn't read her shorthand. It was a little ironic that she was the one who couldn't deal with the switch to something Jim and Emily understood, but she couldn't grasp.

Chapter 25

Dear Natasha,
I'm hosting a potluck gathering in my backyard.
Since we'll be outside, is it okay to use paper plates?
It would make cleanup so much faster!

> *Hostess in Paper Mill Pond, Connecticut*

Dear Hostess,
Paper plates? They're not even appropriate at a
picnic. And please don't put out a giant trash can
for the disposal of paper goods and uneaten food.
You are the hostess. Clean-up is your responsi-
bility.

> *Natasha*

"No more cyber threats?" I asked.

"Jim got that under control. We now have one of the most secure systems there is. No one is hacking in to get our customers' credit cards or bank account numbers. No one! I have seen to that."

The way she said "our customers" caught my attention.

It rolled off her tongue so easily. She felt ownership already.

A couple entered the store.

"I'll get out of your way. Thanks for taking the time to talk with me."

"Just a second." She grabbed a dog treat and handed it to Daisy. "One for the road."

We left the store and hurried to the car. Both of us were panting by the time we got there. I cranked up the air-conditioning for the ride home.

"Good girl, Daisy! I knew Emily would like you."

I drove through the alley behind my house and clicked the garage door opener. I parked the car, closed the door, and let Daisy out. While I walked to the house, she pranced around the yard.

I heard Mochie's cries before I saw him in the living room window. He mewed pitifully and patted the glass with his paw.

He must have jumped down as soon as he heard my key in the door because he was underfoot when I opened it. "Mochie!" I swung him up in my arms. "Were you lonely? We weren't gone very long."

He purred and made no move to be released.

"Poor boy." I turned to call Daisy.

But she appeared to have picked up a scent in the yard. Now I was on alert. It could have been a person. Or, more likely, a squirrel. I was letting Russ's murder get to me.

Daisy finally came inside. She didn't follow a scent in the house. Definitely a squirrel, I decided.

Several hours later, Bernie arrived as I was contemplating which dishes to use for our dinner.

I opened the door for him. "You're early."

"Sorry about that. Maybe I can help you?" he asked, setting a stack of papers on the table.

"Sure. That would be great. Should we eat inside or outside?"

"Inside. Where do you get deliveries?"

I wasn't following him. "Are you asking where I order food from?"

"No. I'm asking where people leave deliveries for you," he said.

"At the front door. Sometimes at the kitchen door. Are you afraid you'll miss our food delivery?"

"Yes. That's exactly right. I need to see who delivers it."

I must have looked perplexed because he said, "I, uh, I might as well tell you what I'm doing."

I had no idea what he meant.

"It appears that someone has set up ghost kitchens that don't exist."

"Isn't that sort of the point of ghost kitchens?"

"Not exactly. They exist. They make the food and have it delivered. The purchaser just doesn't usually know who or where they are. But some of the other chaps with restaurants and I have noticed ghost kitchens listing dishes on new websites that sound remarkably like dishes that we make. It's difficult, of course, because there must be dozens of restaurants in our area selling mac and cheese or hamburgers, right? As you know, at The Laughing Hound we have started offering wood-fired dishes. There are a few other restaurants doing that, but the dishes being offered by some of these new ghost kitchens sound far too similar to mine. Not only that, but the pictures they post of the food look exactly like ours, right down to the positioning of the garnish."

"Okay. So?"

"So we think they're advertising our food, marking up the prices in their online offerings, then they order it from us, slap a different logo on it, and deliver it to their customer."

"Then I don't see the problem. You're getting paid for the food, right?"

"Whoever is behind this is ripping people off. They're adding ten, fifteen, twenty dollars to the price. And the buyer wouldn't know that unless they checked the restaurants' delivery menus and found the same dishes."

"So they're not scamming the restaurants. They're scamming the consumers."

"Exactly. We'd like to know what slimeball is behind this."

"But you don't really know that's what they're doing. They might just be copying your dishes or re-creating them."

"That's what we're trying to figure out tonight."

"Eww. So we won't really know who cooked this food?"

Bernie laughed aloud. "You don't usually know who cooked the food coming from a ghost kitchen. It could have been created in some restaurant you love, or it could be made in a kitchen in a mostly vacant strip mall. But, to figure it out, all the restaurants I ordered from tonight are marking their food to-go with a tiny, unobtrusive red dot on the bottoms of the containers."

"In a vacant strip mall? Are you sure? Don't they need a health inspection?"

"They do. Don't worry, they're inspected. We've heard of a few. It doesn't mean the food is terrible. Not everyone can afford to rent a space for a kitchen. I heard of some guys who rented an apartment and set up a production line there. But most ghost kitchens are like restaurant kitchens. And there's nothing wrong with their food. I'm not anti–ghost kitchen. I just don't want someone buying my food, slapping their own label on it, and charging more for it!"

I had rarely seen Bernie so heated.

"Okay. I'm all in. But you have to explain it to everyone else."

"No problem."

"How many are we?" I asked.

"Nine, I think. Humphrey and Wong came by the restaurant, so I invited them. And someone invited herself."

Of course. "Natasha?"

"Who else?"

I reached for a colorful collection of Fiesta bowl plates. The latest thing in dinnerware, they were like round plates, but curled up at the edges. They really were ideal for dishes with sauces that might roll off a regular dinner plate. They were perfect for pastas and salads, too. Since we were having a variety of dishes, they seemed like just the ticket. Everything would look great on them. I had bought them in a variety of colors so the table would be colorful and fun.

Nina and Mars arrived at the same time. Mars shot me a smile and I knew he was thinking of last night. Nina and I got to work making pitchers of a drink Nina was calling Red Berry Smash, while Bernie opened the door for Wong, Humphrey, Francie, and Betty. Natasha tried to make a grand entrance, but my kitchen had filled up so fast that her arrival almost went unnoticed.

I was standing near the bay window in my kitchen, holding glasses for Nina to fill with the luscious red drink, when I saw the Dinner at Home van stop in front of my house.

Chapter 26

Dear Sophie,
I'm ordering so many things these days and many
of them are delivered right to my door. Am I sup-
posed to tip the drivers of local grocery stores? If
so, how much?
Confused in Tiptop, Virginia

Dear Confused,
It is appropriate to tip delivery drivers. The amount
is five dollars or twenty percent, whichever is greater.
Sophie

Not Charlene! I handed the glasses to Francie and dashed outside to join Bernie, who was marching toward the truck.

It didn't make sense that Charlene would be using other people's food and marking it up. I had been in her ghost kitchen. She was busy baking and cooking.

I caught up to Bernie just as Irv stepped out of the van. "Hi! Remember me? Sophie. You're looking better. I'm delighted to see you're back at work."

"Heh! Barely recognized you without blood all over your dress. Good to see you. You've got quite an order here. Let's see . . ."

Bernie leaned toward me and asked, sotto voce, "This is Charlene's van. Right?"

I nodded. "I don't understand, either. Did you order from Dinner at Home?"

"No. I didn't!" he whispered. Bernie handed me a couple of bags full of food. "So you work for Charlene?" he asked Irv.

"Yep. She's a good cook."

"And this is her delivery truck?" asked Bernie.

"Yep. It's old, but it's holding up okay. I think that's it. Did I get it all?"

I certainly hoped so. There were so many bags that Mars and Humphrey had come outside to help carry them.

"I don't understand," said Bernie. "I ordered these from different places. How come you're delivering all of them?"

Irv froze for a moment. "Really? I wouldn't know about that. I just deliver where they tell me." Irv climbed back into the driver's seat. "Y'all enjoy your dinner!"

Bernie, laden with bags of food, turned and looked at me. "Charlene?"

"I don't know. Did you see the look on his face when you said you ordered from different places? Something's up. He was lying and very uncomfortable. I doubt Charlene is involved. You and Mars delivered for her when Irv was out. So did I. We know she's doing her own cooking."

"Then why did all my orders arrive in her delivery van?"

That was a very good question. And I suspected that Irv knew the answer.

We carried the food into the house, then decided to eat outside after all. The temperature had cooled nicely, and Bernie said that the entire order had arrived.

Nina threw a long tablecloth over the table on my out-door deck. It was actually a portico because it stood alone and had a roof over it. I loved the stone fireplace on one side, but so far it was too warm to use tonight.

We brought out the dishes and silverware. Then Humphrey, Mars, and I unpacked the bags, while Bernie explained to everyone about the ghost kitchen situation. "We think that someone has put up websites for ghost kitchens that do not exist. Instead of cooking food, they are ordering food from local restaurants, but charging more for it. Then Irv delivers it."

"So it's a scam?" asked Nina.

"It's misrepresentation, for one. And secondly, they're cheating the people who order from their phony websites, because they could have the same food delivered to them for a lot less money."

Bernie inspected each container. Most were Styrofoam clamshells. Some were plain, others had logo stickers on them. He examined the bottom of each one for the tiny red dot that indicated it came from The Laughing Hound or one of his friends' restaurants. "Every single one of these came from a restaurant."

"On the bright side, we won't have to worry about the contents or who cooked them. We know they'll be good," I said.

"But it doesn't make sense," said Bernie. "I never thought Charlene was that kind of person. For pity's sake, she asked us to deliver for her!"

"Natasha, is Charlene desperate for money?" asked Bernie. "She doesn't strike me as the type who would pull this kind of stunt."

Natasha looked baffled. "Not that I'm aware of."

"Maybe she got in over her head," said Mars. "She was getting more orders than she could handle?"

"You've got it backward, Mars. This is someone who isn't selling a lot of food. He has to sell someone else's food," said Bernie.

"Charlene is very busy," said Humphrey. "She can hardly keep up."

"There is one other possibility," I said. "Irv could be fleecing Charlene. She may not know that he's delivering food for other ghost kitchens in her van."

"Of course!" said Bernie. "That makes perfect sense. He's driving around anyway. Basically, he's just making more money for something he's already doing."

"And Charlene is picking up the cost of the van and the gas," said Humphrey.

"Wait a minute," I said. "The day Irv was hit over the head, a Dinner at Home cap was on the floor and a package of Natasha's cookies was on Gerrie's dining table. Wong, did you ever find out what happened to Irv that day?"

Wong thought for a moment. I got the feeling she was choosing her words carefully.

"I can't tell you much. The general line of thought is that Irv was hit over the head for cash. He doesn't remember anything, which makes it more difficult."

"Could the person who hit him over the head have taken the cap and stolen the cookies from Irv's van to gain access to Gerrie's house?" I asked.

Wong nodded. "It's a possibility. But so far, we don't have any confirmation of that."

"Or so that he wouldn't be noticed?" suggested Francie. "The hat would've hidden a lot of his face if there were cameras that might have caught him."

"Do you know Irv?" I asked Francie.

"I do," said Betty. "He was one of those people who followed bands around the country."

"A roadie?" asked Mars.

"Yes. That's the word for them. He spent years doing that. I understand he lived quite the life. Gambling, drinking, carrying on with women. Now he needs to augment his income, so he drives a delivery truck for Charlene. It's a win-win situation for both of them."

"If he has been delivering my cookies in Charlene's van, it could mean he has been delivering for other companies all along. And that would be big trouble for Irv," said Natasha.

Using the papers to identify what he had ordered, Bernie stood by the pile of food containers and practically auctioned them off.

I could barely keep track as he handed them out: spaghetti carbonara, chicken-and-bacon empanadas, spicy meatballs with penne, vegetarian quinoa salad, chicken and waffles, sesame beef with broccoli, chicken tikka masala, meatball subs, and lamb korma.

There were more, including some from Bernie's restaurant, but we ultimately passed the containers back and forth, sharing everything and talking about what we liked and which restaurants had actually cooked the various dishes.

Natasha was strangely silent through the entire meal. She picked at her food, like she usually did, but she hadn't said much. She wore a magazine-worthy dress in a rough beige fabric. It had only one shoulder, leaving the other bare, and was nipped in at the waist by a tortoiseshell clip. Her gaze lingered on Mars, and I wondered if she was hoping he might come back to her again.

Nina and I collected the dirty dishes and carried them into the kitchen. We made quick work of rinsing them and stashing them in the dishwasher. I had just removed the panna cottas from the refrigerator when Natasha strode into the kitchen.

Her mouth was drawn tight and she wouldn't look me in the eyes. "I hope you're happy," she said.

I was sorely tempted to respond that I was enjoying my company, but the warring look on her face deterred me.

"What's wrong, Natasha?"

"Remind me to never, ever do you any favors again."

"Is this about your cookies?"

"They are not my cookies anymore. Thanks to you, Natasha's Cookies are dead. They no longer exist."

"Oh, Natasha! I'm sorry about that. They were very popular at the conference." I thought that might console her.

"You just don't get it, do you? If you had not ordered them for your stinky conference, I would not have lost my business."

"You lost your show?" asked Nina.

I knew that couldn't possibly be my fault. We'd had to save her show once before. If the ratings were slipping, it had nothing to do with me.

"Not the show. The people who handle my cookies canceled me. Natasha's Cookies are officially dead. Credit card companies won't accept the charges anymore."

"Because of the fraud," I said. "Of course." I knew it was not my fault. The terrible person who thought up that scam had probably done it before to other brands.

"How on earth can that be Sophie's fault?" asked Nina in an irate tone. "It's not as though she's the scammer."

"They never would have thought of it if she hadn't brought my cookies to the conference."

"If that's the case, then the police should ask Colleen for the names of the attendees," I said.

"Do you know what Wolf told me? That as far as they

can tell, the creep only managed to charge seven thousand dollars' worth of goods. They have no concern whatsoever about the fact that he ruined my brand. Ruined it! My good name was worth a lot more than that." Her eyes narrowed. "Hey! You two are good at solving murders. Why don't you track down that creep so I can clear my reputation?"

Nina leaned against the island and crossed her arms over her chest. "What's in it for us?"

For once, Natasha was at a loss for words.

I flipped the panna cottas onto dessert dishes, ladled the berry sauce over them, and grated just a little chocolate over each one. I placed them on trays, ready to carry outside.

"Do you suppose people will want tea and coffee?" I didn't wait for a response. I wanted tea. Surely, others did, too. Bernie probably would. I put on the kettle and made a pot of decaf coffee as well.

If Charlene was the one perpetrating the restaurant and ghost kitchen scam, Natasha's name would also be brought up as her half sister. There was no question about that. I would hate to hear the fuss in her household when that happened.

"Natasha," I said. "I don't know what we could do. That skunk probably printed the flyers himself. And Wolf said he probably used a throwaway phone to take the orders. If a credit card company can't track him down, then we can't. They have more resources at their disposal. But you have a voice. You have a TV show. Why don't you go public with what happened? I bet you'd get a lot of publicity."

Natasha sucked in a deep breath, clearly appalled. "Are you out of your mind? I would lose my show! Honestly, you have the worst ideas. I was going to ask if you and Nina could help me get Mars back, but you'll probably tell me to walk up to him and tell him I still love him."

I froze.

Nina said, "Good grief, Natasha. It's time to move on already." She looked at me. "We should hook her up with that guy Gerrie went out with last night."

I released my breath slowly. "That's not a bad idea."

I smiled at Natasha and handed her a tray to carry outside.

She pulled her lips back in distaste. "Are you cultivating that look?"

I was still wearing my khaki skirt and white shirt. "There's nothing wrong with this."

"Oh, Sophie," she moaned. "You simply have no taste in clothes. You're hopeless. No wonder you can't attract a man." She set the tray on the counter. "I don't know why you gave me that. I'm not your server." She turned and, without another word, stalked through the living room. We heard the door close behind her.

Nina and I laughed until tears welled in our eyes. We collected ourselves and carried the trays out. Mars, Wong, and Bernie retrieved the mugs, coffeepot, and hot tea. Nina roamed through the liquor cabinet for after-dinner drinks.

Night had fallen outside. Mars lit the fire in the fireplace to ward off any chill.

While we ate dessert, Bernie asked, "How's the murder investigation coming?"

Silence fell over the group. Only the sound of silverware and the crackling of the fire could be heard.

Natasha, who was obviously feeling much cheerier and had already given her dessert to Mars, piped up to answer. "Everyone knows Gerrie was having an affair with Russ.

Her son Todd was upset about it and stabbed Russ when he found him in her house. End of story. I don't know why they haven't arrested Todd yet."

I shook my head. "Why do people think Gerrie was having an affair? She loved her husband. She's devastated by his loss."

"I have to agree with Sophie. Gerrie wouldn't have done that to Edwin. They were true soul mates," Betty chimed in.

"So, who could have done it, then?" asked Mars.

"Todd is certainly on the list," I said. "His brother, Jim, was also at the house that morning. We have to consider Gerrie, of course. Todd's soon-to-be ex-wife, Colleen, dropped by, so she's a contender, too. Their neighbor, Senator Keswick, turned up awfully fast and happened to be home that day, which might or might not have been a coincidence. And there's the possibility of an unknown person who clobbered Irv, Charlene's delivery driver, and may have stolen his cap and delivered Natasha's Cookies to Gerrie's residence."

"Thus gaining entrance to the house because someone inside would have answered the door," said Nina.

"The knife came from Gerrie's kitchen," offered Humphrey.

"Wong, you must know something," said Nina.

"If I did, I couldn't tell you. Sophie did a pretty good roundup. Besides, I don't have anything official to do with that case. I happened to be the first to respond, but it's all in Wolf's hands now."

As they spoke, it dawned on me that I hadn't talked with Charlene or Irv about Russ's death. I mentioned it to her briefly on the day it happened, and she'd been sort of snappy about one of her Dinner at Home caps being found at the crime scene.

Betty and Francie were the first to go home. Humphrey

gallantly offered to escort them. They departed in pairs, until it was just Wong and me, sitting by the fire with Daisy.

"I heard you met Eddie," said Wong.

"I can see why you were infatuated with him. He's very handsome."

"He's the poster child for 'Beauty is only skin deep.'"

Chapter 27

Dear Natasha,
I'm getting married! But I have a budget and I can't believe the prices. How do I get all the fun things I want without blowing my budget?
                    Happy Bride in Groom, Texas

Dear Happy Bride,
Best wishes on your upcoming nuptials. Get ideas from wedding sites, but buy elsewhere for better prices. Shop broadly, and don't overspend on trinkets that will never be used again.
                    Natasha

"You must have loved Eddie once. You kept his name," I said.

"Everyone knew me as Wong. And I thought I might be pregnant at the time we separated and signed the papers. I hated him, but I didn't want to have a different last name than my child."

I didn't want to ask what happened to the baby, for fear it might bring back sad memories.

"Fortunately, I was not pregnant. But I never changed it. I've sort of gotten used to it."

"What is your maiden name?" I asked.

"Well, there is that, too. I didn't mind getting rid of Bacon. Rosa Bacon. My grandmother was named Rosa."

"That's not so bad. It's a pretty name."

"Rosie Bacon? You cannot imagine the teasing. And it doesn't stop with grade school. Grown men cannot resist saying something humorous about it. When I became a cop, all the guys were calling each other by their last names. I guess Daniels and Morales sound more authoritative than Jack and John. I was married then, and my name tag said 'Wong.' It kind of stuck."

We sat by the fire in comfortable silence for a few minutes.

"I hate him," Wong whispered.

I looked over at her.

"If I could change one thing in my life, it would have been meeting Eddie. Since that day, he has manipulated me. Oh my gosh, the lies! The incredible thing about him is that even though he's the one twisting the truth around, he's able to convince you that you're the one who is confused. That you're the one who has it all wrong. That you're the crazy one. That's what narcissists do. They slowly drive you out of your mind."

"Wong, are you afraid of him?"

"I was going to say that I sleep with one eye open and my gun by my side. But I guess that means the same thing. I don't trust him."

"Have you figured out why he came back?" I asked.

"Because he's comfortable here. And he knows he can make some money. He's looking for someone to move in with, and I'm the first on his list, but it's not gonna happen. No way. I am through with that man."

"How cyber smart is he? Any chance that he's the one behind collecting money by selling the food of other restaurants at a marked-up price?"

She shrugged. "Could be. I don't think you'd have to be too clever to have set that up. Eddie never can turn down a good scam. If it is him, I don't think that's the reason he came here, though. He vanished for so long. I feel like something must have changed because he felt like it was safe to return to Old Town."

"Are you sure that he was in town when Russ was murdered?" I asked.

"When it comes to Eddie, nothing is certain."

"Wong, do you want to bunk with me for a while? Just so you can feel safe?"

"I considered staying with my parents. But I don't want to take my troubles to them. If they were harmed, I couldn't live with myself. I'll be okay." She paused. "I envy you. Maybe your marriage to Mars didn't work out, but at least he's a good guy. You've never had to worry about what horrible thing he might do next. I wish Eddie had never come back to Old Town."

My first thought on waking Thursday morning was that it had been a peaceful night. I hoped Wong's night had passed without incident as well.

My second thought was that I had Gerrie's make-up luncheon to look forward to. She always threw such beautiful luncheons, and after what had happened last time, I was certain she would outdo herself.

I dressed quickly in a skort and top and took Daisy out for her morning walk. Rays of sunlight were only beginning to lighten the sky. I left through my front door and noticed something in my mailbox. To my complete horror, I pulled out a flyer for Nataska's Cookies. A chill ran through me just to know that the scammer had walked up to my house to leave the offer for the cookies. I imagined that they were in mailboxes all along the street.

Few cars were out and about yet. As we walked, porch lights turned off and kitchen lights turned on. Through open windows, I caught an occasional whiff of coffee brewing. I kept an eye open for anyone approaching mailboxes.

Daisy paused at the entrance to an alley. A gate creaked and I looked to my right. Gerrie Stansfield quietly closed the gate and scurried along the alley away from us. That stinker! Had her emotional scene, the day before yesterday, been a show? Was she sneaking out to spend her nights with someone?

I turned right and walked along the alley, but I couldn't tell exactly which house she had left. Well! That changed everything!

As Daisy and I emerged from the alley, I heard voices.

"You scum! You told me you were on the straight and narrow."

Was that Wong? It certainly sounded like her. I stepped back, into the shadows.

"Aw, c'mon. I came back here for you. I never stopped loving you, baby."

"Eddie Wong, I am not that innocent girl who was stupid enough to believe you. Give me the rest of those flyers."

"Is that any way to talk to your husband?"

"Ex-husband! *Ex!* Now give them to me and get out of town because they're going to be on your tail for this."

"I'm not scared of cops. I married one!"

"I will not protect you. You have to understand that, Eddie. My job is to look out for the good people of Old Town, to protect *them* from dimwit con artists like you."

"Did you just call me a 'dimwit'?"

"Be glad I didn't call you worse!"

"I am not a *dimwit*. I have a genius IQ."

Wong snorted. "I think you're beginning to believe the crazy stories you make up. If you were smart, you wouldn't need to cheat people."

"Listen, my angel, all I need is three days. That's all. And then I'll leave again."

"Are you so stupid that you're asking me *not* to report you for this cookie scam?"

"Well," he said softly, "maybe you could delay your report. For old times' sake."

"Do not touch me." Wong spoke harshly. "You nearly ruined my life once, but I will not let you do it again."

"I notice that you haven't found anyone to replace me. I'm a tough act to follow."

"Just give me the flyers and get out of my life."

The roar of a car going much too fast drew my attention. I pulled Daisy to me and backed away as far as I could.

A dark sedan shot past me, and I peered after it just in time to see it aiming for Eddie and Wong.

Eddie lunged at Wong, grabbing her, and knocking her off her feet. They fell to the sidewalk and rolled to safety, only seconds before the car careened over the curb, narrowly missing them. But it hit the bag Eddie had dropped. Flyers for Nataska's Cookies flew into the air and fluttered down around them. The car bounced hard as it returned to the pavement and passed underneath a streetlight. On the rear window were written the words *Wash Me!* I squinted in hopes of reading the license plate, but there was none.

"Wong!" I ran toward them. "Are you okay? Should I call an ambulance?"

Eddie moaned and tried to sit up. "Did you see who that was?"

"No. All I know is that it was a dark sedan. And it needed a good washing. Do either of you need help?"

Wong held out her hand. I took it and hoisted her to her feet. "Aw, Eddie. Man! I'm going to be sore all over."

"Are you hurt?" he asked, his voice gentle.

"Yeah, I'm hurt! You jerk!"

"Wong," I said. "I think Eddie saved your life."

"I thought you were immune to men like him. I see he's gotten to you," she snapped.

"It was aiming for Eddie, but you would have been hit, too." I offered a hand to Eddie to help him up.

His eyes met mine and I thought I saw a moment of gratitude flash over his face. He stood, somewhat unsteadily.

"Maybe you should go to the emergency room. You might have broken something," I said.

"No! I'll be all right. I've been worse."

Wong drew herself up as tall and authoritative as she could. "I don't know who you ticked off this time, Eddie, but I want you to leave town. Pack your bags and get out of here. And don't come back. Do you understand me?"

Eddie reached for her hand and clenched it. "There isn't anything I wouldn't do for you, Wong. Except that. I have a little business to take care of." He leaned over and kissed her on the forehead.

Wong stood stoic as a statue. "Get out of here."

He walked away with a definite limp.

"Hey, Eddie!" I called after him.

He stopped and turned to look at me.

"Have you been snooping around my garage and back-yard?"

A sly, coy grin crossed his lips, answering my question.

"Next time I'll call the police."

"You need a better lock on the door leading to your house

from the garage. Next time there could be something in there waiting for you." He turned and limped away.

A shiver ran down my back. "That was a threat!"

"You see what I mean? He's trouble, Sophie."

Wong sucked in air. "He didn't really save me, did he?"

I nodded. "I'm afraid so."

"He makes me so doggone mad. He cheats, lies, and steals, and then he goes and does something heroic, like saving my life."

"Highly irritating." I bent over to help Wong collect the flyers.

"You bet it is! And now somebody is trying to kill him. I can't say *that* comes as a surprise. What do you suppose he's done now? And who has it out for him?"

"You mean besides Natasha, once she figures out that he's the guy behind Nataska's Cookies? Do you need a cup of coffee?"

"Yeah. But I'd better write up a report on this first, while it's fresh in my head. You sure he was aiming for us?"

I nodded. "I'm sorry, Wong. I heard the car gunning its engine, coming way too fast. I pulled Daisy back, and he steered right at you."

"Did you get a license plate number?"

"There wasn't one."

"Oh no. Eddie has gotten himself into a mess this time. I was hoping that it might have been a drunk driver, but if they went to the trouble of taking off the license plate, then that was intentional."

"I wish I could have seen who was driving. It all happened so fast! But someone had written 'Wash me!' in the dirt on the car."

"I know how that is, Sophie. In the heat of the moment, it's hard to see many details."

I felt a little better about missing the driver. "Are you sure that you're okay? Maybe I should walk with you."

Wong brushed off her clothes. "I could use a few minutes of solitude. It'll take some getting used to the idea that Eddie did something decent and good. And that I'm still alive because of it. I'd better gather as many of these flyers as I can, too."

"Daisy and I can collect the ones on our street."

"Thanks." Wong walked away without a limp.

Daisy and I ambled along the street, sneaking flyers out of people's mailboxes. I was quaking inside, and the car hadn't been trying to mow me down. I could only imagine how Wong and Eddie must have felt.

I had a vague memory of it being illegal to remove something from a person's mailbox. Or was that nonsense? In any event, it would be far worse if someone lost money to Eddie's con. I giggled a little when I realized that he must not know Natasha's Cookies had shut down. I hoped other people knew about it and wouldn't call the number on the flyers.

It wasn't until I unlocked my door and was inside my house that I felt better. I made a pot of coffee, showered, and split scrambled eggs with Daisy for breakfast.

Henrietta's comments about the visual importance of table settings gave me food for thought. I spent a few minutes browsing table-setting ideas for upcoming events. While it was possible to spend a ridiculous amount of money on items that one might only use once on a table, I found many less costly items to dress up tables and impart a special theme.

Just before noon, I met Nina on the sidewalk for Gerrie's second attempt at a luncheon. We laughed at our similar 1950s fit and flare–style dresses. Hers had a white background with a purple wisteria pattern, and mine was a soft green background with loud pink peonies around the bottom. I filled her in on Eddie's behavior. As we had before, we walked toward Gerrie's house. But this time, we didn't see her hurrying across the road. She must have replenished her supply of half-and-half.

No one waited before Gerrie's house this time. I banged the knocker.

When Gerrie didn't answer right away, Nina asked, "Are we too early? Maybe she's upstairs and didn't hear the knocker."

She rapped the knocker. Still, no one answered the door.

I tried the door handle, but it was locked. "Should we go around back?"

Nina nodded. We walked around the building and entered through the garden gate in the back of the house. The patio was lovely, with bright geraniums in bloom. But for the heat, I would have liked to have the luncheon outside.

I knocked on the French doors to the kitchen. Nothing moved. Cupping my hands around my eyes, I peered inside. Uh-oh. No plates. No strawberry roll. No messes on the kitchen counters.

Nina peered into the dining room. "The table is set. Sort of."

"So she didn't forget." I tried the kitchen door. It opened quietly, without so much as a squeak.

We stepped inside. I smelled coffee. The glass coffeepot was empty. Only a touch of liquid remained at the bottom. I shut it off so it wouldn't dry out and start a fire. "Gerrie?"

I tried again in a louder voice. "Gerrie?"

I pushed open the interior doors and walked to the foyer, with Nina right behind me. In the elegant foyer, eerily replicated in the mirrors, sat Eddie Wong.

Chapter 28

Dear Natasha,
One of your competitors suggests a complicated scheme for decorating adjoining rooms. What do you suggest to unify the rooms of a home?
Redecorating Again in Pleasant Home, Oregon

Dear Redecorating Again,
Paint all wood trim, kitchen cabinets, and entertainment cabinets sage green. Paint all the walls a light silver gray. Now everything matches, and no matter what you add, everything will flow.
Natasha

I screamed. Nina screamed, too, a second later. A blue knife handle jutted out of Eddie's abdomen. The handle looked just like the one on the knife that had killed Russ. There was no mistaking it. Once again, it had probably come from Gerrie's kitchen.

He was on the floor at the bottom of the stairs, slumped against the wall as though he'd backed up against it, and slid down to a seated position when he was dying.

Nina grabbed hold of me and the two of us stood there in shock.

I swallowed hard. "You call 911. And don't let anyone in. Tell them something. Make up some reason that the luncheon had to be canceled."

"I'll put a note on the door."

"Good idea." I pressed my dress neatly to the backs of my thighs, collected the fabric, and held it in place with one hand so it wouldn't droop and get bloody when I squatted next to Eddie. With my free hand, I reached for his throat. It was a bit of a balancing act, but I managed it. I didn't feel anything. Maybe the EMTs could revive him. I doubted it, though, given the amount of blood.

I rose to my feet and walked through the living room and the dining room in search of Gerrie. The living room looked perfect. But the dining table stopped me cold.

There was no tablecloth. Not even a runner down the center of the table. Each place was set with a dinner plate, a salad plate, a napkin, a soup bowl, then a teacup and saucer all stacked in a pile. Maybe that was her routine in the process of setting a table? She would have to remove everything to put on the tablecloth. Maybe Penelope had been helping her.

"Gerrie?" I called her name, over and over again, as I walked up the stairs. I was tempted to fetch a knife from the kitchen, just in case someone lunged at me, but the police might assume I was the perpetrator if I did that. On the second floor, I spied a fireplace poker. That was better than a knife anyway. At least I hoped so.

I peeked into a bedroom. Pale-pink walls and girlish furniture led me to think it might be Penelope's room when she stayed over. Nothing looked amiss. Farther along the hallway, I entered what had to be the master bedroom, with subtle damask print wallpaper in tones of blue. And on the white comforter, trimmed in matching blue, lay Gerrie, with blood all over her elegant lavender dress.

"Gerrie!" I ran toward her.

I stretched my hand out to check her pulse. Thankfully, I could feel it. Weak, but at least she was alive. That was when I noticed the pills. They lay scattered on the bed. I looked around for a bottle, to know what they were, but didn't see one. A bathroom adjoined the bedroom. I rushed into it, intent on finding the bottle. It wasn't in the trash can. I didn't see any medicine bottles standing around. I checked the floor, just in case one had been dropped and rolled away. Nothing. The place was spotless.

I returned to the bedroom and searched the nightstands. Still, no medicine. I gazed at Gerrie lying on her bed. She wore tan pumps with the lavender dress. Would Gerrie lie on her bed with shoes on? I wouldn't! All the dirt and grime from the street on my comforter? Not a chance!

I studied the bed. It was almost devoid of blood. Her shoes weren't bloody, either. If she had sat on the comforter, she would surely have gotten blood on the edge. It was almost as though she had taken a flying leap and landed in the middle of the bed. And if she had stabbed Eddie, wouldn't there be blood spatter on her shoes? Whoever killed him must have gotten pretty close to drive the knife in.

This was a setup. Gerrie hadn't killed Eddie Wong. She'd been knocked out first, and the blood had been smeared on her dress to make her appear guilty.

Chapter 29

Dear Sophie,
I tried to introduce a summery feeling to my home this year and failed miserably. All those little beachy things just looked like clutter. How do I incorporate a summery atmosphere?
     Nix the Beach! in Summerville, South Carolina

Dear Nix the Beach!
It's not so much about the little things. Swap out wintry items for natural ones. Bring in green plants or cushions with green patterns. And most certainly add items that have the light airy feel of beige sand, like wicker baskets or lamps. Top it off with a few spots of bright pinks, oranges, and turquoise.

     Sophie

"Gerrie," I said, taking her hand into mine, "help is on the way. Everything is going to be okay. You'll be fine. I don't know if you can hear me, but you'll be all right. Hang in there!" I squeezed her hand gently, then released it, and ran down the stairs, hoping I would soon hear the sirens.

They howled in the distance just as I stepped onto the foyer floor. I could hear voices and chattering outside the front door. Nina stood with her back to it, looking terrified.

"Gerrie is alive," I said. "Barely, but I hope the EMTs will be here in time to save her. Come with me."

Nina nodded and followed me into the kitchen, where I paused to look around for a moment. Using a kitchen towel so I wouldn't leave fingerprints, I opened the refrigerator. It was packed. A tall pitcher of gazpacho had been sampled, drips of the vibrant red soup had rolled down the edge of the refrigerator shelves. The plastic wrap on platters of goodies had been lifted in places, as though someone had sampled them. A cake sat on a crystal cake stand with a huge chunk missing. Carafes of iced tea had been made. In true Gerrie style, she had been ready for her luncheon today. But someone had tasted everything. Todd? He should know better.

"A mouse has been tasting things," I said.

"I swear it wasn't me," Nina replied.

I studied the floor. "I'm willing to bet the smeared red spots are gazpacho, not blood."

"You're probably right," said Nina. "I see a wad of paper towels in the trash that look like they were used to wipe up gazpacho."

We left the kitchen door open so we wouldn't add more of our fingerprints, then walked to the street, where a police car and an ambulance were arriving. I motioned them along the alley to the rear of the house.

Wong stepped out of her squad car. "Sophie? What's going on?"

Oh no! Of course, Wong would respond to the call. "Wong, I don't think you should see this."

"I'm a cop, Sophie. I've seen much worse things than you have."

"Have I *ever* asked you not to go into a crime scene before?"

She scowled at me. "No."

"Please. Don't go in this time. There's nothing you can do. Call for someone else to respond."

"This is my job."

"It will be too close to home," I said. "Take my word for it. You will never be able to *un*see this."

Her eyes met mine. She nodded. "Thanks for preparing me."

I didn't think she'd been sufficiently prepared, but what could I do? I waved to the EMTs and showed them through the back patio into the kitchen and led the way to the foyer.

To her credit, Wong did not scream when she saw Eddie on the floor surrounded by blood. I wanted to comfort her, but I knew Gerrie was upstairs, and they might still be able to save her.

"There's another one," I said.

"Another stabbing?" asked an EMT.

She *did* have a lot of blood on her dress. "I don't think so. But she's alive. At least she was a few minutes ago."

He followed me up the stairs and through to the bedroom. Much like I had, he felt her pulse. He nodded at me, then hustled past me to the top of the stairs and yelled something. I could hear the loud footsteps of a second EMT coming upstairs.

While the two of them worked on her, I heard more footsteps. A few seconds later, Wolf walked into the bedroom.

"Hi, Soph." He ignored me as he gazed about the room.

"It's a setup," I said.

"What is?"

"That Gerrie took pills."

"She didn't take pills?" asked one of the EMTs.

"She might have, but I don't think it was voluntarily. There's no empty pill bottle, just the random pills on the bed. And while Gerrie might have taken a nap on top of her comforter, there is no way she wouldn't have taken off her shoes."

A smile crept over Wolf's face. "Are there experts who can testify to that?"

I shot him a dour look. "Don't you see it? There's no blood around her on the comforter. Is she bleeding anywhere?" I asked.

"Not that we've found," said an EMT.

"You see?" I said to Wolf. "The timing had to be just right. Gerrie had to be down and sleepy when Eddie arrived. Then the killer dashed downstairs, let Eddie in, and stabbed him. Whoever it was had to catch Eddie unaware. He was pretty savvy. But he must not have expected to fight anyone off." No sooner had the words come out of my mouth, than I realized, that was significant. *Eddie hadn't expected to be killed.* He had been cautious about meeting with Nina and me, which meant he knew someone was after him. The car aiming for him today hadn't come as a shock to him. He was afraid of someone. But he wasn't afraid of coming to the Stansfields' house, even though he knew Russ had been murdered there.

The EMTs carried Gerrie downstairs on a stretcher. I lingered for a moment. Nope. There was no way she would have ruined that beautiful comforter. I hurried after the EMTs and followed them out into the street, where I was mobbed by a cluster of women wearing elegant summer dresses for a luncheon.

Jenna hugged me to her and whispered in my ear, "I'm so sorry that I introduced you to Eddie. Now she's killed him!" She drew away and faced me, still whispering. "I hope it wasn't because of our meeting with him. Did you tell anyone about it? How would she have found out?"

"Gerrie didn't kill him."

Jenna's eyes widened. She covered her mouth with her hand and backed up a step. "Nooo." It came out as little more than a sigh. "I thought it was over."

"What was over?"

"Gerrie's murder spree. But if it wasn't her, then"—she gazed around in a panic—"who was it? Is he here now? Don't they say criminals return to the scene of the crime? Is he watching as we stand here and talk?"

I was about to calm her, and assure her that was unlikely, when I looked up and saw Senator Keswick in a window. Henrietta Keswick observed from another window. And now that I focused on them, I realized that Elmo was barking at the commotion outside.

It didn't mean one of them had killed Eddie. But it would have been so easy for them. They could be across the street and safely in their own home in seconds. If Henrietta thought something was going on between her husband and Gerrie, she might have wanted to knock her off. It wouldn't be the first time a wife had murdered a husband's paramour. But why kill Eddie?

I excused myself and ran back to the kitchen door. There had to be clues. Small things that the killer had overlooked.

But Wolf was in the kitchen. He opened the door for me, but when I tried to step inside, he said, "Sorry, Sophie. It's a crime scene now."

My disappointment must have shown because he quickly added, "But thanks for your help. Really."

And then he closed the door, and I heard the lock clank. It was such a final sound that I winced.

When I turned to leave, I saw Wong in the garden. She sniffled and wiped her face with both hands.

I held out my arms and hugged her.

She wept on my shoulder. "I'b gedding your dress wet," she said as she let go.

I smiled at her. "I'm so sorry, Wong."

She nodded and blew her nose. "I hated Eddie. You know the grates in sidewalks? There were times I wished he would fall through one and disappear forever. Between the two of us, there might have even been a few times when I wished someone would drive a knife into him. I don't know why I'm crying!" She swiped the backs of her hands across her eyes.

"It was a shock," I said.

"I wished him dead so many times. I never thought I'd care."

"But, Wong, you must have loved him once, or you wouldn't have married him."

"I guess so. He did so many awful things that I've forgotten about the good times. But seeing him like that was horrible. So final. So cruel. Deep down, I guess I knew he would end up this way, but I always hoped he would wake up and leave his life of crime."

"I know," I murmured, holding her close again.

I felt someone on my right and turned my head to see Wolf and a uniformed officer.

Wolf said gently, "Wong, Officer Orlova will drive you home and bring the patrol car back to the station."

"Thank you," she whispered. She walked away with the other cop, probably very glad to be relieved of her duties.

"That was nice of you," I said to Wolf.

"I'm sorry she had to see that. I know they had a miserable marriage, but it rips you up when someone close to you dies, especially like this."

"I tried to stop her."

"She's a good cop. There's nothing you could have done to keep her from going in."

"Wolf, I was out early this morning walking Daisy. Just at dawn. It was still sort of dark outside. I heard a car, a dark sedan, gun forward. I jumped back. It passed me and was heading for Wong and Eddie."

"Did you see who was driving?"

"No. It all happened too fast. Eddie tackled Wong and they rolled on the ground to get out of harm's way."

"I'll check to see if we have any reports about a dark sedan."

"Wolf, it was aiming for them. It wasn't a fluke. The license plate had been removed and someone had written 'Wash Me!' on the back window."

Wolf nodded. "It's hard to keep a black car clean. Everything shows on black paint."

Nina walked up to us. "What did the EMTs say about Gerrie?"

"Not much," said Wolf. "They didn't know what she had ingested."

"We should check on her later," I said to Nina.

"Keep me posted." Wolf returned to the house.

There was no point in standing around in Gerrie's patio in the midday sun. Nina and I walked toward King Street.

"I hate to be petty, given what just transpired, but I'm hungry."

"Look! There's Irv's van."

"Sophie, we can't just help ourselves."

"Of course not. But we could ask Irv a few questions."

"So now I have to smell food, but I can't eat any? Swell."

I grinned. At least some things never changed. We walked up to the van and waited while Irv dropped off bags of food.

He greeted us on his way back to the truck. "Hi, ladies! How was your dinner? That was the biggest order I ever delivered to one place."

"Everything was delicious, thanks. Um, Irv, where did you pick up all those orders?"

Irv rubbed his chin. "Was there something wrong with 'em?"

"Everything was fine. I was just wondering if you went to a lot of ghost kitchens to pick them up."

"I don't really remember. I prob'ly got them from Charlene. She's some cook! Sorry, but I gotta go. People are waiting for their food."

I stepped in front of the driver's-side door. "Irv?"

"Look, I don't want to get into any trouble."

Nina snapped, "We ate that food! We have a right to know where you got it."

"Listen, a friend of mine brought it to me to deliver. That's all."

"Then why are you being cagey about it?" I asked.

Irv gave a small, nervous laugh and crossed his arms over his chest. He looked around frantically and finally blurted, "Because Charlene will fire me if she finds out I deliver for people besides Dinner at Home."

She might if she hadn't had so much trouble replacing him the day he was hurt. But I didn't think I should mention that.

"She already found someone else, for days I don't show up. Skinny guy. Friendly enough, but I gotta be careful. Please don't tell her. I'll lose my job for sure."

"Irv, on the day someone conked you over the head, were you delivering Natasha's Cookies in addition to Charlene's orders?" I asked.

His lips tightened into a thin line. "Yeah."

"So, how does this work?" asked Nina. "Other ghost kitchens call you and say they have deliveries. Then you pick them up and deliver?"

"That's exactly how it works."

"And they pay you for making the delivery?" I asked.

"Aww, come on now. Charlene is real sweet, but I don't make a lot of money. So I do some other deliveries on the side for extra pocket change, you know? I'm not breaking the law or hurting anybody."

"No one except Charlene, who is paying for gas, insurance, and maintenance on this van," I said.

He chewed on his upper lip. "You gonna tell Charlene?"

"Only if you don't," I said.

"I still want to know where you got the food we ate," Nina insisted.

"I told you! A buddy of mine picked it all up, but since it was going to the same address, he asked me to deliver it. Real simple."

"Well, it doesn't sound that unreasonable," said Nina.

"Who is your buddy?" I asked.

Chapter 30

Dear Sophie,
My future in-laws are coming to meet me. There's no time (or much money) to redecorate my house. What can I do fast that will dress it up?
Anxious in Home Gardens, California

Dear Anxious,
I'm sure they'll love you. The one trick that will brighten up every room is flowers! You can buy plants and pop them into any containers or baskets they fit in. As long as they're blooming, those pops of color will make your house look gorgeous.
Sophie

Irv's eyebrows raised, which widened his eyes. "I am not gettin' anyone else in trouble. I was just doin' him a favor, okay? Now I gotta go. This food is gonna get cold or warm or whatever."

I stepped aside.

He climbed into the van and drove away.

"Do you think he'll tell Charlene?" asked Nina.

"Probably not. And he didn't want to tell us his buddy's name, either. What do you bet the buddy is the guy with the websites that are selling food, but getting it from other restaurants?"

"We should tail him." Nina gazed at me hopefully.

"We'd better do it soon, before Charlene cans him."

"Dinnertime tonight," said Nina.

"You're on."

We headed for the bar in The Laughing Hound. The interior was cool and soothing. We took a table in the back and ordered hamburgers and French fries because now and then, you have to have a great burger. We chugged iced tea and it wasn't long before Bernie appeared.

"Rumor had it that you were here. Is it true that Gerrie murdered Wong's ex-husband?"

The words *Gerrie murdered* and *Wong's ex-husband* rang in my ears. I was certain that had not been the case, but I could imagine all the theories, starting with the one that people seemed to jump to about Gerrie, that she was having an affair. For the longest time, I had believed that she truly loved Edwin and that insinuations about her affairs were ridiculous. She was known for being proper and respectable. Was that the reason they jumped to salacious conclusions? Did everyone want to think she wasn't as perfect and untarnished as she presented? Did it make them feel better to imagine she was as flawed as they were? Now that I had caught her sneaking out of someone's yard the back way, at the crack of dawn, I was forced to reconsider.

She'd been a widow for only a few months. True, Eddie Wong was remarkably handsome, but that was no reason to imagine the two of them as a couple. Unless . . . could that be Eddie's reason for returning to Old Town? Did he think he could take advantage of the wealthy widow? But if that had been the case, why would she kill Eddie, now when she was a widow, and had nothing to fear from associating with the man of her choice?

"No. I don't think Gerrie killed Eddie." I said it calmly in spite of my inner irritation.

Bernie pulled up a chair.

Our hamburgers arrived, thick with traditional lettuce, tomato, pickles, and mayonnaise. Before biting into mine, I said, "I honestly don't think she did it." I told Bernie about her bed and her shoes, and how there wasn't any blood on the edges of the white comforter, only in the middle where she had lain.

And then, exactly as I bit into the monstrosity of a burger and juices flowed onto my hands and tomato squirted out, Alex German, my previous beau and Gerrie's attorney, showed up at our table.

Much like Bernie, Alex simply took a seat with the comfort of someone who didn't have to ask. The first thing he did was steal two of my French fries. And then he and Bernie ordered exactly what Nina and I were eating.

I gave him a little nod. My mouth and hands were too full to speak or wave.

"Don't try stealing Nina's fries," warned Bernie. "She's liable to bite your fingers off."

Alex laughed. "I'm aware of Nina's bearlike food-protecting tendencies. I gather you all know that Gerrie is in the hospital?"

I swallowed and asked, "How is she?"

"The last I heard, they were pumping her stomach."

"Eww. We're eating here, you know!" Nina whined.

"Sorry!"

"Sophie doesn't think Gerrie killed Eddie," said Bernie.

"That's the best news I've heard today!" said Alex. "Why not?"

Thankfully, Bernie explained my reasoning, and I tried to be a little daintier about consuming my juicy burger.

"Have you heard anything through the grapevine about what Eddie was up to?" Alex asked Bernie.

"Not a thing. His mom and her sister are frequent customers here. Nice women. His mom told me once that he took after his dad's side of the family."

"Is it possible that he was on the run because of something he did elsewhere?" I asked. "Don't a lot of criminals go somewhere they know well when they want to hide?"

"What did he do?" asked Bernie.

"I haven't the faintest idea," I said. "But according to Wong, that's the way he lived."

The other hamburgers arrived.

Before biting into his, Alex asked, "Does anyone know where Gerrie's sons were this morning?"

I stopped eating. "You think Todd or Jim killed Eddie and Russ?"

Alex swallowed. "I think Todd and Jim stand to inherit a lot of money from Gerrie."

I thought back to the day after Russ was murdered, when Gerrie wanted me to promise that I would come to her first if I thought any of her family could be involved. She'd been frightened. And who would know better than a family member that setting a gargoyle outside the kitchen would terrorize her?

"So when Eddie broke into the house, one of her sons was in the process of killing his mom with pills? Wrong place, wrong time for Eddie?" I asked.

"I'd hate to think that," said Bernie. "Her sons have always been very nice when I've been around them."

"I bet she changed the will!" said Nina. "Didn't they have an early meeting with Edwin's old partner about the will yesterday morning?"

Had she suspected one of her sons all along? Unless something was awry at Moss Restaurant Supply, I didn't think Jim was hard up for money. But his brother, Todd, certainly was.

"Sophie?" asked Bernie.

"Hmm?" I looked up at him.

"Nina said you're staking out Irv tonight."

"We're just going to follow him. He's definitely ripping off Charlene. I could be wrong, but I don't think he's the guy who put up the fake ghost kitchen websites. Hey, does anyone know where Jim Stansfield lives?"

"You think he's involved with the ghost kitchens?" asked Bernie.

"No. I just wondered where he lives."

"It's a nice place over on South Lee," said Alex. "Has a big garden. You can't miss it because you can see part of the garden from the street. He's big on homegrown veggies."

"I didn't know you were tight with Jim," said Nina.

"That might be the wrong word. He's a lawyer, you know. He doesn't practice, but to keep his license, he has to stay current on the law through continuing legal education classes, so I see him around."

"Apparently, his father said flattering things about you," I said.

Alex smiled. "The feeling was mutual. I liked Edwin very much. He was a man of fine character and wry humor. A combination that never misses."

"When Edwin died, was there any undercurrent of foul play?" I asked.

Alex paled. "Not that I heard. I would hate to think that. He didn't pay much attention to his health, so the heart attack didn't come as a big surprise."

We all looked at our plates.

"Oh, come on!" said Nina. "One hamburger and some fries aren't going to hurt us. Edwin clearly ate more than one."

"He was a great guy," said Bernie.

I looked at my watch and signaled for the check. "We'd better get going if we want to look in on Gerrie before we tail Irv."

"It's on the house, Soph," said Bernie.

"No, it's not. I'll have to stop coming here if you never let us pay for a meal." I handed my credit card to the server.

"At least let me pitch in," said Alex.

"Put your money away. Lunch is on me." Frankly, I was glad I'd been able to sit at the same table and eat a meal with Alex without it being awkward. I smiled at him. "Next time, we'll order more and let Bernie pick up the tab," I teased.

"It's a deal," said Bernie.

Nina and I walked home. She wanted to drive her car, but we decided the sleek Jaguar was too eye-catching. Irv was less likely to notice my hybrid SUV.

Half an hour later, we were at the hospital looking for Gerrie's room, when we heard voices coming from a waiting room that was open to the hallway.

"How long have you been seeing her?"

"Is that Colleen?" I whispered.

"Aw, Collie . . ." I could imagine Todd smiling at her, even though she was angry.

"Don't you 'aw, Collie' me. She's a tramp," said Colleen.

"She doesn't say things like that about you," said Todd.

"Because I'm not a tart. I don't want her taking care of Penelope. Heaven knows what she's teaching her," said Colleen.

"Penelope likes her. They go places that are fun," said Todd. "You'll like her, too, if you give her a chance and get to know her."

"Like that's going to happen," said Colleen.

"What could be so bad that Mom would want to kill herself?" a man's voice murmured.

Nina mouthed at me, "Jim?"

"You live there, for Pete's sake. Don't you ever talk with her, Todd?" asked Jim.

"I'm busy, okay? Did you think the two of us sat around the fire having heart-to-heart talks?"

"Were you bugging her for money?" asked Jim.

"No. Let it go, Jim. Besides, she was glad I've been living there. Especially after Dad died."

"Did you know she was taking sleeping pills?"

"No. She was fine. She was . . . Mom."

"Stop it!" a woman's voice said.

Was that Colleen again?

"You're not helping anything by squabbling. When we go in to see her, I don't want either of you carrying on this way. You are going to behave like the gentlemen she raised you to be. I don't care how *you* feel. There will be no arguments in Gerrie's presence. Do you understand me?"

Wow. Colleen had some moxie. I was glad she put them in their place.

I motioned to Nina. We walked into the waiting area.

"Hi. We came to find out how Gerrie is doing," I said.

Colleen jumped up from her seat and hugged me. "I heard you found her."

"Nina called 911."

The brothers murmured their thanks.

"So, how is she?" Nina asked.

"She took a massive overdose of sleeping pills," said Colleen. "They pumped her stomach and put her on a respirator. We're hoping she'll come around soon."

"The doctors are hopeful that she'll make a full recovery," said Jim. "It will take some time, though."

I didn't know how much I should tell them. I was positive she didn't overdose herself. But I wasn't an expert. And I didn't want to say something that might turn out to be false. "Have you seen her?" I asked.

"She looks awful." Jim's mouth pulled tight. "They threw us out. I'm going to stay over with her tonight to keep an eye on her." Jim looked at me. "Do you know something? Why would she do this?"

He looked so sad. Nina nudged me and I relented. "I'm not sure that this was her doing."

Todd, Jim, and Colleen stared at me.

"Hopefully, she'll come around soon and will be able to tell us what happened."

Jim looked to the side and rubbed his forehead. "Mom thinks a lot of you, but I would know if other people were in the house. I've had a security service watching at night, and I had a talk with Mom about not opening the door to people."

Todd snickered. "You did what? I'm there at night, you numbskull."

"As I understand it, you often come home late." Jim didn't look at his brother. "Or not at all."

"I didn't realize it was my job to babysit her."

"It's not. That's why I hired someone."

Surprisingly, Todd did not look annoyed. "Can I get anyone some coffee? Colleen?"

She shot him a look that could have melted steel.

I was ready to get out of that volatile conversation. "Where is Gerrie's room?"

Colleen seemed eager to play tour guide. "I'll show you."

Todd said, "They won't let you in."

Colleen shot back, "Maybe they won't let the two of you in." She hustled us into the hallway. "Honestly, I'm so tired of the bickering that I could scream. She's right this way."

We stopped outside of a room. Colleen quietly opened the door.

We walked in, single file.

Gerrie was barely recognizable with the ventilator covering part of her face. She was frighteningly pale.

"There was almost nothing in her stomach," said Colleen, "except for coffee and the dissolved sleeping medicine."

"So she hadn't eaten any breakfast," said Nina.

"Someone put the sleeping pills in her coffee. Remember the coffeepot I turned off?" I asked Nina. "I hope she makes it." I walked closer and bent to whisper to Gerrie, "We know you didn't do this to yourself. You have to be strong. You have to come back for Penelope. And you have to tell us who did this."

She showed no reaction.

Chapter 31

Dear Natasha,
My sister stopped by my house recently, and three
days later, I discovered she had written "Clean
me!" in the dust on a table in my sunroom! I'm
flabbergasted. Don't you think that was rude?
                              Offended in Dusty, Washington

Dear Offended,
Clearly, someone had to tell you.

                                             Natasha

Shortly after five in the afternoon, Nina and I sat in my
car, waiting for Irv. I had parked on the street, where
we would see him pull out with the loaded van. If he turned
right, we were in business. All I had to do was merge into
traffic. If he turned left, we were sunk.

"It's a fifty-fifty chance," said Nina. "Should we bet on
which way he goes?"

"All right. The loser has to call all the members of A
Healthy Meal to reschedule again."

"Ugh. Couldn't it be something less involved? Like paying for dinner?" Nina asked.

"It could be. But one of us is going to have to pick up the pieces and get organized for the fall."

Nina sighed. "Okay. I say he turns right."

"You're on."

Not fifteen minutes later, the old white van turned right onto the road.

Nina snickered. "That was a really smart bet I made."

I took a deep breath and merged into traffic. Nina had won fair and square.

Irv's first two stops were at a real estate office and a party store.

"The person selling the food of other restaurants could be anyone in those buildings," said Nina.

"True. But he's not bringing food out. He's taking it in. Those looked like normal deliveries to me."

"I see what you mean."

We watched him make six deliveries.

"How can anyone be a private detective?" asked Nina. "This is so boring!"

I had to agree. "Wait a minute. We should have done what Bernie did. If we place an order from one of those fake ghost kitchens, Irv will have to pick it up. Right?"

Nina already had her phone out. "Here's Bernie's wood-fired grilled salmon, but it's listed under a ghost kitchen called Oak Planks."

"Sounds good. There aren't many wood-fire kitchens around."

Nina placed our order online, paying with her credit card.

We watched as Irv delivered a bag of food to a house on Pitt Street. On his way back to the van, he pulled his phone out of his pocket and looked at it. Nodding his head, he checked his watch.

"Could it have happened that fast?" asked Nina. "Is he already being told where and when to pick up an order?"

"Possibly." I put the car in gear and we followed him through three more delivery stops before he doubled back and parked near The Laughing Hound. He returned in minutes, carrying an order that he left on Nina's porch when no one answered the door.

Nina leaped out of my car and retrieved the order. She ran back down the stairs and slid into the passenger seat.

"It smells so good! There's even a scent of the wood." She showed me the clamshell. "There's where he pulled off the label of The Laughing Hound."

A tiny bit of sticky residue marked it. If we hadn't known what was going on, we never would have noticed it.

"We might as well eat it while it's warm," she said.

I nodded and pulled my car around to the alley to park it in my garage.

Daisy and Mochie were overjoyed to see us. I took Daisy outside, while Nina whipped up mango and lemon spritzers. I fed my two furry ones, then brought out leftovers from the previous night's gigantic meal for Nina and me.

"That was a waste of time," I groused.

"No, it wasn't. All we have to do is get hold of Irv's phone."

She was right, of course. "I wonder how Irv gets paid?"

"If I were paying him, I'd send the money online. Like Veem or PayPal or something." Nina devoured an olive. "Maybe Irv hasn't actually met the person."

"Maybe. But he was odd yesterday about revealing who it was, so he must know. Would you work for an anonymous person?"

"That might be very interesting!" Nina took a long drag of her drink. "Actually, I can't imagine why anyone would work for an unknown person. You wouldn't know what kind of crimes they might be perpetrating, and you could get caught up in them. No way!"

"My feelings exactly. Whoever this is has been clever about hiding his identity." I stared at the salmon Nina had purchased. "You paid for this with your credit card. But since the food came from Bernie's restaurant, how did Bernie get paid?"

Nina shrugged. "He used his credit card."

"Which would have revealed his name."

Nina grabbed her phone and called Bernie, putting the phone on speaker. "Sophie and I didn't have much luck tailing Irv. But you should know this guy's name. He must be charging the food on his credit card."

"If only it were that easy. We think he's using a masked card."

Nina looked at me, clearly befuddled. "What's that?"

"Because of all the credit card theft, some banks issue masked or virtual cards. It may be the wave of the future. They give you a temporary number that links back to your real credit card. You can limit how much can be charged for the item that you're buying. That way, the number isn't good for another purchase. It defeats fraud. Some of the masked cards don't reveal your name, and some of them are disposable, good for one-time use, like a burner phone that you throw away. That way, if someone hacks into a business that has your card on file, gets your credit card number, and tries to sell it on the dark web, it's useless."

"How do you know this?" I asked.

"Because I accept credit cards all day long. You can't tell them apart from a regular credit card. My point is that if he doesn't want people to know who he is, he could use a fake name and address."

"I wish people who were this clever would use their brains for something beneficial to mankind instead of trying to fool everyone for monetary gain," I said.

"Thanks for trying," said Bernie. "If you come up with any great ideas, let me know."

Nina disconnected the call. "Well! We're back to square one."

"No, we're not. Irv called that person a friend. If he was paid online, it would go through Irv's bank, and he would have to pay taxes on it. Plus, his friend would have to file a 1040 or a 1099 with the IRS. I bet Irv gets paid cash, under the table. Anyone who is so lazy that he would make money by charging more for meals made by someone else is going to try to cheat all the way around."

Nina swallowed a mouthful of food. "We gave up too soon."

"We sure did."

"Tomorrow we take snacks."

I went to bed that night thinking about Gerrie. I had to be overlooking something. Clearly, Todd, Colleen, and Jim stood to gain the most if Gerrie died. But all this had started with Russ's death. Had one of them hired Russ to kill her? We still didn't know what he was doing at Gerrie's house. I supposed it followed that the same person might have hired Eddie to take care of murdering Gerrie. I was positive that Gerrie had not taken those sleeping pills. No, that whole premise was just wrong, and her comforter proved it.

That begged the question, why did Russ and Eddie go to Gerrie's house? Wong was convinced that Eddie returned here for a reason. Eddie had made Gerrie out to be a Ma Barker type, convincing her sons to commit crimes. But I wasn't buying that. I didn't have any proof of it, and if that were the case, then why was Todd unemployed? How did Jim manage to run a large and successful business?

I had been involved in enough projects with Gerrie to know her better than that. I wasn't buying Eddie's story.

But if she was having an affair, as so many people seemed to think, then her paramour might know what was up.

I got up and went downstairs to my home office. Daisy and Mochie followed me, clearly displeased with the midnight interruption in our routine.

I woke my computer and searched for the street that backed to the alley where I had seen Gerrie. I didn't know whose house I was looking for, but maybe I could narrow it down. I found a site that did exactly what I needed. It listed all the homeowners on a particular street. It was a simple task to scroll through them. I recognized a few names, and then I was pretty certain I found the correct house. It belonged to Louella Everett. That couldn't be a coincidence. Russ Everett's mom, maybe?

I was pleased with myself until I saw a message written in dust on a small table in my office, *Don't you ever clean?*

I could feel my face flooding red with embarrassment. I was willing to bet it was the work of Natasha.

I trudged back upstairs to bed, with a sleepy Daisy and grumpy Mochie behind me. At last, I fell asleep.

On Friday morning, after Daisy's walk, I checked my fridge for strawberries. I found a pound of them, which was all I needed for my strawberry poke cake. The cake itself was fairly simple and quick to put together. Butter, eggs, baking powder, sugar, milk, flour, salt, and a touch of mace for flavor. I poured the batter into a disposable cake pan. When I slid it into the oven, I chose two of the prettiest berries and set them aside. I cooked the rest of the berries and set them aside as I cleaned up the kitchen.

I was thinking of Russ's mother, hoping it was her house I was heading to a little later, when the cake was ready. I pulled it out of the oven and poked holes in it with a bamboo skewer. After saving a little bit of the liquid to flavor the frosting, I slowly poured the remaining liquid from the cooked strawberries over the holes, giving it time to soak in. I spread the remaining cooked strawberries across the top and refrigerated it to cool before I frosted it.

Meanwhile, I sat down at the banquette with a pen and paper to make a list of the people who might have a motive to kill Gerrie, Russ, or Eddie. Eddie had the shortest list. Wong had every reason in the world to be upset with him, but she wouldn't have killed him. I wrote her name under his, but I crossed it off. The other person was unknown. The driver of the car may or may not have been the person who killed him. But someone was out to get him, and Eddie had known it.

Next was Russ. If he was threatening to spill the secrets of women in Old Town to blackmail them, the list could be endless. The only one I knew of for sure was Jenna. She had been very upset. Darting out of Gerrie's house to avoid Wolf had only brought her to everyone's attention. I tended to believe her story, though it could have been a clever ruse to throw us off her trail. I wrote her name under Russ's.

Gerrie was surprisingly easy. Todd, Jim, or Colleen may have wanted her money. Henrietta thought her husband was having an affair with Gerrie.

I studied my list. No name showed up more than once. Frustrated, I sat back and thought about how little we knew. Then I tried a new list. Did I know where everyone was at the time of the murders?

I was fairly certain Jim had been at work when Russ was killed. That would be easy to verify in any event. I wrote his name, but put an asterisk next to it. Todd could have been anywhere. The same went for Colleen.

For the first time, it dawned on me that Colleen and Todd could have been in cahoots. What if all that annoyance with each other was nothing more than a carefully crafted drama? I hoped that wasn't the case. Poor Penelope!

Chapter 32

Dear Sophie,
I love throw pillows, but I have a hard time select-
ing ones that go together. Do you have any rules of
thumb to make it easier?
                    Cushy in Pillow, Pennsylvania

Dear Cushy,
You can use pillows in the same color family with
different designs. For instance, they all can have
the same background color. Or look for pillows
that share a color scheme. Maybe one is a floral
and another is a geometric print, but the design
carries the same color.

                                    Sophie

I returned to my list. Henrietta claimed she was a late riser. That wouldn't stop her from sneaking across the street to kill her neighbor. Was that the reason her husband was home the day Russ died? Could the two of them have planned to kill Gerrie, but had to eliminate Russ when he caught them?

I wrote their names down and immediately crossed them out. Henrietta didn't cook. Not even her morning coffee. She would have bought coffee for Gerrie. The person who tried to kill Gerrie had made a pot of coffee. I assumed the same for the senator, since his driver brought coffee for him to drink on the way to work.

It felt good to eliminate someone.

I rose and checked the cake in the refrigerator. It was cooling nicely. I beat together butter, cream cheese, and the strawberry liquid I had saved for the frosting. I added powdered sugar and let it beat to get a creamy consistency, then frosted the cake. I sliced partway through the two pretty strawberries and fanned them out next to each other on the cake as a decoration.

I refrigerated the cake and changed into a summery pink dress and white sandals. I retrieved the cake from the fridge, snapped on the lid, and left Daisy and Mochie snoozing in the kitchen.

I walked fast in the heat. I didn't want the icing to melt! Hoping someone was home, I tapped the door knocker, in the shape of a golf club, on the door of a two-story house.

The woman who opened the door had to be Russ's mother. She looked just like him.

"Hi. I'm Sophie Winston, one of your neighbors," I fudged. I *was* sort of a neighbor, just a few blocks away. "I just wanted to drop this cake by and tell you how sorry I am for your loss."

"Oh! This is very kind of you." She took the cake. "Please come in."

"You might want to pop that in the fridge. It's very hot outside."

"Of course. It's lovely. Could I offer you an iced coffee?"

"No, thank you." While she disappeared into the kitchen, I gazed around the living room. She had received loads of cards and flowers. And yet, I knew exactly which one probably came from Gerrie. It was the largest and fanciest. I scurried over to it and tried to peer at the card.

Gerrie had handwritten the message. *It is with broken hearts that we share our condolences. Russ was a sweet boy who brought us smiles and love. He will remain in our hearts forever.*

Interestingly, she had not signed it.

"They're beautiful, aren't they?" asked Russ's mom.

"Stunning."

"I think they're from the golf club. No one signed the card."

"An oversight, I'm sure," I lied. "How are you doing?"

"I am shattered. He was my only son. I don't know how to manage without him. He was an adult and didn't live at home, of course, but the world seems so empty without him."

"I'm so sorry. It must be very hard for you."

"My daughter says he tangled with the wrong person again."

"'Wrong person'?" I asked. "'Again'?"

She nodded. "Someone attacked him with a knife a few years ago. He had a long scar on his chest. He was very lucky that time. It was a slash that didn't go deep."

"Really? I don't recall hearing about that. Did the perpetrator go to prison?"

"No. They never could identify who did it."

"Do they think it was the same person this time?"

"They don't know." Her tone was impatient. "It seems likely to me!"

"I don't want to upset you, but do you know if Russ had angered anyone else?" I asked.

"I told that nice policeman that we always thought the previous attack was a fight over a woman."

"Which woman?"

"I never found out. I'll say one thing for Russ, he knew

how to keep a secret. We always thought it must have been a married woman. Russ would have been very careful to keep something like that quiet."

"That makes sense."

"Thank you for the cake. My church group is coming over tonight and I thought I would have to go out to buy something to serve them. Your cake will be perfect."

That was clearly my cue to depart. She opened the door and I stepped outside.

"You are very welcome," I said, and walked away.

I heard the door close behind me and wanted to cry for her. Russ might have been a no-good scoundrel, but he was his mother's beloved son.

My visit hadn't been for naught, though. Clearly, I had been right about Gerrie. She wasn't having an affair after all. She just didn't have the courage to face Russ's mother. Or maybe she had the courage, but thought it would be a terrible affront for her to send anything. But she did anyway. Anonymously, at the break of dawn.

I wondered if Wolf or Wong would tell me anything about the previous attack on Russ. Wong's place wasn't too far away. I probably ought to check on her anyway.

I walked over to Big Daddy's Bakery on King Street. Penelope was inside at one of the tables, chattering excitedly with Nicci over a box of doughnuts. They wouldn't have caught my eye at all, except for the fact that they wore dresses made of the same fabric printed with palm fronds in shades of green.

Nicci didn't have to bend over to show cleavage. The neckline of her dress swung very low. The dress was tight and required high slits along the sides so she could walk. As my mother would say, "It was both too low and too high."

Fortunately, Penelope's dress had an appropriate neckline and very cute flutter sleeves. The skirt portion wasn't tight like Nicci's. It flowed loosely with an asymmetrical hem. Both of them wore glittering green nail polish and matching green enamel bracelets.

Colleen would go ballistic if she knew. I could only imagine the fuss she would make if she saw the two of them dressed alike. Someone—Todd, I would assume— had spent quite a bit of money on those dresses.

I didn't know Penelope well and had only met Nicci once in passing. I decided against asking about Gerri's condition because I didn't know how much Penelope had been told about her beloved grandmother Cookie.

I bought half-a-dozen cupcakes and two large vanilla iced lattes.

"That looks good," said a man's voice behind me.

I turned around to find Wolf. "Good morning. I was just going to drop by Wong's house to see how she's doing."

"Mind if I tag along? I'll bring my own coffee. And I'll carry the cupcakes."

"How could I pass up an offer like that?"

The two of us left the bakery and headed to Wong's house.

"Have you heard anything about Gerrie's condition this morning?" I asked.

"It doesn't look good."

I stopped in my tracks. "But it was just sleeping pills."

"They can cause serious problems. Hopefully, she'll come out of the coma."

"She's in a *coma*!" I screeched.

"And hypothermia. Her body temperature is too low."

We began to walk again.

"How do you know this?" I asked.

"Her daughter-in-law, Colleen, released that information to the media this morning."

"This is terrible! Poor Gerrie. Do you still think she killed Eddie?"

"Not sure."

"Aargh. You're so aggravating. When Nina and I entered the house through the unlocked kitchen door yesterday, the coffeepot was still on. There was hardly anything in it. Either she or the killer made coffee."

He nodded. "I smelled it in the kitchen. But that doesn't prove anything."

"It means the killer was comfortable enough to make coffee in her house."

"How do you know Gerrie didn't make the coffee?"

"Good point. But it still means she was comfortable with the person who killed her."

We had arrived at Wong's house. Her drapes were closed.

I banged her door knocker, in the shape of an amusing fat cat that made me smile.

We could hear shuffling on the other side of the door. It opened and Wong looked out at us wearily. She didn't smile, but then her gaze landed on the cupcakes.

She turned and shuffled away in fuzzy slippers. She wore shorts and a T-shirt that was too large for her.

A rush of footsteps on the stairs drew my attention. Two cats, a large tabby and a smaller orange striped one, came to investigate.

"Dorito and Piglet have come to see who is here. Don't mind them. Eddie is allergic to cats. I figured that was a great way to keep him out of my house."

We followed her into the living room. It was small, but beautifully furnished. White marble surrounded the corner fireplace. Two sets of French doors looked out on a brick patio with a high privacy fence. An oatmeal sofa and two cushy chairs, in an abstract pattern of oatmeal and shades of blue, clustered around an oversize blue ottoman that doubled as a coffee table. A large tray sat on it. Wolf unloaded the cupcakes and the coffee.

I opened my arms and gave Wong a big hug.

She selected a chocolate cupcake and bit into it.

I handed her an iced vanilla latte.

After a swig, she said, "I don't understand why I'm sad. There were so many times I'd have liked to kill him myself."

"It's the end of an era for you, Wong." Wolf sat on one of the chairs. "You lost someone you cared about once. That's hard. Once you love someone, it's rough to lose that person."

His gaze swung toward me as he spoke.

I tried to imagine that remark wasn't directed at me. "I saw Russ's mother this morning. Do either of you know anything about Russ being slashed by a knife a few years ago?"

"Are you serious?" asked Wolf. "Nothing like that came up on his background check."

"His mom said he had a long scar on his chest."

Wong finished her cupcake. "I don't recall anything of the sort."

"In fact, Eddie mentioned a fight at a bar called Ruby's?" I said, watching their expressions.

"I remember that place," said Wong. "It could get rowdy and rough. But mostly I responded to drunk and disorderly there. I don't recall Russ being injured."

Chapter 33

Dear Sophie,
I am put to shame when I receive a beautiful invi-
tation in the mail. Between my job and taking care
of the house and the kids, pretty invitations are the
last thing on my mind. I'm afraid I've ceded to
email. Is that terrible of me?
    Exhausted Mom in Paper Mill Village, Vermont

Dear Exhausted Mom,
You're not terrible, you're saving trees and helping
the environment. While there are some events that
really do require paper invitations, like weddings,
it is acceptable to send email invitations. You can
find a wide variety of beautiful email invitations
online that are every bit as fun and elegant as
printed invitations.

                                                    Sophie

Looking straight at Wong, Wolf said, "We need to double-check police records, and if there's nothing there, then hospital records."

Wong sat up straight, looking better already. "You know that Eddie lied. It wasn't just a cover-up for him. He lied even when it didn't matter. He liked embellishing and saying things he thought might get a reaction from people. It drove me nuts because I never knew what was true. But I'd be willing to follow up on this."

"Sounds good to me. How soon can you get on it?" asked Wolf.

"As soon as I take a shower and get dressed."

Wolf appeared very pleased.

I was pretty impressed that he'd managed to get her out of her funk by simply luring her with research. But it did the trick.

Wolf and I left quickly. When we were out of sight of Wong's house, I turned to him and we high-fived.

"Keep me posted about Gerrie?" I asked.

Wolf smiled at me. "Maybe."

Mars had once pointed out to me that Wolf only gave me information that he wanted me to have. Alas, I knew that was true.

I went home and took care of a few things, like sending Henrietta a thank-you note for the lovely dinner party.

I didn't know when Gerrie would be back on her feet and didn't want to consider the possibility that it might not happen. But school days were coming fast, and we had to get A Healthy Meal in gear. Reluctantly I selected a date and used Jacquie Lawson's gorgeous e-invitations to invite the board to a tea at my house.

But all the while, Gerrie was on my mind. I couldn't do a thing to help her get well, but I could figure out who was behind the deaths at her house and the attempt to murder her. I grabbed my purse and hurried out to the garage.

Remembering Eddie's strange warning about finding things in my garage, I slowed down as I approached it. Eddie was dead, I reasoned. He couldn't hurt anyone now.

But he could have left something in my garage before he died. I unlocked the door with trepidation.

It was cool and dark, and I thought of Wong and the power of suggestion. She had lived with Eddie tormenting her like this. Causing her to worry because she didn't know what he might do. I couldn't imagine that. Here I was, stopping, gazing around, but I didn't know what I was looking for. A bomb? A snake? Once more, I reminded myself that he was dead and pushed the button that opened the garage door behind my car.

The additional daylight was a welcome relief. My car looked just as it had the day before when I left it. I looked around, even up at the ceiling, but nothing seemed out of place.

Everything was fine. I opened the car door, turned on the engine, and sighed with relief. If Wong cried about him anymore, I would tell her about this and remind her of the fear he had brought to her life.

But I made a mental note to buy a more secure lock for the door leading to the garage. There was more than one Eddie in this world.

I drove to the outskirts of Old Town and spied an old building that still bore the sign RUBY'S. I parked my car and peered through the plate glass windows. I could see a bar. There were still chairs and tables inside.

"Looking to rent? She's for sale and for rent. Make a great little restaurant. Let me guess, Italian food?"

The man who spoke was medium height, with a white beard and deep crow's feet. He carried a grocery bag.

"Do you own the place?"

"That, I do. You lookin' to buy?" He unlocked the door and placed his bag of groceries just inside.

"No. Sorry!" I held out my hand. "Sophie Winston."

"Yeah, I figured. You don't look the type. I can't unload

this place. Sam Collins. We don't get out much these days. It's a pleasure to talk with you, even if you're not buyin'."

"Did you run it? Are you Ruby?"

"Ruby is my wife. She loved it. Never would have bought the place if it wasn't for her. She always wanted to own a bar. I think she saw herself as the guy Sam on *Cheers*. Always having a good time with his friends."

"What happened?"

"Ruby's got the arthritis pretty bad. She doesn't like to stand much anymore, and walking is getting harder. I keep telling her she ought to get her knees replaced, but she's afraid it will be worse if she does that. I tried to sell the bar, but I never got any takers. We live in the apartment upstairs. It's not a bad location, but it's getting hard for Ruby to get up and down the stairs, so it's time to move on. Ruby's is just a ghost of her old self now. People having a good time here is just a memory now."

"Do you recall a fight involving Russ Everett?"

He smiled. "I remember Russ. I was awfully sorry to hear that he died."

"He was injured that night. Must have been bleeding a lot."

"I remember it like it was yesterday. They were celebrating. It was some kind of sports team, softball, maybe? I remember that Jim Stansfield, the shorter brother, bought a round of beer and pizza for all of 'em. A while later, Jim carried Russ into the bar, shouting, 'Call 911! Call 911!' Then he put Russ into his truck and drove away."

"He put him in his truck?"

"Must have been a bloody mess. I had to clean up the drips on the floor before anybody slipped on them."

"Did Jim attack Russ?"

"I always assumed he didn't, or he wouldn't have carried him out to the bar area. Jim called me from somewhere and gave me his credit card number. I always thought highly of him for doing that. Most people would have left it up to everyone else to pay and it would have been a big scene. I saw Russ again a few times before we closed, and he seemed all right."

"Did Russ and Jim hang out together at Ruby's often?"

"Jim wasn't a regular. But some of his truck drivers liked to stop in after work. Russ would come with them sometimes."

"Do you know who injured Russ the day Jim carried him out?"

"Naw. People do strange things, you know? They fight over women, sports teams, and money. I guess it's possible that Jim and Russ got into it, and Jim got the better of him, but then regretted it."

"Did the police show up?"

He looked up and to the right. "I'm not sure. We had a nice street cop who used to stop by. My wife always fed him on the house. She said it was good public relations and that anyone up to no good would know not to come here to do their dirty tricks."

"She sounds like a smart lady."

"Oh, she is! I just wish she could figure out how to unload this place."

I felt like he had unlocked a door for me. "Thanks for taking the time to talk with me."

"My pleasure, ma'am."

I stepped into my car and drove over to Moss Restaurant Supply. Russ and Jim had a tangled relationship. Did Jim also have dealings with Eddie Wong?

Luckily, there was a parking space in front of the store. From my car, I could see a sign that hadn't been there before. I stepped out and walked up to the door. A sign saying CLOSED hung on it. A second sign, which looked to be computer printed, was placed beneath it.

We'll be back as soon as we can!
Call our emergency number if you need help
immediately.

Betty had told us that Jim worked too much. He was available around the clock. Was this the first time they had closed except for holidays? I cupped my hands around my eyes and peered inside. Nothing stirred. I didn't even see Hayley.

This was highly unusual. I fervently hoped they had closed because Gerrie was in the hospital, and not because she had died. Jim probably wanted to stay with her. They must have closed for Jim Senior's funeral. And for Edwin's. But where were Emily and Hayley?

I drove home and parked in front of my house. After checking on Daisy and Mochie, and grabbing a cold drink, I jammed a large, framed photograph in my tote, planning to head for the hospital, but decided to swing by Jim's house on the way. I could have called, but the kinds of questions I wanted to ask him usually produced more authentic and detailed responses face-to-face.

I turned south on Lee Street. Alex had said the garden was visible from the street. But I didn't need that as a guide. Just ahead of me, Emily was unloading a car. I pulled up behind it.

"Emily!" I waved at her.

She carried a long dress bag and forced a tight smile at the sight of me.

I hopped out of the car and hurried toward her. "Is Gerrie all right? The store is closed."

"I'm sure you know about Gerrie being in the hospital."

I nodded. "She's not worse, I hope?" I eyed the dress bag.

"I don't think so. At least Jim hasn't said so."

"May I peek?" I didn't wait for her response. Ever so gently, I reached out and unzipped the top a few inches. It contained a gorgeous white wedding dress. I couldn't see all of it, but the lace and pearls gave it away.

"What do you think?" she asked. "I wanted so much to show my mom."

"It's beautiful."

"We were going to elope this weekend. I can't do it anymore, Sophie. Too many people here know me. I'm tired of hiding. I'm worn out from trying to avoid being seen by people I know." She rattled on, as if trying to convince herself. "I just can't make up more lies about being in town because I'm visiting. And now, Jim is distraught about his mother, and I can't even be at the hospital with him! One of these days my parents will find out." Her eyes met mine. "I'd rather be the one to tell them."

"I can understand that."

"It's just easier this way. But I had to have the dress. I really wanted the dress." Tears welled in her eyes.

"Why don't you just tell your parents?"

"We can't. We just can't." Tears breached her lower eyelids.

"Because they like Todd better than Jim?"

"Because my father is having an affair with Jim's mother! I can't put any of them through that, especially not *my* mother. Can you even imagine? It would be like a bad movie. His mother and my father making eyes at each other, with my mom crying in the background? What a lovely memory *that* would be."

"Are you certain about the affair?"

"My mother is. She should know."

"I think she might be wrong. There was someone else your father loved."

"Oh dear." Emily's hand cupped her cheek. "Please don't make it any worse. Please, Sophie!"

I pulled the framed photograph from my tote bag. Senator Albert Keswick and Edwin Stansfield sat in chairs on the Stansfields' patio. Their heads were tilted back, and their mouths were wide open in laughter, as if someone had told a very funny joke. "I was taking this over to the hospital. I thought it might cheer up your mom when she wakes."

Emily studied it and wiped the tears from her cheeks.

"It was in Edwin's office. Your father told me they had a lot in common. Starting with their names. Your dad wasn't an Al, and Edwin wasn't an Ed. Don't you see? They were best friends. Both of them had important positions. I imagine there weren't many people they could confide in or with whom they could discuss their problems. Your dad has been visiting Gerrie because he feels an obligation to watch over her for his old friend Edwin. Gerrie isn't the only one who misses Edwin."

"Are you certain about this?"

"Gerrie lost the love of her life, Emily. She's not running around with other men. She's brokenhearted."

It was as though Emily couldn't take her eyes off the picture.

"Don't do this to your mother. Let her throw you the wedding you've dreamed of. A wedding with Jim's beloved niece, Penelope, walking down the aisle holding Elmo's leash. He can wear a bowtie and carry the wedding rings."

Emily burst into tears. She wrapped her arms around me and sobbed. When she drew away, I was glad to see she was smiling. "Thank you," she said, handing me the photograph.

Chapter 34

Dear Natasha,
My wife read somewhere that she's supposed to bring summer inside the house with plants and fussy baskets. It looks like a greenhouse in here! I stepped barefoot on broken beach shells that the cat knocked off the mantel. Would you please tell my wife to get rid of all that clutter?
 Living in a Jungle in Summerville, South Carolina

Dear Living in a Jungle,
Tell your wife I said she doesn't have to redecorate for every season. The key here is to remove one item at a time so she won't notice. A seashell or two. Then a plant that you hate. Do it slowly so she won't notice. You might also secretly overwater a plant or two. Before long, you will have your house back.

 Natasha

It didn't take me long to drive to the hospital. I headed straight to Gerrie's room. On entering, I stopped for a moment to be certain I had the correct room. Flowers filled every raised surface. Roses were a big favorite, as were bright sunflowers and purple gladiola.

Jim sat in a chair by his mother's bed. "We've asked the nurses to spread them out. Give them to patients who haven't received any flowers."

"It's like a floral competition in here."

"I hope you didn't bring any."

I pulled the photo out of my purse. "I brought this. It was in your dad's office. I thought your mom might like it."

Jim looked at it and smiled. "I've never seen this before. This is how I remember my dad. So many people have told me how stern and serious he was. But this is the man I knew. Maybe Mom will let me make a copy. Thanks, Sophie."

"How's she doing?"

"They say she's better than yesterday. But I can't tell. She's still in a coma, so she looks the same to me. They told me to talk to her, so I've been sitting here telling her all my troubles. I'm guessing that isn't what the nurses meant, but . . ."

"I talked to Emily, if that's one of your woes."

He frowned at me. "What did she say?"

"That she's tired of hiding and that you were going to elope."

Jim took a deep breath. "I love Emily. I wish the situation weren't so complicated. And yet"—he gazed at his mother—"our marriage isn't even the biggest problem. Someone trying to kill my mother trumps everything at the moment."

"Even running the store?"

He looked up at me. "Hayley isn't much help. And Emily wants to be here with me. She's afraid people will recognize her and she'll have to explain to her parents."

"You could call Betty," I said softly.

"*She's* never coming back. I bungled that pretty bad. If my grandfather knew . . ." He gazed up at the ceiling, as if looking toward heaven.

"I think she might return. Especially if she feels needed. I'll sit with your mom if you want to give her a call."

"I guess I've got nothing to lose. But she doesn't know how to work the computer system we have now."

"She can do it the old way for a couple of days. She knows how to arrange deliveries and get repair people out. Right?"

"Better than anyone." Jim punched a number on his phone and strode out the door.

I walked closer to Gerrie and set up the photograph of Edwin and Albert where she might see it when she opened her eyes. Then I leaned over and said, "Hi, Gerrie. It's Sophie here. I hope you can hear me. I think you have a wedding in your future. Maybe very soon. You will adore your new daughter-in-law. She already has the dress! Oh, and she'll be such a beautiful bride. In fact, I think Penelope might be a bridesmaid. We need you to come around so you can help pick out Penelope's dress. You know all the best places to shop for her. Maybe she can even wear a piece of her great-grandmother's jewelry that day! So many things to consider. But they can't even get started without you!"

Jim walked back in, beaming. "You were right. Betty was flattered to be asked. And she was very worried about Mom. I told her she was the only person in the entire world whom I could trust with the store. I offered to put her back on permanently. She said she'd consider it part-time. That would be great. Oh man! I wish Mom could hear this. She was stinking mad at me when she found out Betty left."

"Betty claimed she was fired."

"I heard. But that's not what happened! Moss Restaurant Supply went through changes as the computer era evolved. We had several locations around the Capital Beltway and the paperwork and duplication of documents were getting to be crazy. I invested in a computer system to bring all our locations together, at least where paperwork was concerned. Betty hated it. She's a great lady, but definitely old school. The earliest computer programs were kind of clunky. So we kept updating it, which frustrated her no end, always having to learn a new system.

"I tried to explain that her duties would change because everything was computerized. But she interpreted that as meaning that she was outdated, and we didn't need her anymore. When I called, I told her I was in need of a Brigg's girl. She takes such pride in being a professional secretary. Thanks for giving me the courage to call her. I'm meeting her at the store in two hours to give her the key and open up. Then I'll come back to sit with Mom. If only you could figure out who tried to kill her."

"Do the police have any leads?"

"They thought she was the one who killed Russ and Eddie!" He held out his palms helplessly. "How clueless could they be? You don't think that, do you?"

"No." But I was very worried about Gerrie, because when she came out of her coma, she would be able to tell us who made her coffee that morning. I wasn't sure it would be wise to tell Jim that, though. As it was, he had enough on his mind. And I didn't know him well enough to know how he might react. The killer had to be someone in his circle of friends and acquaintances. I didn't want him blabbing to them—and then the perpetrator would make sure Gerrie didn't live to speak.

Now, how to broach the incident at Ruby's with him? "A couple of people have told me about the incident at Ruby's."

I watched him carefully. His fair face flushed.

"The owner's husband said a softball team had won?"

"I don't see how it could be related to anything that has happened in the last week." He winced and nervously adjusted his watch.

"Russ was injured then, and now he's dead."

Jim left the room and I thought I'd blown my chance. But he returned with a second chair and closed the door behind him.

He sat down on the other side of his mother. "It's a long story. Are you sure you want to hear this?"

"Sure. They said to talk to your mom."

"A couple of years ago, Moss Restaurant Supply was hacked. The hackers sent me an email saying they had the credit card numbers of our customers and they would release them on the dark web if we didn't pay them a ransom.

"I didn't mention it to our employees. My grandfather had already passed on, so it was just me. I went to the two people that I knew I could trust—my old girlfriend, Emily Keswick, and my dad. Emily told us that the hackers probably did not have the credit card numbers. If they did, they would have sold them on the web, and they wouldn't have bothered with a ransom note. All three of us thought it better not to go public because it would damage our reputation. We very quietly mailed notifications to all our customers, letting them know we might have had a breach. We recommended they change credit cards and we offered to pay for credit monitoring. You'd be surprised how few people took us up on that!"

"A lot of companies were being hacked. I remember getting one of those letters from a national chain store," I said.

"I never paid the ransom. But the threats continued. Moss sponsored a local adult softball team. Some of our employees played on it, and after a big win, they went out for drinks and coaxed me to come along to Ruby's. I bought a couple of rounds of beer and pizza for them. At one point, I got up and went to the restroom. Before I entered, I could hear a loud argument between some guys, who sounded totally soused. They were accusing someone of taking their money. They were all yelling. So I flung open the door and barged in. It was one of those times when everything happened incredibly fast. It was utter chaos. They busted past me. There was a bloody knife lying on the floor. I snatched it up and stuck it in my pocket. Russ had a diagonal slash down his shirt and was bleeding like crazy. I picked him up—luckily, he wasn't very big—and I ran through the bar, yelling 'Call 911!' I thought Russ was going to die. I couldn't wait for an ambulance, so I put him in my truck and started driving toward the hospital. I called 911 while I was driving and told them where I was. The ambulance and I met, they transferred Russ over, and they took care of him from there."

"Wow. That took a lot of guts. They could have turned on you."

"It wasn't guts. It was instinct. I didn't even think about it. I saw Russ on the floor, and I knew he needed help.

"I went to my parents' house and told my dad what had happened. He put the knife in his safe. I took a shower and spent the night. When I went home in the morning, my house had been ransacked."

"They were looking for the knife," I said. "You might have been dead if they had found you."

Jim swallowed hard and nodded. "Russ refused to testify against them or identify them. I couldn't believe it. He was protecting them! But he had a point. Technically, it was aggravated assault. But it was likely to be reduced to simple assault and they would have been out of prison in one year or less and steaming mad.

"Dad and I went over to the hospital to check on Russ. Dad closed the door and very calmly told him that he was in possession of the knife, and he should let his attackers know that the knife would not surface. However, if there were any more threats, or attacks on Russ or on us, then the knife would be turned over to the police.

"Dad and I decided not to tell Todd or Mom. Todd would have blabbed it all over town, and Mom would have worried herself to death."

"When did this happen?"

"August, two years ago."

"You must know who they were. You must have seen their faces."

"I wish I had. But the two guys burst past me, nearly knocking me down in their haste. I saw Russ and the knife on the floor.

"Was that before or after you fired Russ?"

"That was *when* I fired Russ. I hated to do it, but Emily was able to track one of the blackmail letters back to Russ."

"Can you do that?" I asked.

"Every computer has an Internet protocol address. She knew how to find out who it belonged to. I think a savvier con artist would have known how to work around that. Obviously, I couldn't keep him in my employ. My mom was furious. First I fired my own brother, and then sweet Russ." Jim let out a sad laugh. "Sometimes you just can't win. I came out looking like the bad guy both times. In spite of his attempted fraud, I sent Russ a nice severance check, since he would be out of work for a while. And then I called Emily and asked her to move down here. She said no. I called her every day until she finally agreed."

I couldn't help smiling at him. "At least she knows how much you love her."

"One good thing came out of this mess."

I tread carefully with my next question. "Are you certain Todd wasn't involved with any of this?"

"I don't know. It, uh . . ." He rubbed his forehead. "I wish my dad were alive." He took a deep breath. "I don't know where Todd was that morning. I left the house to go home, shower, and open the store. Todd has made some terrible life decisions, but I don't think he would murder anyone." Jim stopped talking. "No," he repeated, sounding as if he needed to convince himself.

"Todd is unemployed right now?"

"That's my understanding, but we don't talk much. Actually, the first time we really talked in years was the night before Russ was murdered."

"Did you know that he paid Colleen the back child support he owed?" I asked.

Jim's gaze slid to his mother. "Mom probably helped him out. It wouldn't be the first time. I'm not an expert in family dynamics, but my friends tell me there's always one in every family who needs extra help. In our case, it happens to be Todd."

"Could Todd have been involved in blackmailing Moss Restaurant Supply with Russ?"

"I never considered that." His brow furrowed. "I hope not!"

I leaned toward him. "I think the killer was already in the house with your mom that morning."

"Why would you think that?"

"Gerrie was getting things ready for her luncheon. She

left the house for at least half an hour to buy half-and-half. Gerrie thought she had bought enough. I saw an empty carton in her kitchen trash can. I can't prove it, but I think the killer emptied it so Gerrie would leave the house."

"That makes sense." Jim nodded vigorously. "I think Russ came to get the knife. He probably thought he needed it to protect himself, now that my dad was gone. But I can't prove that, either."

"Then who was in the house and killed Russ?"

Chapter 35

Dear Sophie,
My teacups are so beautiful, but I almost hate to use them because they get brown tea stains on them. How do I get those out? The cups are too delicate for anything harsh.
         Loves Tea Parties in Tea, South Dakota

Dear Loves Tea Parties,
Try a gentle denture-cleaning tablet. Fill the cup with water, add the tablet, and let it soak until the stain is gone.

                                        Sophie

"That's why you're asking questions about Todd," Jim said. "I don't think it was him. We have had terrible arguments. He has stabbed me in the back and nearly wrecked Moss. But there's no way he would have killed anyone. He's totally laid-back. He doesn't care about anything. Nothing gets under his skin. No way. Someone else must have slipped into the house."

"I'm beginning to think that must be the case." I reached in my purse for a card with my number on it and handed it to Jim. "Let me know if I can do anything to help out."

"Thanks, Sophie."

I left him sitting there, staring at his comatose mother.

I parked on the street again when I came home because Nina and I would be leaving soon to tail Irv.

As I was feeding Mochie and Daisy, Nina arrived at my door with snacks. I filled her in on everything, except the part about Emily Keswick. Emily needed to be the one to spring her news on her parents. I had promised not to mention her secret. And for our purposes, it didn't matter because I had no reason to think she was involved with the murders.

I left a light on, and as we had the previous night, we parked on the street that Irv was likely to turn onto. As before, Irv appeared to make legitimate deliveries.

When he stopped to deliver, Nina and I noshed on turkey, Havarti cheese, and spinach mini sandwiches, each topped with a briny black olive.

"Do you think we're wasting our time?" asked Nina.

"No. We know for certain that he delivered the orders. Sooner or later, he has to collect his money."

It was dark when Irv pulled into the location behind Senator Keswick's house where we had found him unconscious.

"If I were him, I sure wouldn't be parking back here," Nina muttered.

The light from the van illuminated Irv when he stepped out. But this time, he didn't open the rear of the van.

"This is it," I hissed. "He doesn't have a bag to deliver."

The two of us followed Irv as quietly as we could. He walked along the path to the street and crossed it.

We were totally exposed by streetlights. If he looked back, he couldn't miss us.

"What's our story?" asked Nina.

"We're out for a walk?" We crossed the street.

"We should have brought Daisy."

"Who knew we would need her?"

Irv approached Gerrie's house and banged the door knocker.

Todd answered the door.

There was no place for us to hide. Nothing to duck behind.

Todd said something I couldn't make out. He pulled a wad of bills from his pocket, counted them out, and handed them to Irv.

The next thing we knew, Irv was walking straight toward us.

"Hi!" I said cheerily. "How's your head, Irv?"

"Good. It's all healed up. What are you two doing?"

"We were walking home from dinner and thought we'd stop by to see how Gerrie is," said Nina.

"Aww. Bad business, that. She was always real nice to me. Well, I best be going."

We said good night and walked along the street a few steps. We waited at Gerrie's doorstep until he disappeared.

"Whew! That was a close one," said Nina. "Should we confront Todd?"

"Are you nuts? Absolutely not. From here on out, Bernie is the one who needs to decide how to handle this."

"What if Todd was paying him, say, a gambling debt?"

"Then he can tell Bernie that."

We walked back to the car and drove home.

"Want to come in for a drink?" I asked as I turned onto our street.

"Absolutely."

I pulled into the alley and hit the garage door opener. The garage light did not turn on as it should have, but when I pulled into the garage, something flew at the car and slammed into my windshield.

Nina and I screamed. A terrifying evil clown face stared through the windshield at us.

We screamed again.

I pulled myself together, but my heart still beat fast. "It's just a Halloween inflatable." I reached for the car door to open it.

Nina grabbed me. "No! Don't get out! Back up! Back up! I'm calling Mars and Bernie."

I didn't think about it long. Maybe she was right. What if someone was in the garage or in my backyard waiting?

"Now! Come to the alley now!" Nina shrieked into the phone.

I put the car in reverse and slowly backed out of my garage. The headlights of my car illuminated the grisly head swinging from the ceiling.

Someone rapped on my window. Nina and I squealed in surprise.

"Are you all right?" asked Mars as he and Bernie looked in at us. The two of them huffed and puffed.

I turned off the engine, opened the door, and nearly fell into Mars's arms.

"What on earth is that?" Bernie asked.

Nina ran around the car and joined us. Mars kindly wrapped an arm around her.

"You're shaking, Nina," said Mars.

I took a deep breath and untangled myself from his embrace. "It's nothing. Just a stupid Halloween inflatable."

Nina clung to Mars as he walked into the garage.

Bernie flicked the light switch but no light came on. "Sophie, would you turn on your headlights, please?"

When I flicked them on, Mars said, "Whoa!" and took a step backward. "What is this about?"

"I'm not sure." I walked into the garage. "Eddie said I

needed a better lock on the garage door. I thought it was a threat."

"But he's dead!" Nina said.

"When were you in here last?"

"Earlier today when I left."

"Maybe we should check out your house," said Mars.

"Daisy! Mochie! I hope they're okay! Mars, turn off the headlights!" I ran to the house and unlocked the French door to the living room.

Happily, Daisy and Mochie heard me and ran to the door before I could open it.

"Hey, guys! I'm so glad you're okay. Daisy, did you hear someone outside in the garage?" I picked up Mochie and held him as I patted Daisy's head. She leaned against my legs.

"Sophie," said Bernie, "I think you should call the police. I know it looks like a goofy prank, but in light of everything that has happened, you should report it."

I went directly to the phone, finally set Mochie down, and dialed Wolf's number. He agreed to come over.

Nina emerged from the dining room with liqueurs in hand. "That stupid thing scared the daylights out of me." She poured them into a blender and added ice cream.

"I suspect it was intended to do exactly that," said Mars. "Maybe you should sit down."

I put the kettle on for tea to calm my nerves but Nina was offering Bernie and Mars Blue Ghosts in martini glasses. The amazing concoction could have been a dessert.

While we waited for Wolf, I told Bernie and Mars about Irv and Todd, as well as the incident at Ruby's. "So, then, if you pare everything down, it's possible that Russ went to get the knife."

"He thought it protected him," said Mars. "But I think what probably kept those heathens away from him and Jim was Edwin. He wasn't a guy to mess with."

A knock on the door made us all jump, even though we were expecting Wolf. It turned out to be Wong.

"You're just in time for tea," I said.

"Or something stronger if you're off duty." Nina raised her glass.

"I'm not officially on duty." She handed me a carton. "I brought homemade strawberry ice cream. I churned it myself."

"Thank heaven it's not cookies," grumbled Mars.

"Since when do you have a thing against cookies?" Nina asked.

"Since Natasha has been bringing him her jalapeño nightmares every day," Bernie teased with a chuckle.

"Every day?" Nina snickered.

"I don't know how to tell her I've had enough without insulting her. Do you want some?"

Nina and I laughed at him.

Wolf knocked on the door and opened it himself. "That thing in your garage definitely falls into the weird category. I'll make a report of it, but I have to say, if it had happened to anyone else, I would think it was a teen prank. Whoever it was unscrewed your lightbulbs. I went ahead and put them back in for you. I'm taking the clown for fingerprints, but I doubt we'll get any, unless it was kids."

While I retrieved spoons and bowls, Wong went outside with Mars to see for herself. They came back soon.

"I put the car in the garage and closed the doors," said Mars, handing me my car fob.

"Yum! This is the best ice cream ever, Wong! You should open your own ice-cream shop," said Nina.

"Thanks, Nina. I'll keep that in mind when I've had enough of police life."

We were quiet for a moment while we ate the ice cream.

"I want to thank you all for being so nice to me about

Eddie," said Wong. "I guess I loved him once and that made it all the more infuriating when he turned out to be a lying, thieving scum ball. I looked up the incident at Ruby's, like you suggested, Wolf. There's a record of the 911 call. There's also a record of the ambulance being dispatched and one at the hospital that confirms Russ was treated in the emergency room and admitted to the hospital."

"No police report?" asked Wolf.

"There's a mention of it, but no follow-up and no details."

"Wong, when did Eddie leave town?" I asked.

"I don't recall the exact date, but it was the end of the summer, about two years ago. Why?"

I looked at Wolf. "I think he was one of the guys who attacked Russ at Ruby's."

"Eddie?" Wong seemed surprised. "Now that I think about it, that fits. He left in a hurry, no looking back. The time frame fits perfectly. I thought someone was after him. I guess someone was. He never should have come back here."

I looked at Wolf. "Do you know who killed him?"

"If I did, I wouldn't be sitting here."

I poured him a mug of decaf coffee and filled a bowl with the superb ice cream, while Mars told him what had happened.

"I'll stay over tonight," said Bernie.

"That's kind of you, but, as Wolf pointed out, it's more like a kid's prank."

"It won't hurt. I'm going to call a meeting at The Laughing Hound tomorrow at one in the bar. Sophie and Nina, since you uncovered the rat, we'd like for you to come."

"You mean you're confronting Todd Stansfield?" I asked.

Bernie nodded. "Wolf, I hope you'll come, too. We've talked to Alex and the whole thing is a little bit sticky, legally speaking. We haven't been cheated or defrauded. But Todd has misrepresented himself to the public."

We were all game. Everyone left, except for Bernie, who helped me with the dishes. He called dibs on the sofa bed in the den. I knew why. It was the only place downstairs to sleep comfortably.

I brought down linens and made sure he had everything he needed.

The night passed uneventfully. Nina came over Saturday morning, still in her bathrobe, to share breakfast waffles with fresh berries.

While the two of them chatted, I stole upstairs to shower.

Bernie had left by the time I returned. I was now dressed in a white shirtdress with a brown belt and brown buttons. We were still at the table when Colleen knocked on the kitchen door.

I invited her in and poured her a mug of coffee.

Colleen joined Nina on the banquette and said, "There is going to be a murder—"

Chapter 36

Dear Natasha,
I ordered some of your cookies online. They were
very tasty and arrived fast enough for the chocolate
to be melty. But they didn't taste anything like your
recipes. There were no jalapeños in them at all.
What gives?

Not Hot Enough in Hothouse, Georgia

Dear Not Hot Enough,
I'm with you. Jalapeños add a zesty spark to my
cookies. I don't know if I'll be selling any more
cookies, but if I do, I'm adding my chocolate chip
cookies with jalapeños and my oatmeal cookies
made with squid ink.

Natasha

I was pretty sure my heart missed a beat. Colleen? She'd been on my list all along, but I never thought she could possibly be the killer. "Last night, I picked up Penelope at Gerrie's house. And she had gotten a tattoo!"

"You mean a fake one, right?"

"I mean one that does not wash off. All I can imagine is that *woman* claimed to be her mother. The nerve of her!"

"How old is Penelope?" asked Nina.

"Twelve!"

"She'll probably be very popular at school for being so cool."

Colleen stared daggers at Nina. "Penelope knows perfectly well that I would not have allowed that. Todd didn't even know about it! But you know Todd, he just laughed it off. What's that *woman* going to do next? Take her to a bar and let her drink? I'm going to see Alex German tomorrow and take Todd to court. I think she sleeps over, and I will not have that in front of Penelope. I will not! I agreed to overnights because I knew she was in Gerrie's house and would be okay. But not anymore! Todd will have to choose between his daughter and that *woman*."

"Where is she now?" asked Nina.

"Staying overnight with a friend, whose mother I will call as a witness if necessary. She was aghast. And why is Todd handing her over to that *woman* anyway? Oh, I'm just beside myself."

And she didn't know the half of it. Her husband was about to face a bunch of angry restaurateurs.

"Any update on Gerrie's condition?" I asked.

"I wish. Jim has someone watching over her at night so he can get some sleep. I'm beginning to lose hope."

"Don't do that. If she were here, none of this would be happening. Todd would dump Penelope on his mom, and she would be well cared for."

Colleen finished her coffee. "I'm so sorry. Normally, I would have gone to Gerrie with my problems. I miss her so much. And the police appear to be stalled in the murder investigation. I just don't understand how someone could walk into her house and murder people. It doesn't make any sense." She checked her watch. "I'm going to try to catch Alex first thing this morning before he gets too busy to see me. Thanks for listening to me."

"Let us know how it goes." I rose and closed the door behind her.

"There really might be another murder. She wasn't kidding," said Nina.

"Never mess with a mama bear," I said.

Nina went home and I went to my office to get some work done.

Just before one, Nina and I strolled over to The Laughing Hound. Bernie ushered us into the bar area.

An old man tried to go with us.

"Sorry, Mr. Jameson," said Bernie. "The bar will be closed for an hour for a private event. Maybe you could come back later?"

"What event?"

"Groom's party."

"Oh." The man frowned. "Then what are they doing here?" He pointed to Nina and me.

Bernie whispered, "Strippers."

The old man looked at us. "Pass." He turned around and left.

Nina and I couldn't stop laughing. But once Todd arrived with Dale, things got very serious. Over a dozen local restaurant owners were present. I knew most of them. Wolf was standing quietly in the rear of the room.

Bernie stood up and said to Todd, "We recently discovered that someone was picking up our food and delivering it to people who thought they had ordered from a ghost kitchen."

Todd leaned back in his chair and listened, not showing any sign of distress.

"It appears that you would be the culprit, Todd."

Todd smiled at the people who had assembled. "All of

you got paid. I don't know why you'd complain. It was more business for all of you."

"But you've been cheating people by charging them more than we charge."

"There is nothing wrong with making a living. If you sold me this chair for twenty dollars and I sold it to someone else for forty dollars, it wouldn't be illegal. That's how business works. Buy low, sell high."

"But you are misrepresenting yourself. People think they're buying food from your ghost kitchens."

Todd said, "And they are. They wouldn't know where the food came from, either way. You make money and I make money. They get the food they paid for. Everybody is happy."

While he was going in circles, I wondered how Todd could have been raised by Edwin, who, by all accounts, was a virtuous man. Todd's suit jacket hung open. He hadn't bothered with a tie.

His friend Dale wore jeans, with a white polo shirt and white knit sneakers that had seen better days. As I gazed at them, I realized that Dale's sneakers weren't old, but they had splotchy stains on them. He must have tried to wash them off, but the knit fabric on top hadn't released whatever had spilled on them.

"Let's go back to this chair again," said Todd. "If I post a photo of it online and ask one hundred dollars for it, then I'm not violating anything, even if it's worth five dollars. This isn't any different."

The restaurateurs were beginning to do some angry murmuring.

"I say we report Todd and his fake ghost kitchens to the police and let them handle the situation," said a red-haired woman. "Deceiving the public is their domain. Besides, we're required to have all kinds of health inspections. How many have you had, Todd?"

"Once again, Marie, I'm not required to have any because I'm not cooking anything."

Bernie stood up. "Thank you for coming. I'm sure we'll see you in court."

Dale grinned and elbowed Todd. The two of them walked out.

When they were gone, Bernie said, "The first thing we do is boycott Irv. No more pickups by Irv."

"Todd will just hire someone else. Like Dale," protested a bald man.

"Then no pickups by Dale, either," said Bernie. "What's going to happen to his websites if he doesn't get food to people? They're going to complain. It's the best way of stopping him from doing this."

"Everyone in?" shouted someone.

Lots of high-fiving took place as they emptied out and went back to work.

"Is it legal to refuse to give someone food they ordered?" Nina asked Bernie.

"Man, this is a tangled mess. I'll have to walk that by Alex."

Nina and I wished Bernie luck and walked home. Nina spun off to her house. I let Daisy out in the yard, even though it was hot. I opened the door to the garage with some trepidation, but it was cool and quiet, like it should be.

Daisy ran inside and sniffed around.

Whoever did this must have done it while my car was out the day before. How did that person get up high enough to attach the clown to something? It dawned on me that it had probably been attached to the garage door opener. Still, to do that, almost anyone would have needed a ladder. He probably helped himself to one of mine. They hung on the garage wall. I examined them and realized one was missing. He'd been sloppy. It leaned against the wall.

I looked at it more closely. There could be fingerprints, I presumed, but other than that, I didn't see anything. No fibers, no hair, nothing caught on a rung.

I was disappointed. I hung the ladder where it was supposed to be. Daisy sniffed under the workbench and then I saw them. Sunglasses! Aviator style. I didn't touch them, but I could tell they weren't cheap. And I suspected I knew to whom they belonged. I had seen him wearing them several times, once outside of Gerrie's house.

I phoned Jim Stansfield.

"Hi, Sophie."

"Hi. How's your mom?"

"About the same."

"Tell her I called, and I need her to help with A Healthy Meal!"

"Will do."

"Jim, you said you hired someone to watch Gerrie's house."

"Yeah. Epler Security. What's up?"

"Are you alone?"

"It's just Mom and me."

"What do you know about a Dale Mancini?"

Jim chuckled. "You are on the ball. Did you see him hanging around my mom's house?"

"Yes. As a matter of fact, I did."

"He works for Epler Security."

That was interesting. I was reeling. Not only did he have a reason to be at Gerrie's house, but he had access to it through his sister, Nicci, and his buddy Todd. I pondered whether to mention the aviator glasses in my garage. Lots of people wore them. They were very popular.

I decided to play coy. "Oh well. That explains everything." A dark thought crossed my mind. "Is he watching your mom at night?"

"No. I hired a nurse to do that. The hospital has security, so I thought a nurse was more important for Mom right now. If anyone is lurking around, the nurse can notify security or call the police."

"That makes sense. Thanks for the information, Jim." I disconnected the call. It would be premature for me to accuse Dale of anything. But . . .

"Daisy, want to go for a ride?"

I slipped her harness over her head and grabbed her leash and my purse, which contained the car fob. We returned to the car and took a trip to the hardware store.

They had a selection of security cameras. I bought a set of four that operated simply on an app and were triggered by motion. Daisy collected a dog cookie and lots of pats from the employees. I also looked at locks. Eddie, for all his faults, had given me sound advice. I purchased a bolt lock for the door.

Back in my garage, I was sorely tempted to install the bolt lock, but I needed to make it easy for the owner of the sunglasses to return for them. I set up a camera that would catch anyone coming through the gate in the backyard. It was small enough that I didn't think anyone would notice it. I placed two in the garage, where they would film the person who came to claim the glasses. I didn't even have to attach them to anything. They sat very nicely by themselves. I added a few gadgets around them to disguise the cameras but made sure the lenses had clear paths. The fourth one I attached to a post in my portico so that it would catch anyone entering or exiting the garage.

Pleased with my efforts, I phoned Wolf and told him what I was doing. Half an hour later, Wong arrived at my door.

"Wolf says you're luring criminals to your house."

Chapter 37

Dear Natasha,
I hate cleaning my refrigerator. On your show,
your refrigerator looks perfect. How do you keep it
that way?
                    Chilling in Hot Springs, Arkansas

Dear Chilling,
There are several easy rules. Never, ever stack food
or containers. There must be at least two inches be-
tween items, so everything is easy to see. Buy only
what you need, never pack your refrigerator full.
And so important, never save leftovers. They are
the biggest clutter culprits.
                                        Natasha

"That's not true! I think the person who hung the clown head in my garage left behind a snazzy pair of aviator sunglasses. I'm guessing he'll be back to collect them."

"They're still in the garage?"

"Right." I pulled up the cameras on my phone and showed her each of the angles.

"That's pretty clever. There won't be a confrontation unless he notices the cameras."

"I thought you were on leave."

"I am. But I've had about enough of Eddie's mom telling me what a wonderful son he was. We picked out his casket yesterday. All I can say is that Humphrey has the patience of an angel. I was ready to run shrieking from the building. I understand what she's going through, and I don't want to be unsympathetic, but I'm having a hard time shaking the bad memories."

I had initially thought Wolf sent Wong to my house to protect me, but now I understood. She needed to vent.

"Do you want to talk about it?"

"Not really. That moment when the car nearly killed us was representative of life with Eddie. Sort of an appropriate ending to that relationship, good and bad all rolled up in one person."

"Nina will probably be over tonight for dinner. Maybe you'd like to join us? You could help me chop things."

"Dinner? I haven't had lunch yet."

"If we chop now, I won't have as much to do later."

"Okay, sure. Who knows when or if this guy will show up? He might not know where he left his glasses."

I checked my refrigerator to be sure that I had everything I needed to make a Cobb salad. It would be refreshing and not too heavy.

Wong and I set to work, boiling the eggs and sautéing the chicken breasts. While they cooked, I minced a garlic clove, then whisked it together with tangy Dijon mustard, balsamic vinegar, a hint of Worcestershire sauce, olive oil, salt, and pepper.

Daisy, Wong, and I made a quick visit to the garden in

the backyard to pick juicy Sweet Million cherry tomatoes. We glanced around and tried not to make any noise in case it was the exact time that Dale might come. I debated whether to tell her who I thought it was, but couldn't see a downside to that.

The tomatoes were warm from the sun. We popped a few in our mouths and hurried back to check on the chicken and eggs. Then we chopped crispy greens and the cucumber and organized them in containers so they would be easy to place in gorgeous colorful rows on a large oval platter later. The eggs were slightly warm when I peeled them. After letting the chicken breasts rest for ten minutes, Wong cut them into cubes and moved them to a container. All that was left was to cook the bacon. I would cut the avocados just before serving so they wouldn't brown. The delicious smell of bacon forced Wong, Daisy, and me to nosh. We had cooked a little extra so we could snack on it.

While we waited, I asked Wong what she knew about the Mancinis.

"Oh swell! I had just gotten Eddie off my mind and here we go again."

"Eddie?"

"Yeah, I know Dale. Let's just say they ran in the same circles."

"Dale works for a security company. Are you saying he's involved in crime?"

"Dale is also a police snitch."

I didn't know what to make of that. "If Dale had been one of the people who attacked Russ at Ruby's, would that account for the meager mention of it in police records?"

"One would hope not."

Nina knocked on the kitchen door and let herself in.

"B-a-c-o-n!" She dragged out the word. "Oh yum! I swear I could smell it from my house."

Wong and I laughed at her excitement. "See what I mean?" asked Wong.

I knew exactly what she was talking about. Her surname. "Nina, you can have a little now and as much as you want for dinner. You're going to make your own salad from everything on the platter."

At that exact moment, my phone made an unfamiliar sound.

Wong and I jumped at the phone.

"What's going on?" asked Nina.

I held the phone out so we could all watch. The gate camera had caught something, as well as the one watching the door to the garage. But so had the ones inside the garage. I went to one of them live.

It was in black and white, but there was no mistaking Dale's face. He turned his back to the cameras, seemingly studying the garage. Taking the sunglasses, he moved out of the camera's view.

I flipped to the other camera. We watched as he unknowingly looked straight at the camera, then scanned the yard and slid on the sunglasses.

Wong was already on the phone to Wolf.

Nina was asking what was happening.

I was sending the taped videos to Wolf.

"Dale is the one who hung the clown head in the garage."

"Why would he do that?" asked Nina.

"To frighten you," said Wong. "I'd bet anything that he was driving the car that nearly hit Eddie and me."

We heard a police siren and the three of us bolted out the door. Squad cars blocked the exit of his car from the alley.

We could hear Dale saying, "But I didn't do anything."
The officer responded, "That's what they all say."

I felt unsettled when Dale was taken to the police station. I was sure he did more than hang a silly clown head in my garage. I remembered his shoes. They were a long shot.

I texted Wolf: **There may be blood or tomato stains on his white shoes. It looks like he tried to get the stains off, but wasn't successful.**

I was glad I had made extra Cobb salad. That evening, Mars, Bernie, Wong, Nina, and I settled at the big table in my backyard for dinner.

Nina brought Muppet and white wine spritzers, with blueberries and strawberries, which were ideal for the warm evening.

I thought of Gerrie when I threw a bright red tablecloth over the table and brought out square white plates. I wondered how she would feel about her beloved house, now that two people had been murdered there. But then, both of our homes dated back to the 1800s. One had to assume that along the way, some people had died in them. Hopefully, not in quite such a horrible manner as Russ and Eddie.

Bernie carried the huge platter to the table. The ingredients formed colorful lines.

Nina filled glasses with the spritzers, while I fed Daisy, Muppet, and Mochie before we sat down to eat.

Each of us selected the components of our own salads, and I made a mental note that this kind of salad was great fun for a casual dinner party. All the picky eaters could simply omit what they didn't like.

Naturally, Dale was the main topic of discussion. We all wondered if he was the one who killed Russ and Eddie. I watched Wong, afraid it might be hard on her, but she seemed fine.

Over dinner, I told them what I'd found out about lawyers not being able to conceal their clients' weapons.

"Whoa! Do you suppose lawyers warn people *before* they turn over murder weapons?" asked Nina. "That's the first thing I would do, you know? What with lawyer confidentiality, I would march the murder weapon straight to a lawyer on the assumption that he could keep it out of police hands. Bummer!"

I laughed at her dismay. "Is there something we should know? Are you planning to knock anyone off?"

"Not at the moment."

"So, what does one do with a murder weapon?" asked Bernie. "Ship it overseas anonymously and hope it gets tossed in the trash somewhere?"

"Ah!" Nina held up her finger. "The Potomac River. I shudder to imagine just how many weapons are at the bottom."

"I know you're kidding around," I said, "but that raises a good question. If Edwin placed that knife in the safe, why did he keep it instead of throwing it in the river?"

"Where is it now?" asked Bernie.

"After Gerrie was poisoned, Jim opened the safe and handed it over to Wolf," said Wong. "But it will take some time to process."

"But it only takes minutes on TV shows," Nina joked.

"And the dead actors all get up and go home to their families, too," said Wong.

"Why would anyone in the family keep it?" asked Mars.

Wong spoke up, saying, "As blackmail."

"You're saying Edwin, who never did anything wrong, was blackmailing someone?" asked Nina.

"Sort of. It was to keep the peace. If those guys messed with Russ or any of the Stansfields again, the knife would be turned in to the cops."

Mars was obsessed with the cameras. "We really should get some of these, Bernie."

"I'm all for that. I'll pick some up tomorrow. How about you, Nina? Would you like us to install them for you?"

"I thought you would never ask!"

Chapter 38

Dear Sophie,
Someone told my neighbor that one shouldn't use paper plates for an outdoor gathering. Please tell me that's not true!
Neighbor in Paper Mill Pond, Connecticut

Dear Neighbor,
It depends on the kind of party. Paper plates wouldn't be right for a formal outdoor gathering, like a wedding dinner or a dinner party. But if you are having a casual party, like a potluck, a neighborhood cookout, or a party for small children, then paper plates and napkins are the way to go. Some of them look as pretty as china!
Sophie

The next two days passed quietly. Wolf called to confirm that I was right about Dale's shoes. The stains were from tomatoes and blood. They were checking to see if the blood matched Russ's or Eddie's.

Gerrie weighed heavily on my mind. I hoped she would recover, but as each day passed, it seemed less likely.

I was walking Daisy very early in the morning to avoid the heat when we passed a house that was having a yard sale. They had just begun to load items on tables. I peeked in boxes, but mostly they contained common household items. And then I saw pink.

I dug a little deeper. They had six Lady Carlyle cups and saucers. "How much for these?" I asked.

They quoted a price that was absurdly low. I had to think of Todd. Was I doing something wrong by taking advantage of a price I knew was lower than their actual value? It was a yard sale, I reminded myself, and readily paid them what they asked.

I felt a little torn about it, but I happily carried them home.

In the afternoon, Nina and I walked down to our favorite place for mani-pedis. The shop was cool and tranquil, with soft music playing. Nina splurged on a foot and leg massage. I was just glad my toenails looked bright and summery.

We were almost done when the door opened, and a very loud voice announced, "We're here!"

Everyone looked at the newcomers. Nicci ushered Penelope inside. They settled in, with everyone hearing every single thing Nicci said.

"What do you think, Penelope? Green again? You can have any color you want, darling."

Penelope stood to examine the colors and I got a good look at her tattoo. I had imagined a tiny, delicate heart, but the thing had to be an inch across. The edges were uneven, like a child had drawn it. And possibly to hide the flaws, a black rim ran all the way around it.

"Soft pink?" Nicci said with disdain. "You don't want

to be cool? How about black? That would freak out your mom."

Penelope did not have a poker face. She was clearly unhappy. "Not black!" She stood her ground, handing the manicurist the bottle of soft pink nail polish.

Nina flashed me a look. I suspected the novelty of fun Nicci had worn off.

Nicci must not have realized that because she blathered nonstop. "The house is fabulous. I simply have to throw a luncheon for you. I just love cooking in her kitchen. The living room isn't my style, though. I managed to talk Todd into taking down the dreadful painting of his parents. I felt like they were looking at me. Judging, you know? I mean, they're dead."

"Cookie isn't dead," said Penelope softly.

"Well, not yet, honey. Any time now, I'm sure. I'll be the next Mrs. Stansfield and Penelope will be my maid of honor."

I was beginning to feel like Penelope. The words *Any time now?* echoed in my head. Is that what a person said to a child about her beloved grandmother? And why would she sound so doggone happy about Gerrie's impending death, when it was most likely caused by her very own brother, Dale? I didn't think I would be talking so casually about it if I were in her shoes.

"What happened to her? Did she have a stroke or something?" asked the manicurist.

"I think she couldn't take going to prison. I made a pot of coffee and took some up to her before I left the house. She seemed fine, but troubled."

I tried not to show my reaction, but at that moment, I knew the truth. It was Nicci who had tried to kill Gerrie. It made so much sense. She probably stayed at Gerrie's house that night. She was already inside and didn't have to break in. She could have opened the door for her brother, Dale. I had suspected the person who made the coffee was responsible. Poor Gerrie probably didn't have any idea that the coffee was laced with sleeping pills.

"The next thing I heard," said Nicci, "she was in the hospital from an overdose of medicine. I bought all new furniture for the master bedroom. You should have seen what it looked like. Old-fashioned and everything was blue. But Todd won't let me change anything else in the living room or the little den on the third floor yet. I've been shopping for it, though."

"Stop!" yelled Penelope. "Why are you so mean?"

Penelope ran from the shop.

The manicurist looked at Nicci. "Aren't you going to get her?"

"My toenails are wet!"

Mine weren't. I dashed out of the shop and looked around for Penelope.

She leaned against a brick wall, sniffling.

I texted Colleen. **Penelope is crying. Can you come get her? We're on King Street. If you can't, I can take her home with me, but she probably won't come unless you say it's okay.**

I walked over to Penelope. "Hi, Penelope. I'm Sophie. I don't know if you remember me—"

Penelope turned and buried her face in my abdomen.

Nina joined us. "I paid your bill. Shall we take her home?"

Penelope looked up at me. "I don't want to go anywhere with Nicci. Please don't make me."

Penelope's phone beeped. She looked at it. "Mom wants a picture of you."

Nina and I leaned our heads together and smiled.

Penelope promptly sent the photo off to Colleen. "Mom

says you're very funny. She wants to know if you would mind walking me over to Beth Ann's house."

"Sure. Is that what you want?"

Penelope nodded.

We stopped for milkshakes on the way and drank them as we walked. They were all melty and slurpy by the time we reached Beth Ann's house. Her friend waited at the door. Penelope ran up the steps and into the house.

That was a good sign, I thought. Maybe she could confide in Beth Ann.

As soon as I got home, I phoned Wolf and told him that Nicci had made the coffee and brought it up to Gerrie.

"Interesting," said Wolf. "But Dale confessed to everything."

"Maybe he's trying to protect his sister."

"A guy like Dale? He murdered his buddies to protect himself. He wouldn't confess to a crime someone else committed."

I had my doubts about that.

I worried about Penelope that night. The bloom was off the rose with Nicci. And now I feared that while Dale had likely murdered Eddie and Russ, Nicci appeared way too interested in Gerrie's demise, not to mention her possessions. I was glad Jim had hired a nurse to watch over Gerrie at night.

The next morning, Penelope phoned me. "Can you come to the house? I can't reach Mom or Dad. It's just not right. It's not right, Sophie."

"Which house? Gerrie's?"

"Yes. Cookie's house!"

I texted Nina, who was waiting on the sidewalk by the time I locked my door. We hurried over to Gerrie's.

Penelope was on the sidewalk, crying. She stood in the

middle of a collection of furniture. "Sophie! They're taking things!"

Indeed, they were. Two brawny men were carrying furniture out to the sidewalk. The beautiful portrait of Gerrie and Edwin leaned against the exterior wall of Gerrie's house. And Nicci was collecting money from people who ambled off with smaller pieces of furniture and bric-a-brac.

I strode up to Nicci. "What's going on?"

"Just a yard sale. Do you see anything you would like?"

"All this belongs to Gerrie."

"She doesn't need it anymore."

I gasped. "Did she die?"

"Soon, very soon."

I texted Wolf, Wong, and Jim about the situation.

Then I walked inside and approached the moving men. "I'm sorry. There has been a change of plan. Would you please bring everything back in?"

I dashed outside and told Nina and Penelope to gather up what they could and carry it back into the house.

Nicci overheard me. "I don't know who you think you are, but you have no business here. Either buy something or move on."

Of course, the reality was that I didn't have any business there. I wasn't a Stansfield. But Penelope was. I hoped I sounded convincing when I said, "Oh, don't worry. The police are on the way to sort this out."

Nicci stared at me. "Why would the police come? This is a family issue."

"I didn't realize that you were a Stansfield," I said sweetly.

"Well, I will be!" she said very loudly, as if she wanted to convince everyone.

"Then I believe, at this very moment, Penelope is the one in charge. And she does not wish to sell anything."

"She's a child."

"But she's the only Stansfield here!"

It was a stupid argument, but it was all I had.

And Penelope was doing a bang-up job of looking authoritative. She stood with her hands on her hips, pointing her finger and entire right arm at the house, and declared, "Everything goes back. And I'm going to tell my father not to marry you."

Nicci looked as if she had been slapped. But that didn't last long. I could almost hear the wheels in her brain turning to Plan B. "Oh, sweetheart, we've had so much fun together. Wouldn't you like a new modern room?"

"No. I want you to leave."

Nicci sighed. "I didn't want to do this. Penelope Stansfield, you go up to your room this minute and don't come down until I come to get you."

"No! This is Cookie's house! Mom!"

Stansfields descended upon us from all directions. Colleen ran to Penelope. Jim raced up the street, and Todd ambled along the sidewalk, completely unperturbed.

Wolf arrived with Wong.

"What's the problem here?" asked Wolf.

Jim yelled, "You're selling the portrait of my parents! What kind of heathen are you?"

Todd just watched.

When most of the furniture had been returned to the house, I took the opportunity to say what I thought. "Nicci Mancini wanted to be Gerrie Stansfield so much that she tried to kill Gerrie."

Todd, ever unflappable, simply looked at Nicci.

But Jim yelled at Todd. "This is your fault. Once again, you have managed to blindly mess everything up! Why did you bring this woman into our lives? Did you pick her up in a bar? Try to impress her? And now, Mom is in a coma because of her!"

"Todd?" said Nicci in a little girl voice.

"Is this true?" he asked.

"No. I just made her coffee and gave her an itty-bitty pill to help her sleep. I didn't know she would have a reaction to it."

She was a liar, just like Eddie.

Wolf took a deep breath.

"Who killed Russ?" I asked.

Nicci's eyes searched the sky for an answer.

Todd peered at her. "You murdered him?"

"I didn't say that! It was your father's fault. He never should have threatened them with that knife," said Nicci.

"Eddie and Dale never should have cut up Russ!" shouted Jim. "They were the ones who started this whole thing."

Wong asked softly, "Did you kill Eddie?"

Nicci's mouth twitched. "That was Dale. We knew Eddie would have ratted him out. We had to have the knife because Dale and Eddie's fingerprints were on it. I had to protect my little brother."

Wolf called a squad car to collect Nicci.

For the first time, Todd appeared uneasy. I was surprised to see Colleen and Penelope stand beside him. Penelope grasped his hand.

Chapter 39

Dear Natasha,
I'm getting engaged! My fiancé's family owns a restaurant and they have offered to have the engagement party there. But it's kind of a pizza place. Not quite as special as I'd like. How do I tell them that?

Bride-to-Be in Celebration, Florida

Dear Bride-to-Be,
If you are footing the bill, you can have it wherever you want. Simply explain that you have already committed to a different venue.

Natasha

One week later, Gerrie Stansfield woke from her coma. The nurses swore her first utterance was, "Have I missed the wedding?"

She was weak, but not too weak to call me to arrange the luncheon for A Healthy Meal. I explained that in her absence we had met at The Laughing Hound. We couldn't bear to have a grand luncheon without her. And we had four new members. Francie and Betty had joined, as well as Colleen and Henrietta.

This year, since she wasn't up to it, I insisted I would throw an afternoon tea party for us. Of course, that meant I really needed to find more Lady Carlyle teacups and saucers. I scoured antiques stores, with no luck at all.

I was back to work full-time and had a veterinary convention coming up in two weeks. But that didn't stop me from planning a wonderful tea. I was looking forward to seeing Gerrie and hoped she would have the strength to attend.

A couple of days before the tea, I heard someone shouting, "Miss! Miss!"

I looked around.

The man from the antiques store across the street from Moss Restaurant Supply ran toward me.

"I've been looking all over for you. Guess what I found!"

"The cups and saucers that match the dishes you sold me?"

"Yes! But there are only six."

"That's all I need." I went straight to the store and bought them.

On Saturday morning, I prepared the table in my dining room for the tea I had promised. I thought a white tablecloth would best set off the vibrant pink of the Lady Carlyle china. Crystal vases held pink roses and baby's breath. With the table set, I brought three-tier cake stands into the kitchen to be filled with three kinds of cupcakes, traditional cucumber sandwiches, chicken salad sandwiches, open-faced salmon sandwiches, miniature croissants, watercress-and-egg-salad sandwiches, petit fours, tiny chocolate cakes, miniature éclairs, cheese biscuits, and, of course, scones with clotted cream.

Nina and Gerrie were the first to arrive, which gave us a

chance to catch up. Gerrie looked great, if still a little bit thin.

"I'm feeling fine," Gerrie said. "Thank you for coming to Penelope's rescue when Nicci tried to sell my belongings. We're still not sure what she sold. I imagine we'll find out over the next few months when we reach for them and they aren't there. I donated my entire knife set to a charity. I couldn't bear looking at those blue handles anymore."

"How's Todd?"

"Oh my. I don't know how he manages to get himself into these things. I have gone around to all the restaurants he was *using*, I don't know what else to call it, and have apologized. Everyone has been very nice. Probably because they knew I was in a coma. I believe you know Irv, the driver? Apparently, Dale bonked him over the head to steal his delivery cap and some cookies to con his way into my house! But it turned out the door was open, and he didn't need to do that. Dale says he didn't come to kill Russ. All he wanted was the knife that he had used against Russ in Ruby's Bar. But then he realized that Russ, who was also there to get the knife, would rat on him, so he ran into my kitchen, grabbed the knife, and killed him." Gerrie sighed. "My beautiful home and all those terrible things happened there. Anyway, when Charlene found out that Irv was taking deliveries from other restaurants as well, she fired him. I wish Edwin were here to advise me, but I bought the Ruby's Bar building. I figure real estate is always a good investment. Irv has moved into the apartment upstairs. Todd will be running the bar downstairs, with Irv's help, which will give Irv the chance to repeatedly tell war stories about having been on the road with various bands. Drawing on his own band experience, Todd will be bringing a band in every Saturday night. I'm very hopeful that Todd might finally have found his calling in life."

"Wow! Those are some big changes," I said.

Gerrie made a funny face. "Hopefully, the bar will keep Todd busy. He can run his own ghost restaurant now if he wants to and he will leave the other restaurants alone! I still can't believe my son perpetrated that kind of scam."

"Have you heard anything about the tests they ran on the knife?" asked Nina.

"Wolf tells me that DNA has confirmed that the blood on it belonged to Russ. But the fingerprints on the handle were matched to my Jim, Eddie Wong, and Dale Mancini, confirming that they were the two men who had attacked Russ at Ruby's."

Five other women arrived simultaneously, and the conversation turned to the break in the heat and what children refused to eat.

We voted unanimously to hire Charlene to prepare A Healthy Meal dishes for the children. She took her job to heart and surprised us with an Almost Healthy Pumpkin Spice Cake, which she cut into squares as dessert for each child's meal.

The following Saturday, I attended an engagement party for Jim and Emily at the Keswicks' house. The invitation was addressed to Mars as well. I felt certain that they knew we were divorced, but it was fine with me. Nina and Humphrey each received one, too.

As I expected, Henrietta had outdone herself. It was held in their garden with stars and fairy lights twinkling overhead. Champagne flowed and dogs with bows or bow ties pranced among the guests.

Senator Keswick remembered my name this time. "Sophie! I understand we have you to thank for this delightful development."

"You're giving me far too much credit. I just pointed out a few things to Emily. That's all."

He gazed at the ground for a moment. "The night you came to dinner, I couldn't figure out where I knew you from. And then I suddenly recognized you. You were at the Stansfields' house when the ambulance arrived. We spoke briefly."

I nodded, uncomfortable now that he admitted remembering where he had seen me.

"I probably seemed awkward. It was a terrible moment for me. You see, my wife was convinced that I was in love with Gerrie Stansfield. That was never the case, but at that moment, I was afraid you would mention my presence at the Stansfields' and it would only feed my wife's unfounded suspicions. Please forgive me if I behaved in a less than gentlemanly manner. I hope you will come back to dine with us soon."

Emily joined us. "Thank you, Sophie. Not only did you keep your promise not to tell my parents I was living here, but you gave me this!" She held her arms out. "You were right. My mom had a long talk with Gerrie. I understand they both cried. I'm only sorry we didn't do this sooner. That way, Edwin could have been part of it. It would have been very special for him to be a proud father-in-law, along with my dad."

The following Saturday brought cold weather and buckets of rain. Wong, Nina, and I gathered in my kitchen for a dinner of vegetable soup and deliciously sinful grilled cheese sandwiches with bacon. Daisy, Muppet, and Mochie lounged comfortably on the floor near a crackling fire. I hadn't planned on bringing up Eddie, but Wong launched into it herself.

"When I look back, I can't believe I married Eddie. Of all the men in the world, you'd think I would have avoided trouble like him."

"He *was* very handsome," Nina said.

"That's no excuse! I meet good-looking men almost every day. Of course, now I'm wary of them," said Wong.

"How are you getting along?" I asked.

"I'm sleeping much better. It's crazy, but Eddie's death was a relief and yet so sad."

"He loved you," I said. "If he didn't, he wouldn't have bothered to push you out of the way when Dale was trying to kill him with that car. You must have known a kinder side of Eddie."

"I think you're right about that." Wong nodded. "Of course, his life didn't have to end that way. Eddie, Dale, and Russ never should have tried to blackmail Moss Restaurant Supply in the first place. The three of them were like a powder keg when they were scheming together. And then they thought Russ was collecting money from Moss and wasn't cutting them in! Did you hear that they're charging Dale for attempted murder in addition to murder? It's for the night Dale and Eddie sliced Russ's chest at Ruby's Bar. If Jim hadn't been there and hustled like crazy to get Russ to the hospital, he would have died."

"But why didn't Russ tell the police who attacked him?" asked Nina.

Wong sipped her iced tea. "Are you kidding? Would you? They would have made bail and been after him. Russ knew that. He told them Edwin had the knife and that it would be delivered to the police if they made any attempt on him. Eddie had the good sense to get out of town. Russ didn't scare him, but Edwin did."

"And that's why he came back." Nina picked up another piece of grilled cheese. "When Edwin died, all three of them wanted the knife. Russ for protection, and Eddie and Dale wanted it so it would never come to light."

"Right." Wong shook her head. "And then Dale's sister smelled money and went after Todd."

Nina's iPhone played a jolly tune. "Oh! I would have forgotten. Natasha is on TV."

"Her show is on in the evening now?" I asked.

Nina turned on the TV in my kitchen. "No, she's on the news or something. I saw it mentioned on Facebook this morning."

On the TV screen, Natasha looked stunning. The anchor, who was equally attractive, was holding up the Nataska's Cookies flyer.

"You can see that it says *Nataska* instead of *Natasha*," Natasha emphasized. "Of course, I spotted that right away."

"She did not!" shouted Nina. "Sophie, you were the one who saw that."

I waved at her to quiet down so we could listen.

"Of course, everyone, just everyone, told me not to go public with this because it would damage my reputation."

"Another lie!" Nina was highly agitated.

"But I couldn't do that to my public," Natasha continued. "I treasure you all so much and felt it was my obligation to tell you about the scams that go on, so you can be on the lookout for them."

"I understand that you have shut down your fabulous cookie business because of this?" said the anchor.

"Yes! I couldn't let people order my cookies anymore, knowing that they might accidentally buy them from a scammer. So I decided to shut it down." Natasha winked at the camera. "But look for new and better Natasha's Cookies in the future!"

Wong, Nina, and I looked at each other and burst into laughter.

"That's our Natasha!" I said.

Daisy raised her head and stared at the kitchen door. She got to her feet and perked her ears.

"Someone's here," whispered Nina.

Seconds later, there was a knock on the door. I flicked on the outdoor light and opened the door to Gerrie.

"We can't come in, we're soaked!"

"Nonsense. Come in out of the rain."

"I'll get towels," said Nina, jumping to her feet.

Gerrie shook her umbrella as well as a smaller one and left them outside when she, Penelope, and a white standard size poodle entered.

Daisy wagged her tail and approached the poodle slowly. They politely sniffed one another and Muppet.

"Who is this?" I asked.

Nina arrived with towels and handed them out. "Wait a minute. I know this dog."

"She's Elsa!" said Penelope.

"I adopted her from the shelter," said Gerrie. "We couldn't be a better match. She's eight-years-old, so she's just my speed. And she knows everything. No house-breaking, no chewing on inappropriate items. She's my angel."

I reached for dog cookies and gave one to each of the dogs. "You're just in time for dessert. Wong baked pumpkin cupcakes." I put the kettle on while they dried off.

Gerrie slid into the banquette, but Penelope sat in the middle of the dogs, stroking all of them.

"What made you finally decide to get a dog?" asked Nina.

"Todd moved out. I didn't realize how much comfort I took from knowing he was there. It's a big house, and after everything that happened, well, I feel much better having Elsa with me. Her hearing is better than mine for starters. But her company is priceless."

"He moved out?" I didn't want to upset Penelope but I was very curious.

"He moved home with mommy and me," said Penelope.

I raised my eyebrows and gazed at Gerrie.

"They're trying to make it work." She crossed her fingers.

"That's wonderful," said Wong.

"But I'm still going to spend the night with Cookie and Elsa all the time!" said Penelope.

I brought dessert plates to the table. "Penelope, would you like hot tea or hot apple cider?"

"Hot apple cider!"

I heated some for her and brought the tea mugs to the table.

When I joined them, they were chatting about how brave Penelope had been. She seemed to take it in stride.

"Gerrie, did you ever figure out who moved the Grumblethorpe statue?"

"Oh, it was that horrible Nicci who tried to kill me. Todd had given her a key and she would sneak into the house and move things, hoping to gaslight me. She was responsible for putting Edwin's death certificate in my purse, too. Apparently driving me mad wasn't getting rid of me fast enough for her taste."

"But she's in jail now," Penelope stated firmly. "Her stinky brother, too. So we're all safe."

I was delighted to hear her speak with such resilience after what she'd been through. Gerrie looked great and smiled at her granddaughter with pride.

Rain pattered on the windows. The fire crackled, keeping us warm and cozy. Wong and Gerrie had been through terror and Gerrie had nearly died. But the future looked bright for both of them.

Recipes

Salmon and Portobello Mushroom Salad with Lemon Dressing

Serves 2–3, depending on serving size.

1 pound red or pink salmon fillet
1–2 portobello mushrooms
2 tablespoons extra-virgin olive oil
1 red pepper
Baby spinach greens
1 red onion
6–9 black olives

Lemon Dressing

¼ cup extra-virgin olive oil
2 tablespoons lemon juice (about 1 lemon)
1 tablespoon honey
2 tablespoons whole grain or Dijon mustard
Salt and pepper

Preheat oven to 350. Line a rimmed baking sheet with aluminum foil.

Wash the salmon and dry. Brush with 1 tablespoon of olive oil on top and on the bottom. Lay on baking sheet skin side down. (If white globs appear, simply wipe them off. It happens. Your fish is perfectly safe to eat.)

Wash and dry the portobello mushroom and cut into ¾-inch-wide slices. Brush with olive oil and place on baking sheet.

Wash and dry the red pepper. Slice in wide sections and place on the baking sheet. You can use separate baking sheets for each, if you prefer.

Bake 15–20 minutes. If you prefer salmon that is not baked through, then bake it a shorter time.

Meanwhile, make the dressing. Pour the oil, lemon juice, honey, and mustard into a small bowl. (Krista's hint: I like to use a Pyrex type–glass measuring cup because they have spouts!) Mix vigorously with a fork or a whisk. Add salt and pepper to taste.

Mound the baby spinach leaves on each plate. Cut the onion in thin slices and arrange 3 on top of the spinach leaves. Drizzle with a little bit of dressing. When the salmon is done, slice it in inch-wide strips (eyeball it) and place the strips on top of the spinach and onions on each plate. Add the portobello mushroom strips. Cut the red peppers into strips and add them. Add 2–3 olives as garnish. Drizzle with the dressing.

Save leftover dressing in the refrigerator.

Cobb Salad

Romaine lettuce
4 hardboiled eggs
½ cucumber
1 avocado
Cherry tomatoes
2 chicken breasts
6 slices bacon
Crumbled Roquefort cheese
¼ cup balsamic vinegar
⅓ cup extra-virgin olive oil
2 tablespoons Dijon mustard
1 garlic clove
Salt and pepper

Eggs

Place large eggs in a single layer in a pot and add enough water to cover by 1 inch. (Krista's hint: Cook more eggs to eat later in the week.) Bring the water to a boil. Place a lid on the pot and turn the heat off. Let it stand with the eggs inside for 9–10 minutes. Meanwhile, prepare a bowl of ice and ice water. After 10 minutes, pour out the hot water and shock the eggs with the ice water. Store the eggs in the refrigerator until ready to use. (Krista's hint: For easy peeling, use old eggs! The fresher they are, the harder they will be to peel.)

Chicken Breasts

Place a skillet (which has a lid) on the stove, turn the temperature to medium, and add 1 tablespoon of olive oil. Add the chicken breasts, swiping each through the olive oil on both sides. Cover the pan with the lid. The bottom part of the chicken breast should begin to turn white. Flip the chicken breasts and place the cover on again. Using a meat thermometer check the temperature of the chicken. (Krista's hint: After killing three thermometers in a year, I finally invested in a Thermapen. It still works—10 years later!) When the thick part of the chicken breasts register 65 degrees, immediately remove from the pan and set aside to cool for 10 minutes before slicing.

Bacon

Place paper towels on a microwave-safe plate. Add 3 slices of bacon, not touching each other. Cover with a paper towel. Microwave for 3 minutes. Remove and repeat with 3 more slices.

Dressing

Makes enough for 3–4 servings. Double if needed.

Crush and mince the garlic clove. Whisk together balsamic vinegar, olive oil, Dijon mustard, and salt and pepper to taste. Add the minced garlic and whisk again.

Serve on a large platter. Slice chicken, avocado, cucumber, and eggs. Lay each ingredient on the platter in a long strip. Vary the colors. Serve the dressing on the side.

Almost Healthy Pumpkin Spice Cake

1⅓ cups sprouted grain spelt flour
1½ teaspoons baking powder
2 teaspoons cinnamon
1 teaspoon nutmeg
Pinch of cloves
½ teaspoon salt
¾ cup pumpkin puree
½ cup oil (mild olive or canola) and extra for greasing the pan
½ cup date sugar (or regular sugar)
⅔ cup maple syrup
2 teaspoons vanilla
3 eggs
7 Medjool dates, pitted and coursely chopped
½ cup finely chopped pecans

Preheat oven to 350. Grease 8x8 pan with oil.

In a bowl, mix together the flour, baking powder, cinnamon, nutmeg, cloves, and salt. Mix well with a whisk or a fork and set aside.

Beat the pumpkin, oil, maple syrup, and vanilla. Add 1 egg at a time, beating on low speed. Add the flour mixture slowly until completely blended. Add the pecans and dates and mix. Pour into pan and bake 45 minutes or until a cake tester comes out clean.

Maple Drizzle

¼ cup powdered sugar
2 tablespoons maple syrup
Drop of water (optional)

Combine powdered sugar with maple syrup to a nice drizzle consistency. If it's too thick, add a drop of water. Drizzle over cake after it cools.

Lemon Meringue Pie

9-inch pie crust, baked
1½ cups sugar
1½ cups water
½ teaspoon salt
½ cup cornstarch
⅓ cup water
4 egg yolks, lightly beaten
½ cup lemon juice (3–4 lemons)
3 tablespoons butter
4 egg whites
½ cup sugar

Preheat oven to 325.

In a heavy-bottomed saucepan, combine the sugar, 1½ cups water, and ½ teaspoon salt in a large pot and heat to boiling.

Mix the cornstarch with ⅓ cup water to a smooth paste and add to the sugar mixture. Stir constantly until it turns thick and clear.

Combine the egg yolks with the lemon juice and stir into the sugar mixture. Cook until it bubbles, then remove from heat and stir in the butter. Cover and set aside to cool.

Meringue

Add salt to the egg whites and beat, adding ½ cup sugar until they hold a soft peak.

Pour the lemon filling into the pie shell. Top with the meringue, smoothing to the edges and leaving some peaks.

Bake 15 minutes.

Cool at least 1–2 hours before serving.

Cherry Chocolate Chip Cookies

1¾ cups flour
1 teaspoon baking powder
½ teaspoon baking soda
½ teaspoon pink sea salt
12 tablespoons unsalted butter (a stick and a half)
½ cup sugar
½ cup light brown sugar
1 large egg
1 teaspoon vanilla
½ cup old-fashioned oatmeal (not quick cooking)
1½ cups dried pitted cherries
⅔ cup semisweet chocolate chips

Preheat oven to 350. Line a baking tray with parchment paper.

In a bowl, mix together the flour, baking powder, baking soda, and salt. Set aside.

Cream the butter with the sugars for about 2 minutes. Add the egg and beat well. Add the vanilla and beat. Mix in the flour, a spoonful at a time, beating on low until it's incorporated. Add the oatmeal and beat briefly. Add the dried cherries and chocolate chips and beat on the lowest speed just to mix.

Spoon onto the prepared baking sheet, keeping them 1 or 2 inches apart. Bake large cookies about 15 minutes and small cookies 12 minutes. Cool on a baking rack.

Easiest-Ever Fruit Salad

This can be served with any meal. It can even be dessert!

1 cantaloupe
1 mango
8 ounces strawberries
8 ounces blackberries
8 ounces blueberries
Juice of ½ lemon
1 tablespoon sugar

Wash the berries and drain. Cut the cantaloupe and mango into bite-size pieces and place in a large bowl. Hull the strawberries. If you have very large strawberries, cut them in half. Sprinkle the sugar over the fruit. Squeeze the lemon over the sugar. Turn the fruit gently to mix. Serve!

Red Berry Smash

½ cup sugar
1 cup water
½ cup blueberries
½ cup blackberries
½ cup raspberries
2 lemons
Berry or lemon vodka
Sparkling water

Make a simple syrup by cooking ½ cup of sugar in 1 cup of water. Bring to a boil and cook until the sugar has dissolved. Set aside to cool. Meanwhile, wash the berries and place them in a pitcher. Squeeze lemons over the berries. Add the simple syrup and 1–2 cup berry or lemon vodka (or to taste). Use a long spoon or a muddler to smash some of the berries and fill with sparkling water. Serve in tall glasses filled with ice.

Panna Cotta

Makes 8 servings.
Plan to make this ahead of time so it will
have adequate time to set.

8 ramekins or dessert glasses
1 envelope unflavored gelatin (2¼ teaspoons)
4 tablespoons cold water
2 cups heavy cream
1 cup nonfat milk
Scant ⅓ cup sugar
1½ teaspoons vanilla

Pour the cold water into a small shallow bowl. Sprinkle with the gelatin. Set aside for at least 5 minutes. Pour the cream, milk, and sugar into a heavy-bottomed pot, stir, and bring to a boil over medium-high heat, stirring occasionally. Keep an eye on it so it won't bubble over. When it boils, remove from the heat and stir in the gelatin and vanilla. Pour into ramekins or dessert glasses and cool. (Be sure the dessert glasses can take the hot filling.) Allow several hours for it to set. Refrigerate until serving.

They can be flipped out on dessert plates or served in a glass. Garnish with berry sauce or fresh berries or fruit.

Berry Sauce

1 pound raspberries (two 8-ounce clamshells)
3 tablespoons sugar (check the sweetness of your berries
    and adjust accordingly)

Pour raspberries into a pot and heat over medium. When they begin to release juices, add the sugar to taste. If you don't like the seeds, put it through a sieve.

Peach Crisp with Oatmeal Crumble

6–7 peaches
1 teaspoon sugar
½ cup rolled oats
⅓ cup dark brown sugar
¼ cup flour
¼ teaspoon nutmeg
¼ teaspoon cinnamon
¼ cup butter at room temperature OR ⅓ cup oil (mild
  olive oil or canola oil)
Vanilla ice cream (optional)

Preheat oven to 375.

Peel the peaches and slice. Place in a baking dish. Sprinkle with the teaspoon of sugar and turn the peaches a few times to mix.

Place the rolled oats, dark brown sugar, flour, nutmeg, and cinnamon in a medium bowl. Add the butter or oil. Use your fingers to mix well. Spread over the peaches. Bake for 30 minutes.

Serve warm plain or with a scoop of vanilla ice cream.

Strawberry Poke Cake

Cake

2¼ cups flour
1 tablespoon baking powder
½ teaspoon salt
½ teaspoon mace (optional)
1 stick (8 tablespoons) unsalted butter at room temperature or softened
1½ cups sugar
3 large eggs at room temperature
1 cup milk
1 teaspoon vanilla

Preheat oven to 350. Grease and flour a 9 x13 baking pan.

Combine flour, baking powder, salt, and mace in a bowl and set aside.

Cream the butter with the sugar. Beat in each egg and the vanilla. Alternate adding the flour mixture and the milk. Bake 25–30 minutes. It should be lightly golden on top and a cake tester should come out clean. While it bakes, prepare the strawberries.

Strawberries

1 pound strawberries
1 cup sugar

Hull and slice the strawberries. Combine with sugar in a pot and cook over medium heat, stirring constantly for about 5 minutes. The sugar should be completely dissolved and there should be liquid in the bottom of the pot. Remove about ⅓ cup of the liquid and save for the frosting. While the cake is still warm, poke holes into it with a wooden skewer. Ladle the liquid over it slowly (if you do it too fast, it will run off to the sides). Spread the cooked strawberries over the cake in an even layer. Cool and refrigerate 1 or 2 hours before frosting.

Frosting

8 tablespoons butter, softened
6 ounces cream cheese, softened
$\frac{1}{3}$ cup of the reserved strawberry liquid
1–2 cups powdered sugar

Beat the butter with the cream cheese and strawberry liquid. Beat in sugar until it reaches the desired consistency and flavor. Beat for 4 to 5 minutes. Spoon it over the strawberries and gently spread with an offset spatula so you don't dislodge the strawberries. Refrigerate.

Peach and Berry Parfait

½ peach per serving, sliced
Berries (raspberries, blueberries, blackberries)
Ice cream (any flavor) OR Greek yogurt
Peach schnapps
Sweetened whipped cream

There's no wrong way to do this. Start with ice cream in the bottom and add berries. Add more ice cream and some peach slices. Then the magic elixir—peach schnapps to taste (about 2 tablespoons per serving). Top with heaping spoonfuls of whipped cream. Garnish with a berry and a slice of peach.

Sweetened Whipped Cream

1 cup heavy whipping cream
⅓ cup powdered sugar
1 teaspoon vanilla

Whip the cream until it begins to hold a shape. Add the powdered sugar and vanilla and whip until it holds a soft peak.

Blue Ghost

Makes 2 servings.

1 jigger (1.5 ounces) blue curaçao
1 jigger coconut rum
1 jigger crème de cacao
Vanilla ice cream

Pour the liqueurs into a mixer and add two large scoops of ice cream. Blend and serve in chilled martini glasses.